EDGAR

WHEN POE'S NIGHTMARES BEGAN

DAVID ALLEN VOYLES

DARK PRESS

Contents

INTRODUCTION

For at least two decades, long before I published my first short story, much less my first book, I have wanted to write a novel about Edgar Allan Poe.

This isn't it.

A strange thing happened when I decided I was finally ready to write the story I had thought about for so long. Instead of the story being about Poe's last days as I had always planned, I was hit with an interesting idea.

What if Poe's best stories were inspired by actual events that happened during one summer when he was a boy living in Richmond, Virginia?

I loved the concept. I got out my anthology of Poe's complete works and re-read all of his short stories to see which ones I thought might be worked into a series of supernatural events. But I needed one of his stories to serve as a connecting thread for the overall plot. It turns out, three stories serve that purpose, but I won't reveal those just yet.

For those of you who are serious Poe fans, you may recognize each of Edgar's adventures throughout the thirteen chapters of the novel relates specifically to one of his stories. Some titles are familiar to every American student who made it to the ninth grade, like "The

Tell-Tale Heart" and "The Fall of the House of Usher"; others are far more obscure, such as "Metzengerstein" and "Some Words with a Mummy." In my "Notes from the Author" at the end of this book, I've provided a list of those stories with explanations of their connections, as well as brief summaries of the original tales for those who might be interested. I also identify which parts of Edgar are historically accurate. I suspect that even ardent fans of Poe may be surprised by some of them.

This whole experience of researching, imagining, and writing about Edgar Allan Poe has been fascinating for me. I've really loved putting myself in 1826 Richmond and walking the old streets (and the cemetery paths, of course) with Edgar and his friends. I trust you'll find this story is much more than a simple re-telling of Poe's work. I honestly can't wait to hear what you think.

There is one limitation, perhaps, to writing a horror novel about a real person. It's kind of like writing any fictional story in first person; you know the protagonist will survive, and while Poe's death is shrouded in mystery, we know he made it past fifteen.

Still, you may have a lingering question about our young writer and his future when you finish the story. Just maybe.

You'll have to let me know.

- DAV, May 2024

1

"His cue, which was to perfect an imitation of myself, lay both in words and in actions; and most admirably did he play his part....and his singular whisper, it grew the very echo of my own."

from "William Wilson"

"There is something in the unselfish and the self-sacrificing love of a brute, which goes directly to the heart of him who has had frequent occasion to test the paltry friendship and gossamer fidelity of mere Man."

from "The Black Cat"

The eyes in the chiseled skull looking back at Edgar felt as empty as his heart.

He dropped his pencil and sketchbook onto the grass beside him, and leaned back against the tombstone. Coming to the graveyard to write poetry and draw usually gave him a sense of peace but, that morning, after yet another argument with his adoptive father, he felt incredibly sad.

The sound of a bird's raucous call nearby caused Edgar to look up; a blur of dark wings disappeared into the foliage. From the corner of his eye he thought he saw something larger move.

"Hello? Is someone there?" Edgar stood and took one cautious step toward the small mausoleum. Its walls were so densely covered in ivy, the stone was nearly invisible. Edgar took another step but stopped when he heard low laughter, or more precisely, someone trying to stifle a chuckle unsuccessfully.

"Robert, is that you? I warn you, I'm not in the mood for one of your pranks." Edgar unclenched his fists and crossed his arms, subconsciously assuming the exact same posture as his father hours earlier.

"Edgar." The hoarse whisper was muffled; it echoed as if it came from within the crypt. Edgar edged his way cautiously over to its entrance and saw the iron gate protecting the wooden door stood unlocked and ajar. The stained-glass window of jewel-toned abstract shapes kept him from being able to see inside.

The sound of more laughter behind the thick door made Edgar's skin crawl, but his unease was quickly replaced by anger as he imagined how his friend would tell the story later. Edgar lifted the iron latch on the door and opened it slowly. He found it difficult to see in the gloom of the crypt at first, but soon he could discern what appeared to be covered enclosures built into the walls on either side that likely held caskets. As he stood in the doorway with the sunlight spilling around him into the dusky room, his breath caught in his chest. Something crouched in the far corner.

At first it appeared to be an inhuman creature, one of many that inhabited Edgar's dreams. But when it stood, Edgar saw it was a man, a boy actually, a few years from adulthood like himself. This person wore clothing like his own and was of similar height and build. As he smiled at Edgar, the grin grew horribly wider and wider--*like the grin of the skull I was sketching*. Edgar thought the boy must be mad.

"And so we meet," the boy said in a hoarse, soft voice barely above a whisper. The speaker tilted his head oddly as he smiled which sent a shiver up Edgar's spine, but then an even more horrifying realization struck Edgar. The boy looked like him. Exactly like him.

Edgar shut his eyes tightly as the sound of crazed giggling bounced off the stone walls, enveloping him like the gloom and wrapping him in its cold embrace so he no longer felt the warmth of the sun on his back. When the laughter faded, Edgar reluctantly opened his eyes and found he was alone.

Edgar spun in the doorway and desperately searched the graveyard for movement but, seeing nothing, forced himself to turn back and look again within the crypt. With his heart pounding, Edgar stepped further into the mausoleum and made his way to the back wall where the boy had been. No sign suggested anyone had been there. The stone floor was clear of any dirt or dust, so the absence of footprints meant little.

Edgar left the crypt and shut the door and the iron gate, frowning for a moment as he paused to stare at the entrance. Shaking his head, he made his way back to the spot where he had been sketching. He picked up his pencil and book from where he had dropped them and stood, surveying the gently rolling hills of the cemetery as he pondered what had happened.

A movement to his right caught his eye: a dark shadow streaked low along the ground before disappearing between two tombstones. Edgar's eyes searched the adjacent crosses and statues, not sure whether he hoped to see the figure again or not.

A small dark shape caught his eye as it jumped up onto the top of a low, flat stone bearing a bronze plaque. With relief Edgar saw it was a cat, solid black except for a small patch of white on its chest. It lay down on the warm stone and licked the top of its paw which it then used to clean its face and right ear. Abruptly it stopped its cleaning and stared at Edgar.

What's wrong with its face?

Edgar took a step toward the cat, but it jumped down from the small memorial and ran quickly off through the cemetery and into the nearby woods.

The familiar pang of loneliness that swelled in Edgar's chest was overwhelming.

"Hello, what's this?"

Edgar's eyes flew open and he sat up from where he had been dozing in the warm summer air against the trunk of a large oak tree.

"Give that back," Edgar said. He reached for the sketchbook Robert had snatched from his lap and held open barely out of Edgar's reach. The book was angled so that the sketch of a ghoulish, crouching figure glared out from its pages. "I thought you were reading."

"This is much more interesting than *The Iliad*," Robert said, ignoring Edgar's extended hand and returning his attention to the sketchbook. "I don't know how anyone is supposed to keep up with all those Greek names. But, seriously, Edgar, these drawings are fantastic. I thought you just wrote sad little poems in here." He flipped the book around to study the picture again. "But I must say, this picture is..." He paused, searching for the right word. "...well, disturbing. What would make you draw such things?" He turned several pages which displayed images of various robed specters and skeletons and then stopped to look at his friend. "I mean, they're all very good, but..." His voice trailed off.

Edgar shrugged. "I don't know. I like drawing them."

Robert studied his friend. "Sometimes you're so withdrawn, so gloomy, I'd think you were brought up in an orphanage run by sadistic nuns if I didn't know otherwise." Edgar frowned. Robert's eyes widened and he raised his hands defensively. "I didn't mean anything by that, Edgar. You know that. But your life is so good. Now with your father's business doing well, you live in the finest house in town. And you're set to be his partner, a man of means yourself. There's not another boy in Richmond who wouldn't trade places with you."

"You have a much rosier view of my future than I do," Edgar said. "It's true, my father's inheritance has changed our lives a great deal. But even with this new wealth, that man can pinch a penny until it bleeds. It is only by my mother's pleading that I have even a small allowance to buy things like that sketchbook. And as far as becoming his business partner..." Edgar shook his head. "I don't see it. And to be honest, I don't think I want it. I don't want to be a merchant; I'd rather pursue the arts. Like my real parents." He picked at a hangnail for a moment before looking up again. "But not a day goes by without him reminding me of my 'questionable' roots."

"I would think your birth parents being famous actors would be something he would be proud of," Robert said.

"I'm not sure you could say they were famous, exactly," Edgar replied. "Maybe my mother. She had quite a following from what my adoptive mother says. But John Allan has no great love for the arts. Actors might--and I emphasize 'might'--rate a step above thieves and harlots in his book."

Robert gave his friend a small smile. "Mrs. Allan seems very kind."

Edgar nodded. "She is. She was friends with my mother." Robert studied his companion for a moment in silence. Deciding to change the subject, he held up the sketch book again with the ghoul facing toward Edgar and asked, "But what about this particular picture? What made you draw it? This would give me nightmares."

Edgar waited before answering, debating whether to tell Robert the truth or not. He took a deep breath and looked into his friend's eyes. "The other day I saw this in the graveyard." Robert's jaw dropped and his eyes widened again but he held his silence and waited for Edgar to continue. "Well, I *thought* I saw this. I was sketching images from some of the tombstones when I heard a voice speak to me."

"Someone had been spying on you?" Robert asked. He leaned toward Edgar, eager to hear more.

"I don't know. That's what I thought. At first, I thought I heard leaves rustling, like someone sneaking around in the graveyard. Then I heard a voice——hardly more than a whisper really——call 'Edgar.'"

"They knew your name?" Robert asked.

"Yes. And then I heard laughter. Not very loud, only a chuckle, as if it were coming from the Blankenship tomb." Edgar paused, and then confessed sheepishly, "I thought it was you."

"Me!" Robert protested. And then he laughed. "Well, that is something I might do. But I swear it wasn't me."

"I know that now."

"Then what did you do?"

"I went inside."

"It was unlocked?" Robert asked. His voice indicated his doubt.

"It was. And I saw something crouching in the corner..." Edgar pointed to the drawing, "...like that." Robert shivered but smiled, encouraging Edgar to continue his story. "But here's what's strange." Robert inched closer as Edgar lowered his voice. "At first, I thought the creature didn't have a human face. Or rather, I should say, a *living* human face. It looked like a skull." In spite of himself, Edgar was clearly enjoying telling Robert his story, and Robert clearly enjoyed hearing it.

"The cemetery would have been a faint image in the dust behind me at that point," Robert said.

"I was terrified." Edgar admitted, "It was as if I were trapped. Frozen. But then the figure slowly stood, and I could see the face had flesh after all. It wasn't a creature; it was a boy, dressed as you and I are. But here's the part that really chills my soul." Edgar blinked and wet his lips. "The boy's face changed." Robert's eyes narrowed as he waited for Edgar to continue. "I saw it looked exactly like me."

Robert stared at Edgar in silence. Eventually Edgar continued, his voice so quiet that Robert had to lean in even further to hear him.

"And then he laughed. It was a horrible, low laugh, so horrible I couldn't stand to hear it. I closed my eyes until the laughter stopped, and when I opened them, he was gone."

"Would you boys like something to drink? A switchel or a lemonade, perhaps?"

Edgar and Robert jumped, startled by the sudden presence of Robert's mother who covered her mouth to hide her smile as the boys stood. They averted eye contact with her as they brushed the grass from their trousers.

"I'm sorry," Jane Stannard said. "I thought you heard me coming. What on earth had you both so captivated?"

"Edgar was just telling me about——" he looked at Edgar who shook his head slightly, "a bear he thought he saw near the river."

Jane's eyes narrowed but she didn't press him for clarification.

"But, Mother," Robert said in a new, playful tone accompanied by a sense of mischief sparkling in his eyes as he held up Edgar's sketchbook. "Did you know that our Edgar is quite an artist?" Edgar's eyes grew big as he silently begged Robert to stop. Robert thumbed a few pages back from the frightening image of the ghoulish boy in the cemetery, and Edgar grew even more nervous.

"Robert, no! Give me that!" Edgar said.

Batting Edgar's hands away, Robert continued. "Mother, you've inspired a budding artist!" He held the book out to his mother so that she could see the portrait of a very pretty woman who obviously resembled her. Edgar's cheeks grew red and he stared at the ground. Jane took the book and read the lines of verse that accompanied the sketch.

> On desperate seas long wont to roam,
> Thy hyacinth hair, thy classic face,
> Thy Naiad airs have brought me home
> To the glory that was Greece,
> And the grandeur that was Rome.

"How wonderful!" she said. "A poem written in ancient, classical style. Did you write this, Edgar?" He nodded and she returned her gaze to the sketchbook where she read more of the poem. "It's about Helen of Troy, if I'm not mistaken. That's hard to do well, Edgar, but you've captured it masterfully." She ran her fingers over the portrait above the verse. "The sketch is beautiful, too. And how clever of you to use local people as models for your subjects, as the Renaissance masters did." Edgar looked up at her, relief clearly evident on his face.

"Should you need a model for a poem about a rowdy, rude boy, I know where to find one." She cast a side glance at Robert but smiled to take the sting out of the mild rebuke.

"Thank you, Mrs. Stannard," Edgar said. He felt something brush against his leg.

"Oh, we have a visitor," Jane said. The three of them looked at the black cat who had stepped from Edgar to Robert and then to Robert's mother, pausing to rub its side briefly against each of them before returning to Edgar. Edgar knelt down and reached out to stroke its head but jerked his hand back when he saw the cat's deformity.

"I've seen that cat here before," said Robert, and Edgar thought back to the cat he had seen in the graveyard. "It must be lost, or maybe someone has abandoned it. I know it's him because of that missing eye." He reached over and rubbed the cat's head, which didn't appear to be troubled in the least by his touch. The cat purred but then turned to rub against Edgar's knee again. Edgar shifted from his kneeling posture and sat fully on the ground, making a lap for the cat of which it took full advantage. It purred contentedly as he petted it and settled in as if it had known him for years.

"I think it's a female," Jane said. "She seems to be looking for a home, poor thing. However she lost that eye, she seems to have adjusted fairly well."

"It's so odd," Robert said as he looked at his mother. "Another one-eyed cat!" Jane frowned.

Edgar asked, "There's been another?"

"My aunt and uncle had a black cat like this..."

"Robert, no," Jane interrupted softly.

"It happened, Mother. You might as well accept it." Turning to Edgar, he explained. "My uncle is an alcoholic. And he's mean when he gets drunk." Jane clenched her lips tight but didn't stop her son from speaking further. Robert settled on the grass beside his friend and continued the story. "My aunt really loved that cat. It had a white spot on its chest just like this one. Well, anyway, one night Uncle Julius came in from another night of drinking at the tavern and the cat made him mad. Aunt Olivia saw it rub against his leg, something cats are prone to do as you can see. Regardless of whether the cat tripped him or he stumbled due to his drunkenness, he fell, hurting his shoulder in the process. Swearing like a sailor, he blamed it on the cat and worked himself into a fury. He grabbed a knife and stabbed it in the head, taking one of its eyes out in the process."

Jane shut her eyes and shook her head. Edgar frowned and continued to pet the cat while murmuring a soft apology to the creature for the cruelty of humans. He raised his head and asked, "But that's not this cat?"

"No, not at all," Robert answered. "Aunt Olivia's cat died from the injury. I buried it for her, so I'm sure this is not the same cat."

"It certainly is odd for another cat like that one, black with a white spot and missing one eye, to show up here," Jane said. She looked down at the cat in Edgar's lap as they stood in silence for a moment. "I'd love to give her a home, but Robert's father has a sensitivity to cats which makes him sneeze. They give him fits. It wouldn't do to have it here."

"He sure seems to like you," Robert said to Edgar. The cat purred loudly, obviously content in Edgar's lap. "Maybe you could adopt it."

Edgar shrugged and raised his eyebrows. "Maybe. My mother would be fine with it, but my father is another story."

"She'd be good at catching rats, I bet," Robert said. "Even with only one eye. Your father ought to like having a cat around, especially in your horse barn."

Edgar nodded. "That's true." The cat looked up at Edgar and reached a paw up tentatively, eventually touching his chin lightly. The three humans looked at each other and laughed. "I think my mother will be able to convince him to let us keep her. She's got such a soft heart; I don't think she could say no to this. I'll take her home with me and we'll see what we can do." Edgar gently moved the cat from his lap as he and Robert rose again.

Edgar turned to Mrs. Stannard and said, "I hope it's still all right if Robert goes with me next week to make that special delivery for my father. I could really use his help."

"I think we can spare him for a day or two. I understand you plan to stay overnight?"

"Yes. I'd rather make camp in the woods near the estate, but my father says Mr. Tamerlane will have a room prepared for us and we shouldn't risk offending his client by not accepting the offer."

"Not a problem for me," Robert said. "I'll never pass up a soft, warm bed over a bedroll on the cold, wet ground."

"Mr. Stannard and I are glad for Robert to be able to help," Jane said, ruffling her son's hair. "And you should both be proud that Mr. Allan is trusting you to carry out this assignment alone."

"Well, he doesn't have to pay us, which I imagine is the greater motivation," Edgar said. "But speaking of my father, I should be checking in with him at the warehouse, I suppose. He doesn't like for me to be idle too long."

"It is always nice seeing you, Edgar," she said. She looked at Edgar with a sad smile for a moment before turning to go back to the house.

The boys said their goodbyes and Edgar picked the cat up and began his walk home. After a few steps the cat squirmed and leapt down to the ground.

"Oh," Edgar said. "Well, walk then, if you want to be that way. I guess we'll see whether you want to live with me or not." He continued across the Stannards' lawn to the dirt street and the cat followed him with its tail pointing skyward.

"I suppose we ought to find you a name," Edgar said looking down at his new companion as he slowed to match the cat's pace.

Morella.

The feminine voice sounded as clearly as if someone had spoken aloud.

2

"We passed through a range of low arches, descended, passed on, and descending again, arrived at a deep crypt, in which the foulness of the air caused our flambeaux rather to glow than flame."

from *"The Cask of Amontillado"*

Edgar stopped in the road and stared at the cat which then stopped to look up at him.

"Did you just speak to me?"

The cat sat on its haunches and cocked its head as it looked at Edgar curiously. Edgar looked around for anyone who might have spoken the name he had heard so distinctly. Seeing no one nearby, he turned back to the cat and regarded the creature with his eyes narrowed. The thought that he was hearing voices again and might at any moment see things that weren't really there terrified him.

The noise of a carriage approaching snapped him out of his reverie and he stepped quickly out of the road to complete his crossing. As he continued his walk to his father's warehouse, he kept an eye on the cat which followed him as the structures along the way changed from homes to places of business.

I suppose Morella is as good a name as any, he thought as he approached the entrance to the business marked John Allan & Company. Gripping the thick brass doorknob, he paused and turned to the cat which looked expectantly at him.

"It might be best if you waited for me out here." He felt a bit foolish speaking to the cat, but somehow it also felt right to do so. "We need to get my mother on our side before we approach him about allowing you to live with us. I have to find out if Father still wants me to deliver something for him. If you're still here when I come out, I guess we'll go from there."

The cat walked over to a large empty crate with several broken slats which sat against the side of the brick building and after inspecting it, settled herself within it. Edgar stood and stared for a moment at the cat's quick and apparently sentient response, and then turned and entered the shop shaking his head.

Motes of dust floated in the slanted beam of sunlight shining through the large, dusty window at the front of the warehouse. The wheels of a leather-backed chair creaked as its occupant swiveled to see who had entered. John Allan leaned back in the chair and set his pipe beside the book in which he had been entering figures. He pulled on the corners of his vest as he stood to greet his son.

"At last. I thought you might have gotten lost in daydreams of fairies and goddesses and forgotten I had work for you today."

"I didn't forget," Edgar said softly. He looked over to the steps leading to the uninhabited living quarters above the shop and warehouse he knew so well. He pictured the small room with a bookcase next to his bed that had housed his first collections of fairy tales and poems. He had lived there with the Allans for several years when they were not in England, before John had inherited a sizable fortune from his uncle, a fellow Scot.

I still miss that room in a way.

Edgar's father flipped through a thick folder as he stepped around one of many stacks of crates in the large room. He stopped, withdrew a paper, and handed it to Edgar.

"Ernest Montresor has already paid me for a cask of special wine I thought I might never be rid of. He'll tell you where he wants the wine to go, but I need for you to be sure to have him sign this receipt of delivery. You shouldn't need the wagon; the hand truck will be sufficient since his shop is only a few blocks from here."

"Yes, the apothecary's," Edgar said. "I know the place."

Mr. Allan pursed his lips as he looked at Edgar. "Yes, I should think so. Your mother certainly frequented the shop enough on your behalf. Always a cough, an earache, a sore throat..."

Mr. Allan reached into his pocket and withdrew a set of keys on a ring. "When you finish, bring the hand truck back, of course, but I'll need you to lock up here. I'm going to the house shortly." Before he set the keys in Edgar's outstretched hand, he looked his son sternly in the eye. "Can I count on you to do all this?"

"Yes, of course," Edgar said.

Mr. Allan continued to study Edgar before handing him the keys. When he finally did, he slid his hands into his trouser pockets and, after pausing thoughtfully for a few seconds, looked Edgar in the eye and said in a softer voice, "I believe I can, Edgar. Not so long ago, this business was known as Ellis & Allan. I look forward to the day when we change the name again, this time to Allan and Son." Edgar looked down at his hands and swallowed hard before looking back up. He was relieved when his father walked over to the hook on the wall beside the entrance where his black frock coat and hat were hung. Rather than putting the coat on, he draped it over one arm and donned the top hat. He turned to Edgar as he opened the door to leave.

"I'll take care of everything," Edgar said with a small nod and an even smaller smile. His father nodded in acknowledgement and left. Edgar put the key ring in his pocket and walked to the back of the front section of the warehouse and through a door which led to another larger area where additional crates and boxes were stored, including the cask of wine Edgar had heard his father complain of on numerous occasions. The wooden hand truck Mr. Allan had mentioned was leaning against the far wall beside the wagon Edgar would not need for this trip.

That's one thing I can be grateful for, Edgar thought. Going to get a horse from their barn, hitching it up, delivering the wine, and then reversing the whole process would be a cumbersome chore, to say the least. *This should be fairly easy.*

Edgar was able to maneuver the cask onto the hand truck with little trouble and worked his way back through the shop to the front door. After he rolled the cask through the front door, he was pleased to see the black cat still sitting on the crate beside the alley.

"Good to see you're still here," Edgar hesitated before saying the name. "...Morella." He waited with raised eyebrows to see how the cat responded. The cat's only acknowledgement was to blink.

"Well then," Edgar said, unsure whether he felt relief or disappointment. "Shall we be off?"

As Edgar rolled the hand cart to Mr. Montresor's, he was grateful that in this section of town the roads were well-maintained. He had little trouble rolling the heavy cask over the hard-packed road with his new companion following along closely. Within a few minutes and only one turn onto a side street, the sign marking the apothecary shop came into view.

"It might be best if you waited––," but before Edgar could finish, the cat had curled up inside an empty fruit box set against the wall of the building. As at Edgar's father's warehouse, an alley ran beside the apothecary shop. The doorway to this shop, however, was not wide enough to accommodate the cask. He hated to leave it outside, but there seemed to be little choice.

I'll watch it for you.

The feminine voice sounded as clear as it had the first time.

Edgar looked up and down the street but the nearest likely speaker was a burly, bearded man in a bloody apron across the street who was far too busy unloading meat into his butcher shop to have even noticed Edgar.

"Did...did you speak to me?" he asked, looking at the cat. The cat blinked at him once more, and then he heard the female voice again although the cat scarcely twitched a whisker.

I said I'd watch the wine for you.

"I don't...did you...I..." Edgar shut his mouth and clinched his eyes for a moment and then opened them as he tried to gather himself.

For someone who wants to be a writer, you seem to have a surprising difficulty with words.

Edgar's jaw dropped and he stared at the cat with his mouth hanging open. When he had regained his composure somewhat, he searched his surroundings for the human who had to be playing him for a fool. Shaking his finger at the cat he spoke in a voice loud enough for the invisible prankster he felt must be hiding nearby as he continued to look around. "All right, now! I have seen sideshow performers who can throw their voices very convincingly. You can come out now and show yourself. You've been very amusing, but the joke's getting old now."

Was this ventriloquist in the graveyard, too?

Edgar felt his skin crawl.

The front door of the shop suddenly opened and a bald head with gray eyebrows as thick as feather dusters above dark, beady eyes and a long, pointed nose emerged. Ernest Montresor supported himself by holding onto the door with one hand and a cane in the other. As the rest of his thin frame came into view, Edgar saw that, in spite of the shopkeeper's attempt to be cheerful, any movement resulted in significant pain.

"Ah, I thought I heard someone." He looked at the cask of wine on the hand cart and his expression brightened. "The Amontillado! As I had hoped! Finally, after waiting for so long!" He turned back to Edgar. "You must be Mr. Allan's boy, um...er..." he grimaced and tapped his forehead as he searched for a name.

"Edgar, sir."

"Edgar. Right, right, right. Well, come in, come in. I need your help getting the wine stored as you can see." He gestured at his cane. Edgar followed the old man between two walls of shelves containing hundreds of glass bottles, jars, and canisters until they reached a counter that ran across the width of the shop. Four tall stools sat in front of the counter. Edgar remembered sitting on those more than once over the course of his childhood in Richmond as he waited with his mother for the old apothecary to prepare treatments for the family's ailments.

And not just on my account, he thought. *I wasn't ill more than anyone else.*

More shelves lined the back wall filled with tinctures, ointments, and liquids. A desk and chair sat on the other side of the counter but facing the front of the shop so Montresor could easily greet customers even if he was working in the back. The fact he had greeted Edgar at the door in spite of his present physical difficulty showed his enthusiasm about the Amontillado. Montresor pushed open a gate to go behind the counter where he opened a drawer at his desk and withdrew a ring of keys much like the ones Edgar had in his own pocket.

"My rheumatism has flared up something fierce today. You'd think something in one of these bottles would provide some relief, wouldn't you?" he said, gesturing with his cane at the shelves. "Well, the cobbler's children go barefoot, as they say, so I'll need your help more than ever." He sat with a grunt before continuing his instruction. "You'll have to take the cask down to the cellar for me. The only entrance is from outside, I'm afraid."

"I'm glad to help." Remembering the receipt, he pulled it from his pocket and said, "My father asked if you would sign this statement saying you received the wine."

"Yes, of course," Montresor said, taking the paper from Edgar and pulling his pen from the inkwell. "I wouldn't expect anything less. Your father is a good businessman. As good as they come." Edgar nodded politely and took the signed document.

"The door to the cellar is around the back. I've wished many times the builder, damn his hide, had made it so I could access the cellar without going outside. But if wishes were horses, beggars would ride. Right, my boy?"

Edgar gave a small smile and nodded again.

"You'll need to be careful taking that cask down the steps. I'd hate to lose this Amontillado after waiting so long to procure it. You'll see some other casks down there. You can set it with those. There is a lantern hanging inside the door if you should need it." He handed Edgar a box of matches, and singled out a dark, tarnished key that looked a bit older than the others on the ring and held it up for Edgar to note before placing the ring in Edgar's hand. "Bring these back once you've locked the cellar up."

"Yes, sir," Edgar said. He put the matches and the keys in a different trouser pocket than the ring with the keys to his father's shop. When he stepped out into the warm sunlight, the black cat was still waiting where he had left her.

"So. Morella, is it?" Edgar asked. The cat yawned, then stood and stretched, but Edgar heard no reply. "Well, whether it's Morella, Midnight, or Muffin, we've got a task to do and we'd best get it done." He wheeled the hand truck with the cask down the alley beside the apothecary shop and around the corner of the building where he found a door in the back with a large padlock as Mr. Montresor had indicated. A raven cawed twice, drawing Edgar's attention momentarily to the boughs of a small maple tree behind the shop before it flew away.

The key worked easily in the lock, but when Edgar pulled the door open, he stood in mute amazement at what he saw. Or more accurately, at what he didn't see. Stone steps descended into pitch darkness, more steps than Edgar had ever seen.

This is not right.

Edgar looked back at the cat whose ears were flattened against her skull as she looked into the cellar. Her tail twitched from side to side.

"Did you just speak to me again?"

I don't think you should go down there.

Edgar found himself totally confused. He didn't know which was more disturbing, steps which seemed to go into a bottomless, dark pit, or the confirmation the cat could indeed talk. He looked from the steps to the cat, and then back to the steps again. As he peered down into the darkness, he thought he could see a faint glimmer.

"I think there is a light down there," he said aloud. "Maybe Mr. Montresor forgot to extinguish the lantern the last time he was there." Edgar realized how ludicrous his statement was even as he said it, for hanging on a hook inside the doorway was the unlit oil lantern Montresor had mentioned.

You shouldn't go down there.

Ignoring the voice, Edgar took the lantern and removed the glass chimney in order to light the wick. Once the flame was burning brightly, he replaced the chimney and carefully set the lantern on the top of the cask. The lip on the cask's lid would keep the lantern from falling as long as Edgar was careful. But if the lantern should fall...

Edgar held his breath and slowly eased the hand truck down the first step. The lantern wobbled a bit but sat steadily enough that Edgar felt confident he could safely descend the steps as long as he took his time. Even after a half-dozen steps, Edgar still could not see the bottom. He could make out only three or four steps at a time from the circle of light projecting from the lantern and after counting a dozen more steps, he still could not see the end.

You should go back.

Even though the voice was in Edgar's head, it startled him as much as if someone had shouted.

"Are you down here, too?"

Against my better judgment.

"Then maybe you should go back up. Cats and stairs are not a good combination."

You don't need to tell me that.

Edgar thought of the story Robert had told him about his drunken uncle earlier that day.

"I'm not going to let a little darkness keep me from doing my job. We're bound to be close to the bottom by now."

Edgar continued easing the hand truck down more steps, and then impossibly down even more steps until he finally came to an open space illuminated by two sputtering torches. He settled the hand truck and took a deep breath as he stretched his aching back. His eyes were wide as he examined his surroundings.

This makes no sense, he thought. *How could there be something this far down? And who lit these torches?*

Nothing else occupied the space he had just entered, but a single tunnel with more flaming torches led off into further darkness. Morella crept with her belly barely above the dirt floor toward the entrance of the tunnel. She peered into it with her ears flattened and her tail straight out behind her. She raised her head to sniff the air, and Edgar thought he heard a soft growl. After a few more moments of peering into the darkness, she moved slowly back to the bottom step.

You should leave the cask here and get out of this place.

"Mr. Montresor said I should put this cask with the others, and I don't see any here. I've got to find where those other casks are."

This place is not right. It is not of your world.

Edgar frowned. "What do you mean? How can something––"

"Edgar."

The faint voice speaking Edgar's name echoed from deep within the tunnel so softly he wasn't sure he had heard it. He took the lantern from the cask and stepped toward the entrance.

Think twice, boy. Nothing good is down there.

"But I need to put this cask––"

"Edgar."

"The whispering voice again," Edgar said. "The voice from the crypt." He took one step into the tunnel and stopped when he thought he saw a pale face in the gloom.

Don't do it, Edgar.

Looking back at the cat, Edgar took a deep breath and then turned back and proceeded deeper into the tunnel. He moved slowly, holding the lantern high. Before long the tunnel opened into another chamber somewhat smaller than the one he had just left. Several tunnels splintered off in different directions, some of which were slightly illuminated by more flickering torches in the distance. Choosing one at random, he held the lantern before him at its entrance. Seeing nothing but gloom, not even the hint of light, he moved to another tunnel, which, like the first, stretched into utter darkness. The third appeared the same.

On the fourth try, he saw a pale face grinning at him from out of the gloom. Its body was invisible, and the head was angled as if the creature peered out from an alcove or cave at the side of the tunnel. The horrible grin was so wide that once again it reminded him of a skull. And yet Edgar was also certain he was seeing his own face.

Think about this, Edgar. This place. These tunnels. They could not possibly exist below the apothecary. This is all wrong.

Edgar looked down at the cat who was peering up at him while thrashing her tail back and forth and then he looked back down the tunnel. The face was gone.

"You don't understand. I have to know who this is. Or what he is." Edgar resisted the urge to run toward where he had last seen the face and settled for walking at a brisk pace down that tunnel with the lantern held before him. Morella followed silently.

As Edgar grew closer to where he thought his double had been, the air grew cool and moist. As Edgar strained to hear any sound that might indicate movement, he became conscious of a steady, rhythmic beat from very far away. *The slow drip of water on a barrel, perhaps?* he thought. *Or the tick of a clock's pendulum?* He could not quite make it out. Soft breezes suddenly flowed through the tunnel with whispers like soft breaths that tickled his ear and swept through his hair as his mother's fingers had done to calm him when he was younger. The voices were so soft he caught only fragments of words and phrases;

he could not quite make out what they were saying although they did seem to be varied, both masculine and feminine. Like the mystery of the dungeon itself, or the existence of his secret double, they excited him; he found it all simultaneously thrilling and frightening.

When Edgar reached the spot where he had seen the face, he held the lantern out to examine it more closely. The earthen wall was scooped out to form a small cell, but it was empty.

"Edgar!"

There it was again—that voice. Even though it was but a whisper, it sounded similar to his own, only rougher, almost guttural.

Go back, Edgar. Nothing good awaits you here.

Morella crouched against the far wall, barely visible with the reflection of the torchlight in her wide-opened, singular eye. Edgar spared her only a quick glance and then continued. A woman's mournful cry echoed from further down the tunnel, a cry that seemed to come from worlds away, a lament filled with sorrow but one this time Edgar could understand. It was a cry mingled with sobs mourning a death.

"Oh, God! Oh, Divine Father! Shall this Conqueror be not once conquered?" The last words of the tearful plea faded in a dying echo.

Footsteps sounded further down the tunnel, and Edgar quickly followed them. The breezes continued to caress him with their ghostly fingers, and the whispering continued as well. He passed another empty cell but did not stop since it, too, was empty except for the faintest suggestion of mist, mere wisps of coiling vapors, and the footsteps leading him further away had not ceased.

In addition to the consistent patter of footsteps, the rhythmic sound grew louder, the one that had been present all along but now finally recognized––a heartbeat! The pounding got louder and louder, until it became so loud, he felt it vibrating in his ear, so loud, he had to stop walking. He thought it must be his own heart beating but it continued, increasing in speed, faster and faster, in spite of the fact Edgar no longer hurried down the tunnel himself.

Suddenly the heartbeat stopped.

A mist floated before him and took a vaguely human shape. He heard a faint, distant male voice cry, "Yes, I hear it, and have heard it. Long––long––long have I heard it––oh, pity me, miserable wretch that I am! I dared not––I dared not speak!" The last word of the echoing voice faded into the depths of the tunnel as the mist dissipated. The fear conveyed in the voice heightened Edgar's own anxiety.

That's not my double, Edgar thought, *but who is it?*

The footsteps resumed, and despite his near-paralyzing fear, Edgar did not hesitate to follow them. He had not noted Morella's presence for some time, but he sensed it might not be wise to call out to her and alert whatever forces lurked in the tunnel to her presence.

She can fend for herself better than I can.

He passed more cells on either side of the tunnel; some contained objects he thought might be bones, but he pushed those thoughts from his mind and pressed on. He stopped and caught his breath when one cell appeared to have a full skeleton held up onto the wall by chains. It wore the remnants of what looked to have once been a multi-colored costume, like something worn by a clown or jester. When Edgar directed the light from his lantern on it, the bones, the rags, and the shackles all disappeared like evaporating smoke. A faint cry, hardly louder than the whispers he could not make out faded with it, but it sounded as if the cry might have been, "For the love of God, Montresor!" accompanied by the faintest sound of tinkling bells.

Edgar leaned against the damp wall of the tunnel and closed his eyes. He took a moment to breathe slowly and collect himself before moving on. In the silence that followed, Edgar turned away from the cell with the ghostly image and held the lantern aloft. He saw that the tunnel took an abrupt turn a short distance away. Then he heard new noises, not footsteps, but rather a sound like someone scraping mud. The sound of the racing heartbeat had stopped some time before, but he could feel his own heart pounding in his chest as if it might burst. Slowly he stepped forward into the tunnel and made the turn. He was surprised to see the tunnel ended abruptly as the walls narrowed into one last cell. Within that cell sat casks similar to the one he had delivered.

Edgar entered the cell and knelt to examine what looked like writing on one of the casks. As he did, he felt a metal clasp close around his ankle followed by the distinct sound of it locking. He turned back to face the entrance to the cell and there before him was the spectral figure he had seen in the crypt. His phantom twin stood there grinning at him. Edgar took a step toward the boy, but the shackle around his ankle bit into the flesh. Edgar realized he was bound as surely as any prisoner in a castle dungeon.

"What are you doing?" Edgar yelled. "Let me go!"

The shadowed figure took a step toward him, and Edgar saw that it held a brick out before him in one hand and a trowel in the other, as if showing Edgar a special treat. His dark alter ego said nothing as he lay the brick down near the opening to the cell. He smiled with the same tilt of his head that had unnerved Edgar in the crypt and then set the trowel down to fetch more bricks from a large pile of them Edgar had not noticed in the gloom and laid them across the entrance to the cell.

"Who are you? Why are you doing this?"

"So many questions," the dark reflection said in the soft, hoarse voice that had frightened Edgar in the graveyard. He grinned as Edgar lunged at him, but the chain securing Edgar in the cell was not long enough to allow him to reach the creature. His doppelgänger fetched more bricks and added them to the line, then picked up the trowel and scooped mortar from the pile beside the bricks. He began a second tier, securing it with the mortar, and a shiver traveled up Edgar's spine as he realized what the villain was doing. Edgar looked for something, another tool or a rock he could throw at his tormentor but he saw only casks which were much too heavy to be used as weapons.

"This is madness," Edgar cried. "What have I done to you to make you wish me harm?"

Edgar's double simply grinned at him and continued his task of enclosing the cell. Edgar pulled and pulled on the chain, but it held fast to the ring that secured it in the stone of the cell floor.

When the tier was nearly waist high, Edgar heard a cat's hiss and a loud snarling howl followed by a thump. Then all was quiet. Edgar saw his own face grinning back at him again as the shade twin continued his task of building the wall.

"What did you do?" Edgar whispered, fearing the worst.

"It's a dangerous place for kitties. They need to keep an eye out for trouble down here." He stopped scraping mortar and looked at Edgar and smiled even wider. "But then, I guess this cat had already done that." He laughed and continued adding more bricks.

The wall grew quickly, casting Edgar into even darker gloom. His mind raced as he frantically searched for something he could do, but there was nothing. The chain held fast; it would not break. He collapsed onto the dirt and sat with his arms crossed over his raised knees and his head on his arms and wept.

Before long, Edgar's shade had only one last brick to place before Edgar would be completely sealed up within his newly made tomb. He could see only his jailer's hands as they placed the stones and patted the mortar into place. As the last brick blotted out the feeble, remaining light, Edgar heard his double's laughter growing. It got louder and louder without ceasing. Edgar put his hands over his ears.

"Stop!" he pleaded. "Isn't it enough that you've sealed me up? Must you torture me with your laughing too?" The laughter became so loud, it seemed it might bring down the cavernous walls and ceiling. "Stop it, you fiend!" Edgar screamed. But the laughter grew even louder, echoing off the walls of the chamber so that it sounded like an army of Edgars.

Edgar felt fear as he had never experienced it before, a claustrophobic fear in the darkness that welled up in him, drowning him, like an ocean of blood filling the cell until his mind could take no more and he collapsed into the void.

When Edgar opened his eyes, he was confused about where he was. He felt at first that he should be in his bed in Moldavia, the Allan mansion on Main Street in Richmond. When he realized he lay upon a hard stone floor, the horror of being imprisoned behind the brick wall returned to him, but he realized as he sat up and looked at his surroundings there was light in this space. Sunlight poured through the doorway at the top of the steps, enough to illuminate the entire cellar whose dimensions were no larger than the shop above it.

The cellar itself was nothing like he remembered. There were no tunnels or torches on the walls. The steps were not excessive in number, no more than a dozen at most. The cellar's only contents were crates arranged neatly along the wall where Edgar had thought a tunnel led out, with wine casks stored against the left wall just as Mr. Montresor had said, including the Amontillado he had brought.

This makes no sense. Where did everything go--the tunnels, the torches? And Morella? Did I imagine her too? Was that cat ever with me? Did I dream that part, as well?

Edgar rubbed his eyes and stood to survey the cellar more closely. He walked around the edges of the room, running his hands over the walls. He found no sign of any doorways, no hidden passageways, no sign of holders for the torches.

It wasn't a dream.

Edgar spun to face the steps and saw the black cat sitting on the bottom step.

"You can hear my thoughts?" Edgar asked aloud.

I can, but it's easier if you speak. Following your thoughts is like keeping kittens in line.

Edgar turned to survey the cellar again and raised both arms out to his sides.

"What...what happened?"

It's difficult to explain.

"Were you hurt?"

I have many lives.

"He...whoever...*whatever* that is...*killed* you?"

Morella moved from the step to rub against Edgar's leg and then hopped up onto a cask where she sat sphynx-like with her tail curled around herself.

I was making a joke. I was knocked unconscious when I tried to help you but, as you see, I recovered. But in truth, we all have many lives. You too.

"I don't understand."

It is difficult to explain. But you should get the hand truck back to your father's warehouse before he wonders where you are.

"Yes, you're right," Edgar said. He turned in a circle and noticed for the first time that the hand truck was missing. "But where is it?" Edgar flapped his hands to his sides in frustration, and patted the pockets on either side that had held the two sets of keys.

"The warehouse keys! They're gone! I have only Mr. Montresor's keys." Edgar looked frantically on the ground where he had been lying. "I had the other set in my right pocket, but now they're gone too. My father will be so angry! I've got to find them!"

Edgar searched the floor of the cellar carefully, even moving the casks and crates to search behind each of them, but his father's keyring was not to be found.

Perhaps they fell out of your pocket on our way here from your house. We can search on our way back.

Edgar nodded, but his face showed his doubt and his anxiety. Morella followed him up the stairs and watched as Edgar extinguished the lantern and replaced it on its hook. Edgar then closed and locked the cellar door relieved to be outside once again despite his anxiety about the missing keys.

"Will you wait here for me while I return Mr. Montresor's keys?" Edgar asked.

Of course.

When Edgar entered the shop, he saw Mr. Montresor dozing at his desk. A small blue bottle sat open beside him. *Hopefully he's found some relief for his rheumatism,* Edgar thought. *I guess there are advantages to being an apothecary.* He pulled the key ring from his pocket and jingled them a bit as he approached the counter so he might awaken the old man without startling him. The old man gave a loud snort and sat up in his chair.

"Hmmm? What? What's that?" He looked about the room, slightly dazed from his abrupt awakening. "Oh, the Allan boy. Yes, yes. Got that cask all secured, I suppose?" He brushed his hands down the front of his shirt and straightened his vest. Noting the open bottle, he picked up the small cork beside it and stopped it up.

"Yes, sir. It's all squared away with the other casks." Edgar reached across the counter and set the keys on the desk. He crossed his arms across his chest and shifted his weight from one foot to the next, anxious to be on his way. "Is there anything else I can do for you?"

"No, no, good job, lad. I'll be sure to tell your father you performed your task admirably. I do wish I had thought to pour a bit of that Amontillado into a decanter before you took it down, but my thinking's a bit fuzzy today." He slipped the bottle into his pocket.

"I suppose I'll be off then. Good day, Mr. Montresor." When Edgar had made his way about halfway across the shop, he stopped and turned back to the old apothecary.

"I do have one question for you, if you don't mind, sir."

"Yes?"

"Were there ever tunnels under this house?"

"Tunnels? No, no, nothing like that. Tunnels. What an idea! I've certainly never heard of such. Why?"

"No reason, really. I, uh, I just thought it would certainly have been a good place for, um, buried treasure, or a robber's hiding place." He paused briefly, and then added, "Or a murderer to bury a victim."

"Oh, my! Well, your father did say you have quite an imagination. But nothing like that, most certainly."

"Yes. Well, I thought I'd ask. Have a good day, Mr. Montresor. I hope you're feeling better soon."

Edgar exited the shop and rejoined Morella who was patiently waiting where he had left her.

"That was fortunate," Edgar said as they walked toward Main Street. "Mr. Montresor had fallen asleep so he wasn't aware of how long I'd taken to store the wine. But my father will be furious when he realizes the warehouse isn't locked up and I've lost the keys." The cat followed silently, her gaze directed at a raven who flitted from tree to tree along the avenue as if it were tracking them.

Within a quarter of an hour, he and Morella approached the front entrance to Moldavia. Edgar paused as Morella eyed him curiously.

"About you living here with us. It might be best if I go in alone first to assess my father's mood."

I can amuse myself. There are plenty of mice here, I am certain. But I wouldn't turn away from a saucer of milk and a bit of sausage.

Edgar smiled wanly, but his anxiety increased as he mounted the steps and crossed the large, covered front porch, pausing before entering the house to watch his new feline friend hop onto a wide railing. Before Edgar could open the front door, his father emerged.

"Ah, Edgar!" he said with a smile, quite uncharacteristically to Edgar's mind. "I thought I'd take a short walk before dinner." As he crossed the porch, he spied Morella on the railing, and asked not unkindly, "What have we here?" Edgar was surprised to find his father in such extraordinarily good humor, but decided to address the issue of providing a home for the cat before owning up to the disaster of the lost keys. *Best to strike while the iron is hot,* he thought.

My thoughts exactly.

Edgar jumped slightly and then eyed his father to see if Mr. Allan had heard Morella's response. Noting that his father simply waited for a response, he answered.

"Um, well, this cat has been abandoned, it seems. It has been visiting the Stannards, and they have been feeding it. They say it's a really good rat-catcher, in spite of only having one eye." Mr. Allan stepped over and held his hand out to Morella. She sniffed his fingers and then rubbed her face against his hand, purring loudly. Mr. Allan ran his hand down her sleek fur. Encouraged by their interaction, Edgar continued. "They'd like to keep it, but Mr. Stannard has an allergy that won't allow it." He paused and drew a breath for the big question. "Mrs. Stannard thought maybe we would take it."

"Mrs. Stannard thought so," Mr. Allan said with a knowing smile.

Edgar smiled back sheepishly. "Well, I was hoping so too."

"We could use a good mouser," Edgar's father said. "Let's regard this as a reward for you doing such a good job today."

Edgar offered his father a tight-lipped smile, the most his guilt would allow. He drew a breath as he prepared to address his failure, dreading how his father would react. Before he could speak, his father continued.

"I especially appreciate how you carried out this assignment today, Edgar. You did exactly as I asked, promptly and efficiently. It gives me confidence in sending you on the special delivery to Frederick Tamerlane's next week."

Edgar's frown grew even deeper, the reason for which his father misinterpreted.

"Surely you haven't forgotten about that already?"

"No. No, sir. I haven't."

Before Edgar could say more, his father stepped down onto the first step. As he did so, he put his hands in his pockets as he was wont to do when walking, and Edgar heard a metallic jingling. "Oh, that reminds me," his father said, turning back to Edgar while reaching into his pocket. "Would you put these back in my desk for me?" He withdrew the ring containing the warehouse keys and handed them to Edgar. "I forgot to put them away after you gave them to me earlier."

Edgar's gaze went from his father's retreating back to the keys in his hand. A loud corvid call from a crow or raven carried across the yard from the boughs of the old oak whose branches shaded the porch. To Edgar it sounded like laughter.

3

Robert stroked the cat napping beside him on the folded blanket in the back of the wagon and fought the urge to fall asleep himself. He sat with his back against the side of the wagon and his feet pushing against one of the two crates that took up most of the space. Noting how Edgar gathered the reins in one hand and rubbed his eyes with the other, he said, "I can take over for a bit if you'd like."

Edgar turned to look at his friend and smiled before returning his gaze to the horse in front of him. "I'm good for now, thanks. We can take a break, though, if you'd like to stretch your legs. It's still a few hours before we get to Tamworth. And Pluto could use some water, I imagine." The horse snorted as if in agreement.

"My legs are good but my bladder might be grateful for a stop," Robert said.

"Mine, too. There's a stand of trees ahead with a stream for Pluto."

After Edgar had directed the wagon onto the grassy patch beside the road, he remained on the driver's seat as he waited for Robert to return to the wagon before taking his turn. He watched a raven fly from a branch of a birch to another tree deeper into the stand. Morella lifted her head and blinked her one eye as she inspected their new surroundings, then stood, yawned, and stretched before turning around twice and settling herself back into the folds of the blanket. Robert returned buttoning his trousers and took the reins from Edgar and climbed up to take his place on the driver's seat as Edgar hopped down and got the pail from the back before walking to the stand of trees.

After relieving himself, Edgar picked up the pail and made his way to the stream. Over the gurgling of the water as it filled the pail, he heard movement behind him. He rose from kneeling and was surprised to find Robert was not there. At the edge of his vision, he sensed a blur; a dark shape slipped into the shadow behind one of the trunks further out. He froze and stared at the area carefully.

"Hello?"

Robert called back from the wagon in a mocking voice. "What's the matter, Edgar? You need help finding it?"

Ignoring his friend, Edgar walked to the tree where he thought he had seen something move. When he got there, he saw nothing, no sign anyone had been there at all. He turned in a circle to survey the whole area, then slowly made his way back to the wagon, throwing an occasional backwards glance as he went.

"What's the matter?" Robert asked.

"I thought I saw someone." Edgar looked out into the trees as he set the pail of water before Pluto.

"Your double again?" Robert's voice gave no hint of mockery this time.

Edgar shook his head. "I don't know. I couldn't see them very clearly. Don't know if I even saw anyone at all, to tell the truth."

"We can both take a closer look if you want."

Edgar stared a bit longer and then took a big breath. "No, let's not waste any more time over something I may have just imagined. I'd like to get to the Tamerlanes before dark if we can. Let's move on." He emptied the rest of the water on the ground, returned the pail to the back of the wagon and jumped up beside Robert on the driver's seat.

Robert clicked his tongue and popped the reins causing Pluto to snort and shake his head as he pulled the wagon back onto the road. Edgar turned to check on Morella, who jumped over the back of the seat and made herself comfortable in Edgar's lap. She gazed up at Edgar's face and looked him directly in the eyes.

It was him.

Edgar's frown deepened, and he inspected the landscape carefully as they moved along. They traveled for several moments before Robert spoke.

"What exactly do you think is going on?"

Edgar waited before speaking, and looked at Morella when he finally did.

"I wish I knew."

"That business at the apothecary's," Robert said, keeping his eyes on the road before them, the reins now loose in his hands. "Are you sure you didn't dream all that?"

"How did my father get the keys to the warehouse if I dreamed it?" Edgar said.

Robert shrugged. "Maybe, you simply don't remember giving them to him. Maybe you were, I don't know, sleepwalking."

Morella turned to stare at Robert.

He's an idiot.

Edgar chuckled in spite of himself.

"What?" Robert said, his voice rising. "It's possible. More possible than what you described. I mean, those voices? And the skeletons? Another Edgar sealing you up in the wall?"

"Yes, it's much more likely," Edgar agreed. "All I know is I wasn't sleeping. I can't explain how it all happened; I just know it did."

"Whatever you say, my friend," Robert said, the doubt evident in his voice. After a brief awkward silence, he raised his face to the sky. "I don't much like the way those clouds are gathering."

Edgar noted the dark band stretching across the horizon. "Let's hope we don't have to use our rain gear.

Edgar's hopes were to no avail. By the time the wagon approached the entrance to the Tamerlane estate, a steady rain dripped from the brims of their oilskin hats and ran in rivulets down their coats. Morella huddled in the back within a shelter of blankets Edgar had stretched across the bags which held the boys' extra clothes and provisions. They had been traveling through a forest of sickly trees in near darkness for the last quarter hour, and neither boy could recall the last time they had seen or heard signs of wildlife.

As they crested a small hill, a roofline consisting of at least a dozen gables came into view as the blighted trees around them thinned into a clearing, and gradually the entire house was visible in the fading light. Two still ponds sat on either side of the road that led to the house and outbuildings, giving the impression the house sat on an island.

There is great evil here.

Edgar looked into the back of the wagon to find Morella looking back at him. As if he had heard the cat's silent communication, Robert said, "I don't know about this place, Edgar."

"At least we have refuge from the rain," Edgar said. "We'll deliver these crates, get a warm dinner and a dry bed and be back on the road in the morning."

As they slogged their way through the muddy road, bouncing on the hard seat of the wagon, they both noted the many broken tombstones leaning on either side of the road.

"That's certainly a cheery entrance any family would love," Robert said as he guided the wagon between the two ponds. "I wonder if there are alligators in this moat." Edgar shook his head but smiled at Robert's attempt to make light of their situation.

"My father said not to expect servants here," Edgar said as he pointed to a broken structure that might once have served as a carriage house. "From what he told me, Mr. Tamerlane lives alone here with his sister." Robert gave Edgar a quizzical look, which Edgar responded to with a simple shrug. "Let's store the wagon and see if we can get Pluto fed and secured. Then we can look for Mr. Tamerlane."

Morella had followed them into the carriage house and watched from a nearly dilapidated counter running along parts of one wall. After unhitching the horse, they found a stall suitable for him and spied a pile in a darkened corner that appeared to be sacks of feed. As they approached it, several large rats squealed and scattered in different directions. Grimacing, he attempted to lift the top bag which disintegrated in his grip, spilling its rotted contents on the dirt floor. He dug further into the pile until he saw some feed he thought would be acceptable, and using a rusty trowel, scooped some into a trough at the head of the stall.

"I saw a pump on our way in," Robert said, holding a bucket he had found. "I'll see to Pluto."

"Good. I'll get our gear." Edgar walked to the back of the wagon and pulled both bags out and set them on the ground near Morella.

"Not the best accommodations out here, I'm afraid," Edgar said.

Not to worry. I have no intention of sleeping here.

"But our hosts may not——"

They'll never know I'm there.

Edgar raised one eyebrow then nodded.

"So, are we ready to make our way to the house now?" Robert asked, wiping his hands together in a fruitless attempt to clean them. He grabbed his bag as Edgar took his. Morella ceased licking her fur long enough to watch as the boys stepped back out into the rain to make their way to the massive stone house.

Rain poured in torrents from the many eaves and caused small rivers for the boys to wade through as they made their trek to the large, oaken door. They passed places where rooms jutted outward rather than following a single plane, a feature that added to the singularity of the mansion's architecture. As Edgar looked up to see how many floors the house contained, a brilliant flash of lightning seared the image of a snarling gargoyle against the gray sky into his brain. Immediately a blast of thunder shook the ground, and Edgar feared the massive structure might crumble and crush him right there. He stood for a second, dazed, as he gathered his wits.

"Good thing my pants are already soaked," Robert said behind him, "since I'm fairly sure I just made them even wetter."

Together they made their way to the portico before the main entrance to the house, grateful for the respite the covering gave them from the torrential rain. They climbed the stone steps to the front door but, before Edgar could lift the large iron ring to announce their arrival, the door opened. A pale face with a halo of wispy, blonde hair floating around his head glowed in the darkness of the house like a ghost. His beard appeared as unkempt as his hair, as if it had not seen a comb in days or weeks. He wore a robe of rich, dark fabric with a long, soft gray scarf wound around his neck and tucked into the front of the robe. The loose-fitting trousers which showed below the small expanse from the robe to the floor seemed to Edgar like something possibly worn in India. He wore soft slippers rather than shoes, which made Edgar wonder how often he stepped outside, if ever.

"Young Mr. Allan, I presume?"

"Um, actually it's Poe, sir. Edgar Poe. John Allan is my adoptive father. And this is Robert Stannard, my friend who was gracious enough to offer to help me with the delivery of your, uh..." Edgar stuttered, realizing he could not identify the contents they had brought. "...with the delivery."

"Yes. Well. About that. I certainly want to get you boys out of this weather but first, I'm afraid, I need your help. I have no servants and..." his voice trailed off. "I need your help in getting those crates inside." He looked down at his frail form and gestured weakly at Edgar and Robert. "I'm afraid my health––"

"Certainly," Edgar said, cheerfully. "We can do that. Where shall we put them?"

"They'll need to go in my cellar; there's another entrance around the back of the house. I'll go through and open it from inside and meet you there."

"Fine. They're rather large, as I'm sure you know," Edgar said. "It will take both of us to move one. We'll have to bring them in one at a time."

"I understand," Mr. Tamerlane said. "Once we get them inside, I'll need your help to unpack them. I hope you don't mind."

"Not at all," Edgar said. He looked down and water poured from his hat onto the stone floor. He smiled at Frederick Tamerlane. "We'll meet you around back then."

"No servants," Robert said when they were out of hearing. "I guess that means no one will be warming bath water for us. And I was so looking forward to a hot soak to take the chill from my bones."

"Getting dried out before a fire and getting food in my belly will be good enough for me." Another flash of light and roar of thunder made both boys jump, and they broke into a jog to the carriage house. They found that although the crates were by no means light, they could manage one crate between the two of them easily enough. The boxes were about six feet long and two feet in height. They carried the first box sideways between them so neither had to walk backwards on the unknown terrain.

"It would have to be a mansion," Robert grumbled as they wound their way through the rain and around to the back of the house.

Eventually they saw a mound with two doors thrown back to reveal several steps leading down under the house. A light flickered in the darkness and they saw their host was far enough within to be out of the worst of the rain. He motioned them in and they stepped down into a cellar larger than anything Edgar had ever seen before.

"It's like a dungeon in a castle," Robert said as Edgar winced at the thoughtlessness of his words.

The room did have the looks of what Edgar imagined a dungeon would resemble. Thick columns stood throughout, stretching up to a vaulted ceiling. Stone arches led off to other rooms whose contents were too dark to discern. Frederick Tamerlane held a lantern and gestured to an area against one wall. "You can put them both here," Frederick said. Once they had set the crate where their host had indicated, they exited the cellar to fetch the other crate.

"What do you suppose is in these boxes?" Robert asked.

"I have no idea. But I think we're about to find out."

When they had fetched the other crate and placed it beside its fellow, Robert took a towel from a pile he found in a basket near the door and wiped up their muddy footprints from the steps and started to clean up the mess from around the crates as well.

"You can leave that," Frederick said. "But I do have one last task for you. If you could unpack these for me, I would be so grateful." He held out a hammer and a crowbar suitable for prying open the crates.

Edgar took the tools and set to work prying apart the boards of the first crate. Within a matter of minutes, the boys found to their amazement they had delivered an elaborately decorated coffin. And judging from the similarity of the crates, most likely, two coffins.

"I procured these with your father's help," Frederick said looking at Edgar. "When I was in better health." He ran his fingers lightly over the embossed carved image of ivy entwined with skulls on the one nearest him. "I fear I've depleted the last of our inheritance in getting them. Our family has long used the best Italian craftsmen to make our sepulchers and caskets. My sister and I are the last of our line, so it seemed only right we continue the tradition." Edgar and Robert could think of nothing to say in reply and stood in awkward silence for a moment before Edgar started in on the second crate. The revealed coffin matched the one Edgar had unpacked.

"If you would, I'd like to have these placed with the others."

Others?

A chill raced up Edgar's spine, but he nodded to Robert who looked at Edgar with wide eyes, and they went to opposite ends of the coffin they had unpacked and lifted it by handles located on each end. Frederick led them through the dark cellar and into one of the adjacent rooms with his lantern held high before him. As the light illuminated the room, Edgar saw each wall had a number of niches carved out, several of which contained coffins. Frederick made his way to two of the empty spaces, one above the other, and rested his hand on the upper one.

"Perhaps the first one here," he said. The boys set the coffin on the dusty floor briefly and readjusted their grips in order to better lift the coffin shoulder high and then into the niche. Once they had slid it into place, they followed Frederick back into the main room to fetch the second coffin.

"I can't thank you enough," Frederick said once both coffins had been placed in their respective resting places. The light from the candle flickered across his wan face, creating shadows that made his face seem cadaverous in spite of his faint smile. "I imagine you'd like to get out of those wet clothes. I'll show you to the room you'll be sharing tonight and then you can join me in my study where we can have our dinner, such as it is." When Frederick saw the boys shoot a questioning look at each other, he explained further. "As I said, I have no servants, but the parson's wife has been bringing some food each week since..." He paused. "Since recent developments." He turned and began an ascent up a stairway before the boys could ask further questions.

Frederick paused when they reached the first floor in what appeared to be a large foyer where two candles made a feeble attempt to push back the darkness. He pointed to an open doorway in which another faint light flickered. "That is my study. After you've changed, you can join me there for what repast I can offer." He then continued up the stairs, and the boys followed after exchanging mutual worried looks.

The stairs continued up to yet another level, but Frederick turned to enter a very dark hallway on the second floor. Edgar tried to peer past his host to see how many rooms the hallway contained, but Frederick stopped at the first doorway and entered, which threw the hallway into even more darkness. Light flickered across the room as Frederick crossed to the mantle above a large, empty fireplace where another lantern sat. As Frederick worked to light the second lantern, Edgar and Robert examined the room where they would be spending the night. One large four-poster bed jutted out from the wall to their left. Heavy curtains on the wall opposite the doorway suggested a large window might offer some relief from the blackness of the room which otherwise enveloped them like a cloak. A pitcher and basin sat on a bedside table. Two matching portraits of a stern-faced man and woman in Puritan attire were barely visible above the mantle; the dim candlelight made the faces appear more ghoulish than human.

With the second lantern lit, Frederick walked back to the doorway and turned to face the boys. "Once you are comfortable, please make your way to the study where you'll find the fruit and bread I've left. I'll hopefully be awaiting you there but, first, I must see to my sister." The boys stood in silence as he exited and listened as Frederick's soft footsteps faded on the stairway before speaking.

"What on earth have you gotten me into, Edgar?" Robert asked in a low voice.

"I have no idea. But regardless, I'm glad you're here."

When the boys had changed into dry clothes and draped their damp items over the few pieces of furniture in the room to dry, Edgar took the lantern from the mantle and moved toward the door. "Wait," Robert called. Robert searched the drawer in the small stand by the bed and held up a box of matches. "In case ours are wet."

Edgar nodded.

A rare demonstration of foresight.

Edgar flinched at the voice in his mind.

"Morella?"

The cat sat on its haunches on the bed with her eyes narrowed and tail twitching.

"How'd you get in here?" Edgar asked. He approached the bed and reached out to stroke the cat's head.

You left the cellar door open. Fortunately.

"Maybe Mr. Frederick let her in," Robert suggested.

And back to imbecile so quickly. Morella rubbed against Edgar's leg and purred.

"Stay close to us, girl," Edgar said as he reached down to stroke her back. "But maybe stay out of Mr. Tamerlane's sight if you can. He may not want cats inside the house."

In this dark house that will be easy to do.

"Let's go down," Robert said, tapping on the doorframe impatiently. "I'm starving."

The boys closed the door behind them and quickly made their way downstairs to the study. The light from the lantern they brought with them added enough illumination to see an extensive library of books lining the walls. Several unframed paintings were tacked onto some of the shelves around the room. An easel set up in another dark corner of the study with the beginnings of another image on its canvas suggested at least one of the Tamerlanes was the creator of the paintings.

Edgar crossed over to examine the one closest to him. The face was easily recognizable as Frederick's due to the wild, thin hair and sparse beard sprinkled liberally with streaks of gray and the gaunt, sunken cheeks. The dark, hollow eyes pleaded to the viewer for release from immeasurable suffering. Across the room, Robert looked at a portrait of a woman, most likely Angeline, Frederik's sister. She looked as miserable as her brother, but even more emaciated.

"Why would Mr. Tamerlane have painted her this way?" Robert asked. "Why not show her as she must have been in better health? She was likely a beautiful woman."

Edgar shook his head. "Maybe it was a self-portrait," he said. "I wonder how recently they were painted." He held the lantern up to examine the next one more closely, and what he saw made him catch his breath. The painting was dark––as dark as the hallways they had been walking, with dashes of paint only slightly paler to indicate dozens of long, ghostly faces peeking around corners and out of doorways.

"That's this house," Robert whispered over Edgar's shoulder. Edgar nodded silently and then moved the lantern over to examine the painting on the easel with Robert close behind. Although it was unfinished, there was little doubt due to the screaming faces within the mad slashes of red, yellow, and orange of the artist's intent. "That's Hell," Robert said even more quietly than he had spoken before. He pointed out two of the faces and added, "And there are the Tamerlanes again." Edgar released the breath he hadn't realized he'd been holding and, turning his back to the paintings, shined the light on the rest of the room in hopes of seeing something less disturbing. Edgar noted a bust of the goddess Athena in a small alcove over the doorway.

Seems like her brother Apollo might have been the more appropriate choice given Mr. Tamerlane's interest in the arts.

Edgar lowered the lantern; the light reflected in Morella's eye, revealing her safe space under another worn, stuffed chair. Edgar raised an eyebrow at his feline companion, surprised by the cat's erudition. Morella stared at him and blinked slowly.

Further examination revealed a guitar displayed in a stand in the corner, while a harpsichord, its keys covered in dust, was situated across from a large writing desk. Both supported Morella's observation of Frederick's tastes. A decanter partially filled with a dark liquid sat beside two glasses on the desk. Two couches formed a right angle with a stuffed, worn, high-backed chair between them which completed the sitting area. A bowl of fruit and a platter of bread sat next to a pitcher and two more glasses on a low table in the midst of the couches and chairs.

"At last," Robert said, grabbing an apple from the bowl.

"Maybe we should wait for--"

"Achhh!" Robert spit the bit of apple he had bitten off into his hand. "This apple is rotten." He crossed to the empty fireplace and flung the sodden piece into it. Edgar looked more closely at the remaining fruit.

"Looks like it's all been here for a while," he said. He tore off a chunk of bread and sniffed it. "The bread is a bit stale, but I think it's probably fine." He popped it into his mouth while Robert warily tore off a piece for himself. "So much for a meal to warm our bellies." He gestured to Robert and smiled. "Bon appétit, mon ami."

There are plenty of mice.

Morella hopped up onto the seat of the chair and turned about in a circle, preparing to settle herself when she stopped suddenly and stared at the doorway. With her ears flared back she jumped down and crept into the shadow under the harpsichord. Soon the boys heard the sound of Frederick's slow, slippered footfalls on the stairs, and then he stood before them in the doorway. His hair stood out in even more disarray than it had previously, and his mouth hung agape. He looked about the room, but he seemed to be seeing nothing.

"Mr. Tamerlane? Are you all right?" Edgar asked.

Frederick turned to face Edgar and looked at him vacantly, as if he didn't know who Edgar was, or even where he was. Taking his distraught host by the elbow, Edgar guided him to one of the stuffed chairs. He sat on the couch near him and Robert placed himself beside Edgar.

"She...she's gone," Frederick said.

"Your sister?" Edgar asked. Frederick didn't answer, but stared into the space before him. Turning to Robert, he pointed to the desk and said, "Pour him a glass of whatever's in that decanter." Robert did, and Edgar took the glass from him and after sniffing it, offered it to Frederick. "Perhaps a bit of brandy, Mr. Tamerlane?"

Frederick took a sip and closed his eyes. A tear ran down his cheek.

"I knew it would be soon," he said, seeming to address the room rather than Edgar or Robert, "but I didn't think..." He shook his head.

"I'm so sorry," Edgar said. "If there's anything Robert and I can do..."

Frederick looked at Edgar as if just then noticing him. He nodded and took another sip of brandy. He took a deep breath and let it out in a long, shuddering exhalation. "I will need help," he said. "We'll need to take her to the cellar."

Edgar looked at Robert, who looked back with eyes as wide as saucers.

"Shouldn't we get a doctor?"

"There's no need," Frederick said. "I know she's gone. You'll see. The doctor was here only days ago. He said she would not last long, but I thought she had longer."

"What was her illness?" Robert asked. "Is it safe for us to--"

"It's all right," Edgar interrupted, quieting Robert with a look of disapproval. "We'll help you. But we should check on her."

Frederick nodded. "I need to get her to her coffin."

Edgar frowned. "Perhaps we should wait until the doctor--"

"No!" Frederick spoke with more energy than the boys had yet seen. "We must place her in the coffin as soon as possible. Now!"

Edgar looked at Robert who seemed more frightened than ever.

You should do as he says. And quickly.

Edgar could see only the candlelight reflected in Morella's eye where she sat under the harpsichord. Edgar couldn't explain it, but he felt he should follow her advice.

"All right, Mr. Tamerlane. Tell us what you'd like us to do."

"I'll take you to her," he repeated firmly." He drained the glass and set it on the table and then slowly stood with Edgar's help. "I'll be fine, now, I think," he said in a gentler voice. "I am grateful you're here." He took up his lantern and the boys followed him out of the study and back to the stairs where they made a procession with Morella bringing up the rear to the third floor.

"Angelina preferred being on the top floor," Frederick said. "She said she liked being able to see out beyond the family cemetery." They climbed in silence for the rest of the way and then walked down a hallway identical to the one on which Edgar and Robert were staying. This time they walked the entire length of the hall before reaching the only room with an open door.

Edgar took a breath as he followed Frederick into the room. Sheer white bed curtains hanging from a canopy were gathered at each bedpost. Another lantern flickered on the mantle above the fireplace like the one in the boys' room. Thunder roared as a light flashed across the room, illuminating the stark, nearly skeletal face framed in long dark hair streaked with gray. Her mouth stood partially open, and her eyes stared out defiantly. Frederick set his own lantern on the small table beside the bed and gently ran his hand over his sister's eyes to close them, putting her to rest.

"She hardly weighs a thing," he said. "She's wasted away for so long." He looked at her through tears brimming in his eyes. "As have I."

He pulled the covers down past her bony feet and then to Edgar and Roberts' amazement, he slid one arm under her knees and wrapped the other around her shoulders. He lifted her from the bed and straightened. Edgar touched his arm, an offer to help, but Frederick shook his head.

"I can manage, thank you."

He exited the room, carrying his sister with her head leaning against his chest, and began his descent down the three flights of steps. When they got to the foyer, he crossed over to the steps that led to the cellar and turned to Edgar. "You go first." His voice showed the toll the exertion was taking. Edgar quickly led the way with Frederick's lantern while Robert followed Frederick with the other lantern from their room. Morella stayed out of sight in the rear.

When Edgar entered the chamber where the family coffins lay, a black, winged shape darted at his face with a raucous cawing that caused Edgar to duck and fling one arm over his head. The light from the careening lantern in his other hand threw the room into a whirling disorientation of shadow and light. He felt the raven's wings brush his face and looking back into the main room, he saw the bird fly up the steps toward the first floor. Frederick, too, had ducked, but the weight he carried threw him off balance and caused him to drop to his knees. Only the greatest effort allowed him to avoid dropping his sister's body. Robert gripped the older man and helped him to his feet again and, after an exchange of baffled looks with his friend, the trio moved on to the newly placed coffins.

Edgar had no problem opening the coffin. The clasps were not locked and the coffin was situated for the lid, when opened, to rest against the wall.

Edgar straightened Angeline's gown as Frederick lay his sister in the coffin, and Frederick gently arranged her hair so that it gracefully framed her gaunt face on the pillow. He whispered something to her that Edgar and Robert could not hear, kissed her forehead, and then closed the lid. Frederick secured the five clasps that locked the coffin lid, one on either end and three along the length, and then he pulled violently up on the lid several times, testing it Edgar assumed, to make sure it was locked. Frederick then stood in silence with his eyes closed and hands clasped prayerfully before the coffin, his body shaking in his near silent grief. When another boom of thunder shook the house, Edgar thought of the outside cellar doors, but was surprised again, pleasantly this time, to see Robert had apparently had the same thought and was already moving to secure them. And yet, Edgar noticed, Robert paused at the foot of those steps, staring down.

"What is it?" Edgar asked. Robert pointed. Beside the wet paw prints which showed Morella's earlier entrance into the house, another set of wet, muddy footprints, obviously human, led down the steps into the cellar.

4

The boys looked at each other for a moment, and then Edgar went to shut the doors. He threw the latch which secured them and came back to Robert who looked at him with raised eyebrows.

"I don't know," Edgar said, addressing the unspoken question in a low voice. "But for now we'll see to Mr. Tamerlane." He walked slowly to where his host stood, stopped, and cleared his throat quietly. Frederick raised his head to regard Edgar and looked at the boy with eyes so sorrowful Edgar thought the man might not be talked into ever leaving the cellar. "Shall we return to your study, sir?" Edgar said, gently tugging on Frederick's elbow. Frederick allowed himself to be guided back to the steps leading upstairs and Robert followed solemnly behind.

Back in the study, Edgar settled his host into what seemed to be Frederick's favorite chair, then he and Robert sat on either side of him. A rustling behind them made both boys jump. The raven from the cellar perched on the top of the easel preening the ebony feathers which made it nearly invisible in the gloom.

"Open the front door, Robert!" Edgar said, rising from the couch. Robert dashed out of the study as Edgar jumped up and waved his arms, yelling at the bird in an attempt to shoo it out of the study, but it simply flew noisily to the bust of Athena above the door and cawed angrily back at Edgar.

"Let it be," Frederick said wearily. Another crash of thunder, and a blinding simultaneous flash of light bleached all the color from the entry hall and study for a fraction of a second, as if they had slipped momentarily into another monochromatic world and then back again. Robert slowly closed the front door and took his place again beside Frederick.

"What can we do for you, Mr. Tamerlane?" Edgar said. "Would you like some brandy?"

The older man shook his head. "There is nothing left for me, I fear. Or the Tamerlane lineage. My sister and I were the last of our line."

Edgar and Robert looked at each other helplessly with only the sound of the torrential rain hitting the windows. Finally, Robert ventured a question.

"Why didn't either of you marry?"

Frederick lifted his head and looked straight ahead rather than at either of the boys as he answered. "We were a strange family due to a cruel twist of fate. My mother died when Angeline was a baby, and I was only ten. My father lived for five more years, but he grieved so deeply he did not offer much as a parent. I took care of my sister to the point I think she came to look at me as a parent. And I loved her as much as any father ever loved his daughter. I feel our bond was much stronger than it would have been had both our parents lived and we regarded each other only as brother and sister." Getting Mr. Tamerlane to talk was perhaps a stroke of luck. Once the well was tapped, the stream of memories poured easily.

"I suppose some might have viewed our relationship as unnatural, and it was in many ways. Angeline was a very quiet child. She rarely spoke, and when she did, it was usually a question. She thought deeply about many things; I often found her gazing at the night sky for hours at a time."

"You have quite a library here," Edgar said as he looked about the room. "Was your sister interested in books as well?"

Frederick smiled sadly. "In some of them, yes. In theology and mythology more than science. She was fascinated by Milton's *Paradise Lost*. I think she felt sorry for Lucifer. To her, the fallen angel was the hero of the story."

"Which of you is the artist?" Robert asked. Edgar winced, fearing that directing Frederick's attention to the dark subjects depicted in the paintings might worsen his pain. His fears appeared justified as Frederick's expression fell.

"Those are mine," he answered in a low voice. "An attempt to exorcize my demons."

"Do you suffer from your sister's malady as well?" Edgar asked. He looked at Frederick intently, hoping his host heard the empathy he felt for Frederick and his sister.

Frederick looked down at his feet; he seemed to be studying the intricate patterns in the carpet, but eventually he spoke.

"Yes, I believe I do. It's nothing doctors can treat. No medicine, no potion, or salve for a melancholy that affects the heart, it would appear. My sister simply quit eating no matter how much I implored her. I begged her to take at least the smallest morsel to keep herself alive, but she would not do even that." He paused. "I understand now how she must have felt, for I, too, no longer feel the will to continue." Frederick looked from Edgar to Robert, the pain evident in his eyes. "Might I ever find peace?" he cried. "When might I see my beloved sister again?" From atop its perch on the bust, the raven spoke a single word, as clearly as any human might.

"Nevermore."

Frederick took an apple from the bowl and threw it at the bird. Although he missed, the raven did leave its perch. After circling the room once, it flew out of the study and into the darkness of the house. Frederick held his head in his hands and sobbed. Edgar rested a hand on his host's shoulder and said, "We can chase the bird out of the house."

"No," Frederick said, wiping his eyes. "You boys should retire to your room. There's nothing more you can do tonight. In the morning you might get the coroner in Tamworth. But until then..."

"Let's do as he says," Robert said, touching Edgar's arm. Edgar reluctantly straightened and nodded.

"If you're sure, Mr. Tamerlane," he said. Frederick nodded and offered a weak wave of dismissal.

Robert took one of the lanterns and he and Edgar left the study. The darkness of the house seemed denser than before, as though it were a thick cloud. The light barely was enough to see their way up the stairs, and the sound of the rain was so loud they could scarcely hear their footsteps. Once inside the room, Edgar voiced the thought weighing heavy on his heart. "I'm not sure it's right to leave Mr. Tamerlane in this state. He's so despondent, what if...?"

Robert shrugged. "But what can we do? We might as well get some rest since there is much to do tomorrow. One of us will have to report

Miss Tamerlane's death. I'd like to get that done as soon as possible so we can get back to Richmond. I don't want to spend another minute longer here than we have to."

Edgar nodded. "That makes sense. I just don't feel good about leaving Mr. Tamerlane alone. I'm going to go back down to sit with him, but you can stay up here and get some sleep. He's bound to be exhausted, too, so I'll likely be able to sleep a bit in the study. I know I won't rest if I'm worrying about him up here." He went to the mantle and lit a large candle on a thick base from the lantern as Robert pulled his trousers off and turned down the bed cover. "I'll see you in the morning if not before," he said and headed out into the pitch-black hallway.

Without the glass shield of a lantern, Edgar was forced to walk much more slowly down the stairs, cupping the flame of the candle to keep it from blowing out. As he approached the bottom floor, he saw a dark shape at the foot of the stairs. Morella growled softly behind him.

"Mr. Tamerlane?" A low, familiar chuckle answered and Edgar's candle went out. Edgar froze on the stairs and called out again. "Mr. Tamerlane, could you step out into the foyer?" As Edgar heard Frederick rise from his chair, the silhouette before him outlined by the dim light coming from the study came closer, rising slowly step by step in sync with Frederick's slow steps from the study. When they stopped, Edgar felt a breath on his face accompanied by a soft whisper.

"Hello, Edgar."

The dark shadow standing before Edgar dissolved as the light from Frederick's lantern grew brighter and Frederick stepped into the foyer.

"What is it, Edgar?" He looked up to where Edgar stood.

"Um, nothing, really, I guess." Edgar cleared his throat and took a deep breath. "I'm sorry. I thought it might be better if I sat with you, if that's all right, but I lost my light."

"Thank you. That's very kind. Is your friend with you?"

Edgar descended the rest of the steps and joined Frederick in the doorway of the study. "No, I left him in our room. I wasn't really sleepy. Too wound up from the storm, I guess. I'll only keep him awake, and one of us needs to be fresh enough to go into Tamworth tomorrow to notify them of...everything."

Frederick nodded and turned to go back to his seat in the study, and Edgar followed. The rain lashed furiously at the windows which shook in their frames at times from the wind and the vibrations of the frequent peals of thunder. When Frederick was settled, Edgar said, "Since it appears neither of us can sleep, perhaps you'd find it calming if I read aloud from one of your books? Or I can tell you one of my stories. Robert says I can put anyone to sleep."

"Either would be welcome. You decide."

Edgar ran his hand over the spines of several books, but none seemed to offer what he felt might be needed. Deciding one of his own original stories might be too dark under the present circumstances, he decided to tell Frederick about the time Robert accidentally locked himself in the Stannards' cellar. He seemed to have hit upon a good idea, for before long, Frederick was actually smiling slightly as Edgar related how frustrated Robert had become when Edgar couldn't find anyone to unlock the door.

"He was pounding on the door so hard that––"

"Shhh!" Frederick started up suddenly in his chair. "Did you hear that?"

Edgar answered with a puzzled look. "The thunder?"

"The pounding noise! You didn't hear it?"

Edgar sat still for a moment, but then shook his head. "I hear nothing but the storm."

He's right. There is something.

Edgar's eyes grew big, surprised by Morella's abrupt mental intrusion. He remained quiet and strained to listen, but still he heard nothing. He saw that Morella sat under the easel again, crouched with her tail around herself and her ears laid back, and hoped Frederick wouldn't notice her.

"It's stopped," Frederick said. He remained as still as the bust above the door, staring into the darkness beyond the study doorway but then, after a moment, eased back into his chair although his frown remained. "Perhaps I...Please, continue with your story." The brief moment of levity Edgar had been able to achieve seemed lost, but he made a valiant effort to regain the moment.

"Well, Robert was fit to be tied. He kept screaming at me to find the key, but I had already searched the kitchen cabinets and drawers where he had told me to look. I had no idea where it might be, and there was no one else at his home I could ask. 'If you don't find it, I'll have to break the door down!' he shouted. And then he threw himself against the door several times until I heard a splintering crash––." As Edgar described Robert bursting through his cellar door an undeniable loud crash came from deep within the house.

"Angeline!" Frederick cried.

"It's only something disturbed from the storm," Edgar said, trying his best to reassure his host with his tone. "An open window has allowed the wind to blow something over." As if in answer to his statement, thunder rolled in the distance and rumbled through the house.

"It's Angeline, I tell you! We've trapped her within the coffin!"

"I'm sure it's just the storm!" Edgar answered. He moved to comfort Frederick who had risen from his chair. "But we can check on her if doing so will calm you."

That's not a good idea, Edgar.

"Yes, we must go to her!" Frederick said, his eyes wide and crazed. Before they could move toward the foyer, a crash of thunder with a brilliant flash of light revealed a stark white figure with long hair streaming down past her shoulders standing in the doorway. Edgar tried to make sense of what had to be an illusion caused by the play of light but even in the dim lantern light, he could tell someone did stand there. Another crash of thunder and the light showed Angeline looking even more ghastly than the image depicted in Frederick's painting. Her eyes stared out much as they had when Edgar had beheld her dead in her bed, but she raised both of her skeletal arms and stepped stiffly toward Frederick as if to encircle him in a loving embrace.

Run, Edgar! Run!

Edgar snatched the lantern from the table before them and gave a brief thought to grabbing Frederick and yanking him back––to what safe place he had no idea––but instead he backed himself slowly away from Frederick, afraid even as he did he might be drawing Angeline's attention to himself. She kept her vacant, unblinking stare focused entirely on her brother. Her bare feet made no sound, although anything would have been hard to hear over the din of the howling storm which was rising in intensity by the minute. She seemed not to see Edgar, who took her focus on Frederick as his chance to dash behind her through the doorway and up the stairs to warn Robert.

Edgar threw the door to their bedroom open and ran to the bed where Robert lay on his side facing the far wall. Edgar gripped his friend's shoulder and shook him. Fighting the impulse to shout, he spoke in a low but urgent voice.

"Robert, wake up! We have to leave!"

Robert jerked and turned toward Edgar, but Edgar's racing heart skipped a beat as he realized the person in the bed wasn't Robert at all. For a second, he thought he looked into his own grinning face, but then a flash of lightning illuminated instead an old, balding man's deathly pale, wrinkled face. He gaped at Edgar blindly as saliva dripped from his nearly toothless mouth onto his stained nightgown, squinting as he searched the darkness for something that obviously terrified him. Edgar could see only one ghastly translucent eye which held the slightest tinge of blue.

"Who's there?" the old man cried.

He turned his head frantically from side to side as he clutched the bedspread to his bony chest. Edgar backed away from the bed and bumped into a table he was certain had not been there when he and Robert had first settled in the room. As he looked about, he noticed none of the furniture was as he remembered. The fireplace was on a different wall, impossibly situated where the window had been before. A dresser he did not recall stood opposite the bed, and a single cane-backed wooden chair sat in the corner.

Leave, Edgar.

Edgar needed no encouragement to follow Morella's advice, for he was already backing out of the room. He retreated to the stairway and was astonished to find he was somehow on the third-floor landing. As there was no time to contemplate how he had gotten there, how he had managed to climb an extra flight of stairs without realizing it, Edgar hurried down the stairs to the next floor and rushed to the room he shared with Robert. A pulsing orange/yellow glow seeped out from the cracks under and around the closed door. *A fire?* he thought, but when he cautiously touched the handle, it felt cool to his touch.

When Edgar threw open the door, he saw an expansive room much larger than was physically possible even when considering the massive structure of the Tamerlane mansion. This was a ballroom illuminated with candles--hundreds of candles. The walls, curtains, and table-cloths were all of one single hue, a deep crimson. A tall hooded figure in a black robe that nearly reached the floor stood in the middle of the room with its back to Edgar. All around the room, the bodies of people in costumes and masks as if dressed for Mardi Gras were strewn. Some lay crumpled on the floor, others face down across the tables. They all had one thing in common--their faces appeared to be painted in blood. As the robed figure turned slowly to face Edgar, he saw it, too, wore a mask, one that covered its face entirely but, instead of depicting a scowling or smiling face, it was blank, completely devoid of any suggestion of emotion. Edgar thought it odd for the mask to be yellow, but he reasoned the coloring could have been due to the play of the candlelight. The figure raised its hands slowly, theatrically, to push back its hood and remove the mask. Edgar saw what he had feared most, his own face. Light from his lantern showed that, like the bodies on the floor, blood covered much of this face too. Obsidian eyes without a hint of white bore deeply into Edgar's own as his double stepped toward him.

Edgar fought to make his legs work as he backed slowly out of the room. He slammed the door shut and ran to the stairway. He was mystified to find himself yet again on the third landing, the highest floor of the Tamerlane house. "This can't be!" he cried as he looked down the stairs. "What is happening?"

No time to think. Find Robert! Morella was already several steps below where Edgar stood.

Edgar hurried down to the second landing, pausing only to peer over the banister to confirm the area below was actually the foyer.

Satisfied the house's geography seemed normal once more, he jogged to their room. No light whatsoever emanated from around the closed door this time.

Edgar didn't want to enter but, knowing he had no choice, he steadied himself and turned the doorknob. This time the room was a bedroom at least, but it was nothing like the room he shared with Robert. Like the ballroom, it, too, had numerous candles which illuminated the gold tapestries and paintings hanging on each wall. The bed looked as if it belonged in a bridal suite with its trappings of white fabric covering the canopy. The woman who sat up against the headboard had piercing blue eyes, a fair complexion, and an abundance of light brown curls which fell to her shoulders.

Suddenly it struck him. He was in Angeline's room, although it looked much different in this light than he had seen it when he came with Frederick to fetch her body.

Frederick's sister turned to look at Edgar. With her round, innocent face she appeared to be not much older than him. But then her appearance began to change. Her face grew longer, not grotesquely so, at least, not at first, but enough to give her a look of greater maturity. Her eyes darkened, as did her hair, her locks straightening as they grew longer with gray strands mixed in with the lusterless brown. These darker eyes shone intensely, and Edgar intuited––he didn't know how–– that they held great knowledge, a forbidden knowledge, of things most mortals did not care to know. Edgar winced as he remembered how Frederick had said she felt Lucifer was the hero in the story of *Paradise Lost*.

Her smile grew bigger, frighteningly so, for it reminded Edgar of the uncanny manner in which his double grinned at him. The woman's change did not make her less beautiful at first, only a different kind of beauty, a darker beauty. But her transition did not stop. Her eyes grew larger as they sunk deeper into her head until they disappeared, and her cheeks became more pronounced. As Edgar watched, the skin grew tighter and her lips drew back until eventually her face was little more than a skull.

These are only visions, Edgar. You must not let them overwhelm you.

The sound of the cat's voice broke Edgar's trance, and he left the room quickly, slamming the door behind him. "How long will this continue?" he asked. "When will this nightmare end?" From deep within the house a single word echoed.

"Nevermore."

It will end. Keep going, Edgar. As with any nightmare, you will wake up. But you must keep going.

As he could think of no other course of action, Edgar simply followed Morella down the stairs to their second-floor bedroom again, wondering how long his sanity could take these endless visions.

Once Edgar opened the door, he found himself inexplicably standing in total darkness. The lamp he had managed to cling onto throughout his search for Robert had vanished. The air was cooler and damp, and he could smell a familiar odor of mold and earth. A flash of lightning momentarily illuminated the space enough for him to see he was in the dank, crypt-like cellar where they had interred Angeline hours before. He stood well within the main chamber, and was dumbfounded as to how he could be within the walls of *any* room since he had taken no steps once opening the door to the bedroom.

Get out, Edgar!

"I can't see the door!"

You need to get to the stairs.

In the darkness, he heard a scraping sound of metal on metal, of unoiled hinges and latches being worked after years of disuse. He strained to make out what was happening beyond the gothic arches that led to other chambers in the cellar. He thought he could sense some movement in those spaces. The rustle of fabric followed by the soft repetitive sound of slow footsteps––many footsteps––sliding across the stone floor, added to Edgar's feeling there was some movement of shadows within the greater darkness of the outlying chambers but still, Edgar could not make out what might be approaching from the gloom.

Suddenly the doors leading to the outside, doors which Edgar himself had latched, burst open with a deafening boom of thunder and a tremendous flash of lightning which threw the chamber into stark relief. Edgar briefly glimpsed a host of decayed corpses, deceased Tamerlanes from decades past, shuffling toward him in the fine suits and dresses in which they had been laid to rest in their coffins. But then all was dark again. Leading the host Edgar thought he had seen his grinning double. A second thundering flash confirmed it. The visions Edgar had of the skeletal entourage were made worse by their brevity; not being able to see them in the blackness that followed each explosion of light paralyzed him with fear.

Edgar, run!

Thunder continued to rumble like some ancient, infernal beast roused from its slumber as Edgar responded to Morella's plea. He fled, praying he was not running toward the shambling horrors but toward the steps to the main floor. He stumbled onto the moist, cold stairs, scraping his shin and hands on the hard, stony edges, but he managed to scramble upward on all fours until he felt the sturdy oak door and tumbled out onto the carpeted foyer of the mansion. Morella ran past the study to the other set of stairs leading up to the second floor.

Hurry!

Edgar glanced toward the study, dreading what the Tamerlanes might do if they saw him.

Don't think about them. Hurry up the stairs.

Edgar pulled himself up, shut the door to the cellar, and directed his focus only on getting to Robert on the second floor even though he dreaded what he might find there. Enough light shone from the study to allow him to see the stairs. Keeping his eyes on the floor in front of his feet, he made his way to the steps. When he came to the landing, he turned to the right and felt his way along the wall to what he hoped was their room.

As he opened the door——*The same door? Or are these different doors?*——he released the breath he had been holding as the glow from the low-burning lantern by the bed brought Robert's profile to light where he lay face up in the bed. He rushed to his friend's side and shook him. "Robert, wake up! We have to leave!" A wave of déjà vu chilled Edgar as he remembered how this scene played out before but, this time, Robert didn't change into the horrible old man. But neither would he wake up. Edgar shouted into Robert's face, "Wake up! Wake up!" He slapped his friend's cheek lightly with no result. Edgar could see his chest rising and falling, so he knew his friend was alive, but he was helpless as to what to do.

You must get help.

"How? From whom? I don't want to go back down there where Mr. Tamerlane..." He couldn't finish the thought.

It seems quiet now. I'll go downstairs.

Edgar looked at his friend who snored lightly beside him and then back at Morella. "I'll watch Robert."

The cat trotted out of the room and into the darkness. The rain beat steadily on the window, but it had lessened in intensity and the thunder seemed to have ceased.

When Morella hopped lightly up onto the bed, Edgar jumped.

It is quiet. And no one is in the study. You should be able to leave by the front door with no problem.

"And leave Robert here? And you? Where would I even go? What would I tell anyone?

Frederick mentioned Tamworth. It can't be far. You can ride Pluto. Someone there can help you. I'll wait here with Robert.

Edgar shook his head. He simply wanted to wait in the bedroom for Robert to wake up, and then they both could leave and put all this behind them.

You must go.

Edgar took a deep breath and then stood and gathered his coat and hat which were still wet. "I don't know who I'll find, or what I will tell them, but I'll find someone, I guess." He took the lantern he had brought from the study which left one burning for Robert in case he should wake before Edgar returned.

Morella curled up on the bed beside Robert and watched as Edgar left the room. Edgar stepped lightly as he descended, worried the sound of his footsteps would bring some new terror before he could get out of the house.

His fears proved to be unfounded, for nothing came out of the gloom, either in the house or as he made his way to the carriage house. He did not have a saddle for Pluto since they had used him to pull the wagon, but he had ridden bareback before. The rain had nearly stopped, and Edgar could see a faint pink streak on the horizon. The thought of the storm being over and daylight approaching heartened him, and he set himself to the task of finding someone in Tamworth who could help with a renewed sense of purpose and hope.

Edgar brought Pluto to a trot as they passed the tombstones on either side of the drive between the two ponds in front of the mansion. With all he had seen that night, he felt he would not have been surprised to see skeletons crawling out of the ground, but all the dead who had served past generations of Tamerlanes stayed in their graves as Edgar passed.

Edgar had ridden for less than a quarter of an hour when he came upon the first house. The rain had stopped soon after he had left the Tamerlane property, and the sky was getting lighter. He saw a light through a window he thought might likely have been the kitchen, so he didn't feel too badly about knocking on their door.

A thin man with sharp features dressed in farm clothes stepped out onto the porch and scowled as he looked at the boy who nervously twisted the brim of the hat he held. "Yes?"

"I'm sorry to trouble you, but I desperately need help. I made a delivery to the Tamerlanes and I fear something awful happened. I think Miss Tamerlane is dead––at least, I thought she was––and her brother may be in trouble, too. Can you help me or tell me where I could go for help?"

A woman who looked as lean and wiry as her husband approached from behind him.

"You say you came from the Tamerlane place?" she asked.

"Yes. They...they're not well. And something's happened to my friend. I can't wake him up."

"Sounds like you need a doctor," the man said. He studied Edgar with squinted eyes and then turned to his wife with a questioning look.

"Yes, maybe," Edgar said. "And possibly the sheriff. I...It's all been so strange! I don't know what to do, to tell the truth." It was all Edgar could do not to break down. He wanted nothing more than to be taken into the house and have somebody take over the whole mess. The farm wife's features softened as she sensed Edgar's distress.

"Caleb," she said. "Take the boy back there and see what's happened. When you get back we can see about getting Doc Holmes or whoever else is needed. *If* they're needed." Caleb nodded and went back into the house. "Step inside, boy. Let me fetch you some tea to warm your bones while my husband pulls himself together." Once Edgar had wrapped his hands around a hot mug, the woman continued. They both sat at a small, crude table in a kitchen that offered a comfort in its normalcy more warming than the tea. "Those are strange folks, to be sure. Always kept to themselves, servants, too, even before they lost their fortune. Odd for brother and sister to live together like that and never marry, but there's no accounting for some folks. The reverend's wife has arranged some charity for them. We gave 'em part of a hog we slaughtered last year."

Caleb came into the kitchen wearing a coat and hat and bearing a rifle. "Follow me, boy, and we'll see what's the matter."

Edgar followed Caleb out of the house and waited with Pluto for Caleb to get his horse from the barn nearby. Within minutes they were galloping back down the road to the Tamerlane mansion. By the time they arrived dawn had broken fully and Edgar could see the house more clearly than he had before. He noted for the first time a massive crack running up the stonework of one wall from the ground nearly to the roofline. They rode past the dismal ponds to the portico and tied their horses up to a rail near the steps leading up to the entrance of the house. Before they had reached the massive front door, it opened and Frederick stepped out. Much to Edgar's surprise, he stood tall and seemed much stronger, with even a healthy pink to his cheeks.

"Mr. Gilmore? This is a surprise. I see you've met our guest, Mr. Poe."

"Mr. Tamerlane! You're...all right?" Edgar sputtered. "But how...?"

"Yes, I'm fine, of course. I thought you were still upstairs with Mr. Stannard." He turned to Caleb. "That was some storm last night, eh, Mr. Gilmore?"

"'Twas, indeed," Caleb said, looking at Edgar warily. "The boy here seemed to think you were in some sort of trouble."

Both men studied Edgar who still gaped, unable to come up with a suitable explanation, but turned when Angeline Tamerlane stepped out behind her brother onto the porch, a look of concern evident on her face. She pulled the dark blue robe tighter around her and, like her brother, while thin, seemed in good health. Edgar felt the blood rush to his feet and tottered as the world seemed to swim around him.

"Edgar, are you all right? I think you better come in and sit down." Frederick took Edgar by the elbow, an eerie feeling for Edgar as he remembered doing the same for Frederick the night before, and they stepped inside and took seats in the study. Angeline poured a bit of brandy into a glass and handed it to Edgar. "It's a bit early for such a libation but, under the circumstances, it might do you some good."

Edgar took a small sip and winced as the fiery liquid traveled down his gullet. "I don't know what to say."

"The boy said Miss Tamerlane was dead," Caleb said bluntly.

Frederick and Angeline raised their eyebrows. "Well, I'm happy to report I'm alive and well," Angeline said.

"But, during the storm," Edgar turned toward Frederick. "You...you said your sister had passed, and we...Robert and I...we assisted you in taking her down to the cellar where you put her in..." Edgar couldn't bring himself to say the rest.

"It sounds like someone had quite a vivid dream," Angeline said. "But quite understandable with such a storm. And many people find this house a bit, well, unnerving."

"Have you seen Robert? My friend?" Edgar asked. He had difficulty looking Angeline in the eyes, so he directed the question to Frederick.

"Not since last night when the two of you went up to retire. You remember when you said you were going to bed?" Frederick asked.

"Yes, but then…" Edgar shook his head. "I suppose I should check on Robert and we can be on our way."

"I'll have the balance of my payment for you to take to your father when you come back down." Frederick turned to Caleb. "And Mr. Gilmore, I appreciate your kindness in coming with the boy. I'm sorry he troubled you." He smiled. "The imagination of youth. I suppose we were once a bit fanciful ourselves in our day."

Caleb grunted. "I'll be on my way then. Cora will be worried." He put his hat back on and Edgar avoided his gaze.

When Edgar entered the room on the second floor, Robert stirred. Morella was still lying beside him in the same position Edgar remembered from when he had left an hour or so before.

"You're all right!" Edgar exclaimed.

Robert rubbed his eyes and shifted into a sitting position. "Why shouldn't I be? Although I could use a few more hours of sleep."

"We couldn't wake you earlier." He turned to Morella. "And you've been asleep since I left?

Yes. Something strange about that. She stood, stretched, and hopped down off the bed.

Thinking Edgar had addressed him with his last question, Robert said, "I didn't know you had gone anywhere. Where did you go?" He yawned and threw the bed covers back and spun his legs over the side of the bed. "I don't suppose there's a breakfast waiting for us downstairs?" He stood and retrieved his trousers from where he had draped them over a chair.

"Robert, do you remember what happened with Miss Tamerlane?"

"I didn't ever see her? Did you?"

"You don't remember Mr. Tamerlane saying that she...that she died?"

Robert froze. "That she *what*?"

He doesn't remember.

Edgar looked at Morella. He directed his next question at her silently.

Do you?

Everything, she answered. *Including the events on the third floor.*

"I think we should leave as soon as possible," Edgar said. "We can eat the rest of the snacks my mother prepared for us on our way."

"It would be rude to turn down a breakfast if they've prepared one for us, Edgar."

"I think we can be fairly certain there will be no meal prepared." Edgar rummaged in his pack and retrieved a paper from an envelope carefully wrapped to protect it from the weather.

"I need to give Mr. Tamerlane his receipt for the rest of his payment for the coffins." He turned to Robert. "You do remember the coffins, don't you?"

"Oh, yes. Most likely the most morbid delivery I'll ever be involved with. At least, I hope so. And that cellar. More like a tomb if you ask me."

"That's exactly what it was, Robert."

"Well, I'm so sleepy it's all a bit of a blur to me."

Once they had gathered their gear, including the wet clothes from the day before, they left the room and descended to find Frederick and Angeline having tea in the study. Frederick stood and pulled an envelope from a pocket within his robe which he then handed to Edgar. "The balance for my purchase. I appreciate your help with this delivery, Edgar. And you, Robert. It was nice to meet both of you."

Edgar smiled weakly and handed Frederick the envelope he had brought. "And your receipt." The painting of Frederick stood right behind him, and Edgar was struck by the extreme contrast between the man and his self-portrait. He turned to Angeline and nodded. The contrast with her and her portrait was even more disturbing. "Glad to have been of help. And I'm sorry for, um, my confusion." With a small nod he and Robert left the study and stepped gratefully into the morning light.

Edgar untied Pluto from the rail out front and they led him to the carriage house where Robert stored their gear. Edgar readied the wagon and soon they were back on the road to Richmond, with Morella settled on the driest blankets they could find and the Tamerlane estate out of view behind them.

"That was the strangest experience I've ever had," Edgar said. Robert shrugged and smiled as he gripped the reins with one hand and tried to get comfortable against the hard back panel of the driver's seat for the first leg of the long ride back.

Bra-a-ack!

The loud squawk made the boys turn around. Morella stared wide-eyed at the raven perched on the back board of the wagon.

Edgar groaned and said, "When are we going to be rid of him?"

"Nevermore," the bird croaked.

5

✦

*"How is it that from beauty I have derived a type of
unloveliness? From the covenant of peace, a simile of
sorrow?"*

from "Berenice"

"Is he here?"

Edgar scanned the rows and rows of monuments from where he
sat in the shade with his back against a tombstone and his sketchbook
open on his knees to the drawing he had made of a raven. Morella lay
in the sun on her side atop her favorite stone memorial but fully alert.

I think not.

"You can't hear his thoughts?"

No.

Or the raven's?

No. Nor can they hear mine.

"But they seem to know what I'm thinking."

You have not learned to shield yourself. You are an open book.

"Can you teach me?

Perhaps.

"Well, will you try?"

I have tried. You can be quite stubborn.

Edgar's eyebrows shot up. "I don't mean to be."

Old lessons are hard to unlearn. She paused. *When you were young you had need of walls, so you created them. Most humans do. But they have kept you from hearing.* They sat in silence for a few moments as Morella gave herself a bath while Edgar pondered what the cat had said.

"Does this raven have a name?"

You should ask the next time you see it.

"I'm not sure I want that kind of relationship. He seems to be connected to my double." Edgar turned to face the cat more directly as a thought struck him. "Is the raven to my double as you are to me?" Morella continued to clean her back. Edgar wondered by her silence if he had offended her but, after a bit, she paused, frozen in a seemingly uncomfortable posture the way cats so often do while licking. Just as abruptly, as if becoming unstuck in time, she shifted to a sitting position to face Edgar and addressed his question.

He could be. But I do not know for certain. It is something I have not experienced before.

"But he is more than a raven."

Yes. Just as your double is more than a boy.

"And you are more than a cat."

Aren't we all the special ones? Morella squinted as she looked up into the sunlight with her one good eye. To Edgar it seemed like she was smiling. He decided it might be a good time to broach a possibly sensitive subject he had been wanting to ask about for a while.

"What happened to your eye?"

It has always been thus.

"You are not the cat injured by Robert's uncle?"

No.

"But it's hard to think of your appearance at the Stannard home following that other cat's death as a simple coincidence."

It would be, yes.

Edgar threw his arms up in exasperation. "Well, is it?"

Is it what?

"A coincidence!" Edgar was almost yelling.

There is no such thing as coincidence.

Edgar shook his head. After a moment he decided to try another approach. "About my double...who is he? *What* is he? What does he want?"

You are the only person who can answer that.

"But I don't know! That's why I'm asking!"

Bra-a-ack!

A shadow flew over them as they heard the familiar raucous call. A chill ran down Edgar's spine as the raven settled on one of the lower boughs of the spindly pine two rows of headstones away.

Ask.

Morella stared at Edgar as the tip of her tail twitched repeatedly.

"Ask what?"

Whatever you want to know.

Edgar cleared his throat and directed his question as if he were asking a question of a schoolmaster.

"Who are you?"

Bra-a-ack!

The raven stretched its feathers as it called and resettled itself on the branch.

"Is that all you can say?"

The bird turned its head to the side to look at Edgar, but did not answer.

"Why are you following me?"

The raven shuffled its feet, but it did not fly away.

Perhaps it's hungry.

Edgar looked at Morella, and then opened the leather pouch in which he had packed bread and cheese. He tore off a chunk of the bread and tossed it toward the raven.

Bra-a-ack!

The bird flew down to the ground, snatched the morsel, and then flew back to its perch in the pine. In one swift flick of its head, the bread disappeared down the raven's gullet.

Bra-a-ack!

"You're welcome," Edgar said. "Perhaps we can be friends now."

Bra-a-ack! "Nevermore!" Bra-a-ack!

Well, he did at least answer.

Edgar frowned. "Can you say anything besides 'Nevermore?'"

"Edgar." Bra-a-ack! "Edgar."

Edgar's eyes widened. "Is this a warning? Who is it from? Who are you warning?

Bra-a-ack! "Nevermore." Bra-a-ack!

Edgar stood and took a step closer to the pine tree. "Me? You said 'Edgar' before. Are you talking about me, or the other Edgar? And is 'Nevermore' a threat or a warning?"

Bra-a-ack!

With this last call, the raven launched itself from the branch and sailed across the cemetery disappearing into the surrounding trees.

Morella's eye narrowed and her tail twitched more violently. *Too many questions, Edgar. Think before you speak. God forbid you find a genie in a lamp. You'd wish us all into oblivion.*

Edgar crossed his arms over his chest and stared into the woods where the raven had flown. "It knows my name, Morella! What do you make of that?"

I'm glad he didn't speak mine.

On their return from the cemetery, Edgar slowed as they approached a house with a garden filled with a mix of blooming roses.

Looking for someone special?

Edgar did not answer, but when he noticed a girl about his age smiling at him from the porch, he nodded to her and slowed even more. The girl stood, walked over to the rail and, leaning out, she called.

"Are you Edgar Poe?"

Edgar stopped, surprised at the question. "Yes, I am. Forgive me, but..."

"Elmira," the girl replied. She reached up and pulled one shiny, dark brown curl that lay on her shoulder as she grinned at him. "Elmira Royster. We haven't met, but I have heard about you." Edgar felt his cheeks redden.

"Um, you have?"

That's it, Edgar. Dazzle her with your brilliant wit.

"Please, come into the yard," Elmira said. When she saw Morella following Edgar, her face lit up. "Is this your cat? It's beautiful!" Morella trotted up the steps and leapt up onto the rail where Elmira stood. When the girl ran her hand down Morella's back, the cat responded by rubbing her head and side against Elmira's body. "But it's missing an eye! What happened to the poor thing?"

"I don't know. Suddenly she was here. She seems to be a part of our family now."

"What's her name?"

"Morella."

"How pretty! A pretty name for a pretty cat. How did you come up with that?"

"Um, well..." Edgar's mind raced for a suitable answer. "It just...came to me."

Elmira continued to pet Morella and even kissed the top of her head after the cat deftly turned on the rail and rubbed against the girl again.

Smart girl. Obviously appreciates beauty and grace.

"I'm curious about something, if you don't mind me asking," Elmira said, keeping her eyes focused on the cat.

"Please," Edgar said, squinting as he looked into the sun but grinning widely.

"Did you really swim seven miles up the James River?" Elmira looked shyly up from her petting.

"How did you hear about that?" Edgar asked.

"Robert Stannard told me," she replied. "You're good friends with him, aren't you?"

"Yes, when he's not irritating me. Which is most of the time." Elmira chuckled. "But I'm not sure it was quite that far. I swam from Ludlam's Wharf to the one at Warwick."

"Still, quite a feat! And upstream! What on earth would possess you to ever try such a thing?"

Indeed! Did you fall from a boat?

Edgar winced slightly in annoyance and shook his head as if clearing his mind from Morella's intrusion. He smiled again as he looked up at Elmira.

"I read how the poet Byron once swam the Hellespont after he read the Greek myth of how Leander used to swim it every night in order to see his love, the fair Hero. Byron wanted to prove it could be done.

When I told Robert about that, he said Byron's deed was likely a myth too. That it was impossible. I suppose I've got a bit of a stubborn streak, so I, um, well, I decided to prove him wrong and Byron right."

"How impressive!"

Hmmm. Not as smart as I thought. Morella hopped down from the rail and found a sunny spot on the porch in which to lie. Edgar beamed.

"Do you walk this way often?" Elmira asked.

"I do. I often walk and sketch and write poems in the cemetery down near the river, so I pass by here quite regularly." He held up his sketchbook, and then immediately swept it behind his back, fearing Elmira might ask to see his drawings.

"The cemetery!" Elmira frowned briefly, then smiled as she continued. "A dreary place for a walk, I would think."

"Oh, no, it's beautiful," Edgar said, his enthusiasm obvious. "You should come with--"

The door to the house opened and a tall, heavyset man with a full mustache and dark eyebrows nearly as thick as his side whiskers joined Elmira by the railing. Morella darted off the porch and curled herself around Edgar's leg. "Well, who have we here?"

"This is Edgar Poe, Papa. He lives near here."

"I've seen you in John Allan's warehouse, if I'm not mistaken," Mr. Royster said.

"Yes, he's...he's my father," Edgar stammered. Mr. Royster's eyes narrowed.

"I remember when John and Francis adopted," he said. "Very kind of them. Before John's good fortune allowed him to purchase--what does he call that house? Moldavia, I believe?" Edgar nodded. Elmira's father studied Edgar for a moment, and Edgar felt the heat rising in his face. "Your mother was...a performer, as I recall."

"An actress, yes," Edgar replied. He raised his chin and spoke firmly. "She was regarded as one of the best." Royster and Edgar regarded each other in silence until Royster turned to his daughter.

"Your mother could use some help in the kitchen." He turned to Edgar and with a small dismissive smile said, "Nice to meet you."

"And you, sir." Mr. Royster had turned to go back into the house before Edgar had even finished his brief reply. Elmira wrung her hands and smiled weakly at Edgar.

"He can be abrupt sometimes," she said.

Edgar smiled. "My father is the same way." The two looked at each other awkwardly, and then Edgar summoned his courage. "I'll likely be going to the cemetery again tomorrow at noon. If you'd like, I could show you why I find it so beautiful. It's really like a park. But with dead people." He winced again in instant regret at his wording, but Elmira's laugh poured over him like a spring shower, washing away his embarrassment. He had never seen a smile he liked more. Her teeth shone like pearls in the sunlight and he wondered what it would be like to kiss her full lips. He felt his face grow hot again as he tried to push away those awkward feelings.

"That would be nice," she said. "But perhaps you'll refrain from making any introductions to the residents while we're there." Edgar chuckled and nodded. "Where shall I find you?

"There's a spot right near the entrance. We'll be easy to see."

"We?"

Edgar gestured to the cat at his feet. "Morella and I. That is, if her highness deems us worthy of her company."

That remains to be seen.

"Until then?" Edgar asked.

Elmira nodded. "Until then." She disappeared into the house and Edgar turned, smiling, and left the yard.

I like her.

"So do I," Edgar said.

"I knew she wouldn't be here. I should have been here hours ago." Edgar clenched his fists and turned in a circle to survey the graves around him once more.

You needed to see to be sure. Now we go to her house.

Bra-a-ack! Bra-a-ack! Bra-a-ack!

The raven flew so close to Edgar's head it caused him to duck. It called loudly as it soared through the open gates, mocking Edgar it seemed to him.

It was a short walk to the house on Pearl Street. Edgar fought the urge to run, but still walked more briskly than his usual gait. Morella kept pace beside him but trotted to do so. As they turned the corner and the Royster's back yard came into view, Edgar spied Elmira folding the last of the items she had removed from the clothesline. When she saw Edgar, she gathered the clothes and with an obvious frown walked briskly toward the back door.

"Elmira, wait!" Edgar called.

She paused only to glare at him for a second and then quickened her pace to the house. The door slammed shut before Edgar had even reached the picket fence around the property. Edgar stared at the house with his mouth hanging open.

As he made his way to the front of the house, Morella's telepathic voice stopped him in his tracks.

I wouldn't. She obviously needs more time to calm down.

"But I couldn't help being late. My father--"

It doesn't matter why. She feels she's been insulted. She's hurt. It will be better tomorrow.

Francis Allan set her cup down and looked at Edgar across the table before speaking. Although she smiled, her concern shone in her eyes.

"You hardly touched your breakfast. And you didn't eat much dinner. What's wrong, Edgar?"

He looked up from the cold eggs on his plate, unaware he had been staring at them. "It's nothing, really." He gave his mother a little smile which faded quickly. He bunched his napkin and set it beside his plate.

Mrs. Allan reached across the table and gripped his hand. "Is it your father? Have you been quarreling again?"

"No, no. It isn't that. We're fine." He paused. "I suppose." He stared at his plate as he struggled with whether to continue sharing his thoughts. "I think I hurt someone's feelings. Someone I just met."

"Oh!" Francis withdrew her hand and straightened in her chair, feeling both relieved her husband and Edgar had not had a disagreement and glad Edgar had finally confided something personal to her. She pushed her plate aside and crossed her arms on the table before her, leaning in further as she waited for Edgar to say more.

Edgar continued to look down as he spoke. "I met a girl the other day when I was walking home from the graveyard. Elmira. Elmira Royster. She seemed interested when I told her I liked to sketch and write. So I invited her to meet me in the cemetery yesterday." Realizing how awkward that sounded, Edgar looked up at his mother. "To show her the statues and carvings I like to draw. But then I wasn't able to go because Father insisted I help him with the inventory." Edgar rubbed his brow. "If I had known, I wouldn't have told Elmira to meet me. I went to the graveyard as soon as I could but she wasn't there. When I passed by her house on my way home, I saw her in the yard, but she wouldn't respond when I called out to her. She just hurried into the house."

"I see," Francis said. "She thinks you didn't take her seriously. That you dismissed her as unimportant. No one likes that."

"I hate that warehouse!" Edgar said as he fell back into his chair. The unexpected force of Edgar's sudden outburst practically pushed Francis back into hers. "I'm sorry," Edgar apologized, sensing her surprise but still scowling. "It's just that working there always seems to be keeping me from what *I* want! Everything is always about what *he* wants."

Francis gave Edgar a minute to calm himself, and then spoke. "You know your father wants you to benefit from the business he's built up. If he pushes you, it's because he wants you to be successful. It's really a sign of how much he cares about you."

"Oh, yes! 'How much he cares.' Well, sometimes I wish he didn't care so much."

"Edgar, you don't mean that. You know we both care the world for you and want the very best for you. We chose for you to come and live with us, Edgar. Most parents don't have a choice when they have a baby, but we *chose* you! Your father did too."

Edgar sat quietly, his lips drawn tight. Francis smiled sadly as she studied him. "Since your father has gone to Charlottesville and won't be needing you, why don't you go to Elmira's house and ask to speak with her? I'm sure her parents will make sure she sees you if you ask to see her politely and formally. Then you can explain what happened.

I'm sure she'll understand." Edgar nodded and rose to take the remains of his breakfast to the kitchen.

Morella was sunning herself in the morning light on the wide front porch when Edgar emerged with his sketchbook and a sack containing bread, jam, fruit and nuts, a lunch with enough to share which Francis had prepared for him. She fell in behind Edgar as he made his way to the street.

Your mother is a wise woman.

"She's very sweet," Edgar agreed. "I think I love her as much as I would have loved my actual birth mother. Possibly more." They walked in silence, nodding at the people they passed along Main Street. As they turned onto Pearl Street, Edgar said, "Now we find out how forgiving Elmira is."

The woman who answered Edgar's knock seemed as stern as her father. Her thin eyebrows met over her narrowed eyes and her lips were pressed tightly under an upturned nose. "Young Edgar, I believe?"

"Yes," Edgar said. "I wonder if I might speak with Elmira, please?"

"I don't think my daughter--"

"It's all right, Mother, I'll talk to him." Elmira stepped out from behind her mother, her eyes piercing Edgar with their intensity. Her mother frowned, but stepped aside. Elmira stepped out onto the porch with Edgar and shut the door behind them. She pointed to a wooden chair with a tall woven back for Edgar and took her place on an identical one. Edgar set his sketchbook and sack on a round table between the chairs. When Morella jumped into Elmira's lap, the girl's expression softened and she automatically began to stroke the cat's back. Morella settled herself and purred loudly enough for Edgar to hear her as well.

"I'm so sorry about yesterday," Edgar began. "I had every intention of being there, but my father suddenly required me to help him with counting––"

"Wait!" Elmira held a hand out as if to stop Edgar physically. "You sound as if I didn't see you yesterday."

"Well, I saw you in your backyard, but you obviously didn't want––"

"No, I mean before that. In the graveyard."

"That's right. My father made me help with inventory and I didn't make it there until you had already left."

Elmira's brow furrowed in confusion. "You didn't meet me in the graveyard?"

Edgar's expression mirrored Elmira's. "No. I'm trying to explain why."

"Edgar, I saw you in the cemetery."

Think of what happened with your father's keys, Edgar. After the incident in the apothecary's cellar. Edgar felt spidery fingers crawling up his spine.

"You saw me? In the cemetery?"

"Yes! And you behaved...well...." Rather than finishing her statement, she looked down at Morella as she continued to stroke the cat's back.

"Elmira, this is going to sound strange, I know, but trust me when I tell you this is only one of many strange things happening to me lately. But first, please tell me what you think I did in the graveyard."

"It's not what *I think* you did, it's what you did!"

Edgar closed his eyes briefly and nodded.

"Please, tell me."

"Well, at first, you were fine. I thought it was strange you didn't have your sketchbook, since that's what you said you like to do there, and that Morella wasn't with you." The cat looked up at her with an exceptionally loud purring noise, which made Elmira smile gently in spite of her subject. "But I didn't think much about it. You were nice; you told me..." Elmira paused without looking up at him.

"I told you what?" Edgar prodded.

Elmira took a breath and continued, "You told me I was pretty." She glanced briefly at Edgar and then she directed her eyes back to her hands.

"Well, you are," Edgar said softly with a sheepish grin. "But I don't think I would have had the courage to say that." Edgar thought he saw a trace of a smile but, when she looked up, he saw her eyes had turned hard again.

"Well, you did say it. More than once. And it was strange, Edgar. Not right. The way you smiled at me. Not like you did just now. It was scary. Like a madman almost. And you kept talking about *my* smile."

"Your smile?" Edgar felt a twinge of guilt, remembering how much he had enjoyed seeing Elmira's smile at their first meeting, and hearing her laugh when he had first mentioned his enthusiasm for the grave-yard, how it was like a park with dead people.

"Yes. You kept talking about what beautiful teeth I had. The most perfect teeth you, or anyone, had ever seen. And you kept saying it. Many times. Edgar. That simply isn't right."

"I...I don't know what to say. I agree. That is very strange. And not right. But I assure you, it wasn't me." As Elmira looked at Edgar, he saw the muscles in her jaw clench.

"Edgar, unless I dreamed it, it was you." She continued to stroke Morella's fur, an action which she realized was more for her own benefit than the cat's. Morella shifted in Elmira's lap to look directly at Edgar.

Tell her about the keys.

"I don't think it was a dream, but I have an idea, or maybe just the beginning of an idea of what might have happened. I need to tell you about what's happened to me within the last few weeks."

Elmira stopped petting Morella and sat perfectly still, ready to hear what Edgar wanted to say and surprised that she actually wanted to hear him offer some kind of explanation.

"About two weeks ago, I think it's been, I made a delivery of wine to Mr. Montresor, the apothecary. He had me take it down to his cellar below the shop. But when I got there, the cellar was, I don't know quite how to say it. It was...all wrong."

"'All wrong?' What does that mean?"

"It wasn't a cellar; it was a huge underground dungeon. With tunnels and cells. I heard voices and saw people who were there and then not there. Elmira, it didn't make sense. I knew logically what I was seeing couldn't be real, but there it was."

"It sounds very frightening."

"It was. But that wasn't the worst of it." Elmira's eyes grew bigger. "I saw someone who looked just like me. And he grinned at me exactly as you said I grinned at you in the graveyard. It's a terrifying grin."

"This sounds like a dream."

"It does. And that's what I thought too." Edgar thought it best not to tell her all of the details of the encounter, of how his spectral rival imprisoned him and sealed him up in the wall, for fear it would prove to be too extreme, too much for Elmira to accept. "At one point I passed out and, when I came to, the cellar was as you would expect any shop cellar to be. There were no tunnels or dungeon cells. The wine I had delivered was there with other casks. But the hand truck was gone, and the keys I was carrying to my father's warehouse weren't in my pocket. I had them when I left the warehouse with the wine. I knew, because I distinctly remembered locking the warehouse up when I went there to get the hand truck. But when I woke up after the--well, let's call it a dream--I knew I had lost the keys and the hand truck. I was terrified about how my father would react."

Elmira's face had softened. In her eyes Edgar saw what he thought were signs of sympathy.

"But here's the point. When I got home, my father wasn't angry. In fact, he was very happy with me! He said he was proud of me for doing such a good job. And then he reached into his pocket and gave me the very keys I had lost. He said he had not put them away after I had given them to him earlier and asked me if I would do so for him then. Elmira, *I never gave him the keys!*"

Elmira's hand went to her mouth. "You're saying there are two of you? There's another Edgar?"

Edgar nodded. "And it's not the only time I've seen him. I saw him first when I was sketching in the cemetery, and he called to me from one of the crypts. I was so scared I had to close my eyes. When I opened them, he was gone." Edgar stopped, relieved to see Elmira seemed to be believing him. "There were other times, too, terrifying things that happened last week when Robert and I delivered caskets to a man in Tamworth; I saw glimpses of the double then, as well."

"What do you think this Dark Edgar wants of you?"

Morella turned in Elmira's lap to look at Edgar.

'Dark Edgar.' She's got it exactly. And she believes you. This is a special girl, Edgar.

"I don't know," Edgar answered. "But now you are the second person besides me who has seen it. At least, you're the only ones I know of who have. I've told Robert about my first encounter with Dark Edgar, as you call him, and as I said, he saw strange things at the Tamerlane mansion, horrible things that encourage him to believe me, but he hasn't ever actually seen it. My father, of course, doesn't know it wasn't me who gave him the keys." Edgar wiped his hands on his trousers as he debated how much of his turmoil he wanted to share with Elmira. "I've felt like I was going mad for the last two weeks.

"Oh, Edgar." As she leaned over to reach across the table, Morella jumped down from her lap. "I'm so sorry." She gripped Edgar's arm and squeezed it lightly.

"Do you believe me?"

"I believe you believe it. As for me, I don't know what to believe," Elmira said. "Not yet. But I have an idea." Edgar's eyebrows shot up. "Let's go to the cemetery."

"This is the crypt where I first saw him," Edgar said as they stood before its gates. Morella stood next to Edgar with her side brushing his leg.

"It's beautiful." Elmira's eyes were wide as she surveyed the ivy-colored walls and the stained glass on the door behind the iron gates. "It belongs in an old German tale, the final resting place for a young girl who died pining away after the death of her lover."

Your kind of girl.

Edgar looked down at Morella and smiled despite his nervousness.

Elmira reached through strands of ivy and took hold of the gate and pulled. The screech of rusty iron filled the graveyard like a banshee's wail as the gate opened. As before, the latch on the door was unlocked as well. With only a glance at Edgar, Elmira entered. Edgar felt his heart racing as he followed her into the gloom.

"This is where you first saw him?" Elmira asked as she turned to view all the walls of the crypt.

"Right over there." Edgar pointed to the corner where his double had crouched. "At first, he seemed more like a skeleton than a flesh-and-blood boy. But then his face changed until I saw he looked like me. Except his smile. It still looked like the grin on a skull."

"That smile is terrifying," Elmira agreed with her back to Edgar who remained near the door. She moved to the corner Edgar had indicated and squatted down to study the floor with no apparent regard for how any dust or spiderwebs might soil the bottom of her dress. "I don't see any sign––"

"So pretty." The voice was soft, a whisper on a breeze, although the air in the crypt was still.

"Did you hear that?" Elmira whispered, her dark eyes large and luminous in the shadows of the crypt. Edgar nodded. Morella crouched in a corner, her eyes wide and ears laid back and flat against her skull.

He's here.

"Your teeth...like pearls."

Edgar's skin crawled as he remembered how he had privately made the same observation. Elmira stood, her eyes narrowed until she looked as intense as when she had greeted Edgar in anger only an hour before.

"You heard that too?" Edgar asked softly.

"Oh, yes," Elmira answered in a voice as low as Edgar's. "And he's still talking about my teeth. I don't like it, Edgar." She then turned her head up and spoke in a louder, defiant voice, "I said, I don't like it!"

The door to the crypt slammed shut and they heard the gate screech again. The room was thrown into more shadows and it was harder to make out the small altar on the far wall and the contents of the alcoves within the walls. The meager light filtering through the stained glass did allow for them to see each other. Elmira moved to stand next to Edgar and gripped his arm with both hands. It seemed to him she did so more from excitement than fear.

The girl has spirit. But perhaps tell her not to yell at it again. Morella's unblinking eye shone green from the corner where she remained.

"Some of these caskets are filled, no doubt," Elmira said much more quietly than her defiant shout before.

"No doubt," Edgar agreed.

"Do you think he's in one of them?"

Edgar shivered. "You're not suggesting we--"

"No, of course not!" Edgar could tell she was visually examining each of the alcoves just as he was, although neither moved from their spot in the center of the crypt. "That would be wrong. Disrespectful. Still, I wonder..."

I don't sense him anymore. I don't think he's in here.

Edgar moved to the entrance, guiding Elmira with one hand at her back. The latch lifted easily and he opened the door which allowed a bit more light into the tomb much to Edgar's relief. "Shall we look outside?" When Elmira nodded, he pushed the gate open which filled the graveyard with another metallic creak and the couple stepped out into the sunlight.

The sound of flapping wings right above them made Edgar jump. Elmira noted how intently Edgar watched the bird's flight. It landed on the top of a cross near where the graveyard bordered the trees. Edgar continued to stare at it as it expanded its wings and hopped from one arm of the cross to the other.

Bra-a-ack!

"Something special about that crow?" Elmira asked.

"I believe it's a raven but, yes, I think he's connected to my double. I've seen him nearly every time I've seen the other Edgar." Elmira started walking toward the cross.

"Wait!" Edgar said, still trying to keep his voice low. "I'm not sure that's a good idea."

Elmira continued on her path across the graves. Edgar shook his head and moved to follow her, but before he had taken his first step, something grabbed his shirt collar and yanked him back into the crypt. He lost his balance and struck his head as he fell onto the stone floor, vaguely aware of the sound of the gate and the door slamming shut once again as he lost consciousness.

Surprised at hearing the crypt sounds again, Elmira stopped and turned to see Edgar with his back to her, gripping the gate. "What are you doing?" she called. When he didn't answer immediately, she stepped toward him. He turned slowly. Once Elmira could see his face, she saw he seemed dazed.

"I'm not sure," he said, frowning. "I feel a bit dizzy."

Once she reached him, she gripped his arm and peered into his eyes. "Perhaps you should sit down." She walked him over to the stone memorial where they had left their lunch. "Are you ill? Should I get someone to help us?"

"No, no," Edgar said, rubbing his forehead. "I think I'll be fine in a moment. I don't know what came over me."

A low, feline growl made Elmira start. Morella crouched in front of the tombstone where Edgar frequently rested as he sketched. She wrapped her tail around herself with her ears laid back. "Poor, Morella. She's worried about you too!" Suddenly the cat darted from her spot to the crypt, squeezed her body through the iron bars of the gate, and stood on her hind legs to scratch on the crypt door. "How odd!" Elmira said.

"Probably thinks there's a rat in there. She does that sometimes." Edgar smiled and took Elmira's hand in his own. "Thank you for taking care of me."

"Of course," Elmira said. "You're feeling better then?"

"Much."

Elmira smiled back, but began to feel uncomfortable as Edgar continued to gaze at her. And smile. She patted the hand that held hers and tried to pull it back, but Edgar tightened his grip. "You do have such a remarkable smile," he said. He reached up with his free hand and ran a finger down her cheek and across her jaw. "And such beautiful teeth."

Elmira jerked her hand from Edgar's grip and stood. "I don't like that, Edgar."

"I'm sorry," he said, smiling up at her. "Please forgive me." His smile grew wider and Elmira took a step backwards.

"I'd like to go home now," she said.

"But I'm feeling better now. And it's so nice here in the graveyard. I told you, it's like a park, isn't it?" Edgar's smile grew even wider, so wide he no longer seemed human. He stood and started moving toward her.

"Stay away from me!"

"Don't be afraid," he said as he continued to approach her, his arms spread wide on either side. His grin seemed too wide for his face.

Elmira turned away from him and stepped quickly toward the entrance to the cemetery. When she threw a glance back over her shoulder, she saw Edgar was moving faster than she was and would quickly overtake her. Gathering her dress to free her steps, she broke into a run. She didn't need to look back to know that Edgar, too, pursued her at a run. Suddenly she heard a cat screech, followed by a thump and a loud curse. She risked a look back and saw Edgar had fallen. A shadow darted along the ground and behind a tombstone. As

Edgar gathered himself, Elmira resumed her flight out of the cemetery. She ran without risking another look behind her and without regard for the strange looks from the few passersby on the street until she saw a familiar face.

"Robert!" she gasped, surprising him further by gripping his arm. "I need your help! I think Edgar's in trouble."

"What is it? What's happened?"

"There's no time to explain. We need to go to the graveyard!"

"But, what--?"

"No time for that! We have to hurry." Elmira tugged on Robert's arm until he began to move with her back down the street in the direction from which she'd come. When they got to the entrance of the cemetery, there was no sign of Edgar. Elmira hurried to the crypt with Robert following in her wake where they found Morella pacing back and forth in front of the gate. Elmira yanked the gate open so quickly it hardly screeched. She quickly unlatched the door and they saw Edgar lying crumpled, face down on the stone floor. Morella meowed and ran to where he lay.

"Edgar!" Elmira called as she knelt beside him. Robert knelt on the other side and together they rolled him over to his back.

"He's breathing, at least," Robert said.

"Edgar, can you hear me? Edgar?" Elmira patted Edgar's cheeks as she tried to wake him. Gradually he began to stir, and finally his eyes fluttered open.

"Elmira! And...Robert? What...what happened?"

"That's what we were going to ask you," Robert said, smiling with relief.

"We were following that bird, or at least I was, when something odd happened," Elmira said. "Do you think you could sit up?" Edgar nodded and Robert helped Elmira pull Edgar to a sitting position.

Morella walked back and forth around him, rubbing her body against his arms and back as she purred loudly.

"What do you remember?" Elmira asked.

"I was about to follow you toward the raven on the cross when something pulled me into the crypt. I fell, and..." Edgar's hand went to his forehead where blood trickled from a cut in the middle of a swollen bump which was beginning to turn blue. "I must have hit my head."

Elmira looked at Robert and then back to Edgar. "I heard the door close and then the gate. But you were standing outside the crypt, holding the gate as if you'd shut it."

"I don't remember doing that."

It was him. He attacked you, Edgar.

"You acted so strangely I had you sit down on that big stone block."

"What was strange about him?" Robert asked. "I mean, more than usual." Edgar smiled in spite of himself but then winced as he touched his bump lightly.

Elmira found Robert less amusing. She looked at Edgar as she spoke. "Remember how I said you behaved when I saw you yesterday here in the graveyard? Well, you were like that. You smiled in a way that made me...uncomfortable. And you touched my face."

"That doesn't sound so scary," Robert said.

"It wasn't right!" Elmira snapped. "And then you said something again about my smile." She paused. "And my teeth."

"Your teeth?" Robert snorted. "That does sound like Edgar. Complimenting a girl like he's describing a horse."

"This is serious!" Elmira's dark eyes flashed. She turned back to Edgar and her expression softened. She reached out to lightly touch his injury but then pulled her hand back.

"It wasn't me," Edgar said. His eyes pleaded with her to believe him.

"I know it wasn't. But that smile, it was just as you had described it. Like a skull. It was hideous! If it wasn't for Morella, I don't know what would have happened."

"Morella! What did she do?" Edgar asked.

I tripped the bastard.

"I think she got tangled up in his feet."

It was no accident.

Edgar turned to look at Robert. "How did you get here?"

"She brought me," he said, nodding toward Elmira. "She was flying down the street like Artemis chasing a deer and grabbed me."

"Do you think you can get to your feet?" Elmira asked. "Perhaps we should get you to Dr. Tarr."

"I can stand, I think." Robert and Elmira each took an arm and together they helped Edgar up. "I'd really like to get out of this tomb."

Once out in the sunshine and fresh air again, Edgar did feel better. His friends walked with him over to Morella's stone where he sat. They stood before him, watching carefully for any signs his injuries might be more serious than he claimed.

"It's only a bump," he said, touching the wound again lightly. "Not much blood, as you can see. Good thing I didn't hit anything serious. Only my head." He smiled at them, hoping to ease their concerns.

"Such a big target," Robert said. "You could draw a life-size sketch of the Colossus of Rhodes on that forehead."

"If this bump keeps swelling, maybe so." In spite of her jest, Elmira's eyes betrayed her worry. "Do you think you could eat something?" She turned to Robert and pointed to the sack. "See what's in there, Robert."

"Gladly," Robert said. "Looks like there's some bread. And fruit. Would you like some grapes, Edgar?"

"I'm not hungry. But you—" Robert was already happily munching several.

"I'll have some," Elmira said, snatching the cluster from Robert's hand. "But I think if you're up to it," she said turning to Edgar, "we should probably get you home where you can lie down."

Edgar nodded and stood. As the threesome started to make their way to the entrance of the cemetery, Edgar stopped. "That's odd," he said. "I didn't notice that before."

Robert and Elmira followed Edgar's gaze to a mound of dirt on a grave past the cross where the raven had perched earlier. "Neither did I," Elmira said. She walked to it and the others followed. As they got closer, Robert gasped and looked away.

"That's horrible," Elmira said. Edgar stared at the unmarked open grave in horror. A plain, wooden coffin little more than an oblong box lay fully exposed, its simple lid pried open revealing only the stained burial cloth that had likely wrapped the missing human remains.

"This is where paupers are buried," Edgar said. When Robert gave him a puzzled look, Edgar explained further. "Those who can't afford a stone or other memorial are buried here. The caretaker showed me this area some time ago. I always felt so sorry for them. They have no one to come and mourn for them, to pay their respects."

"This needs to be reported," Elmira said.

"My father is out of town," Edgar said. "Robert and I can go with you to your house."

"Are you sure?" Elmira asked. "Don't you think—"

"I'm fine, Edgar said. "And right now it might be best if we stay together. Dark Edgar doesn't seem to like being seen by more than one person at a time."

As they moved toward the entrance, they noticed Robert lagged behind. He had managed to force himself to look again at the grave, and he stood staring at it in stony silence. Edgar stepped back to his friend and rested a hand on Robert's shoulder.

"Come on," he said gently. "Let's go."

When they got to the Royster home and ascended the steps to her porch, Elmira noticed a small sack sitting on the round wooden table between the two high-backed chairs, not unlike the one Edgar's mother had packed their lunch in. Robert looked at the sack in his hand as Elmira went to the other one. She picked it up and bounced it in her hand with a quizzical look on her face.

"Someone leave you a bag of marbles?" Robert asked, a reasonable guess given the sound when Elmira had jiggled it.

She loosened the strings which secured it and upended the sack, dumping its contents which clattered onto the table.

The three friends gaped as they realized what the sack had held.

Thirty-two human teeth polished to shine like pearls gleamed in the sunlight.

6

"The box in question was, as I say, oblong. It was about six feet in length by two and a half in breadth; I observed it attentively, and like to be precise."

from "The Oblong Box"

"...Doctor Ponnonner was preparing his instruments for dissection...when someone suggested an experiment or two with the Voltaic pile."

from "Some Words with a Mummy"

As Edgar climbed the steps onto the Stannards' front porch, Robert rose from his rocking chair with a greeting Edgar noted was warm but lacking its usual jocularity. Edgar found it odd that Robert didn't offer him a seat.

"Hello, Robert. Is everything alright?"

"Yes. I'm fine." Robert nodded but looked back toward the house while answering in a pleasant tone that seemed forced to Edgar. Edgar frowned slightly as he looked at his friend. Morella circled around Edgar's legs, pausing to rub against him at intervals.

"You're sure? The business in the graveyard?" Edgar asked, his eyebrows raised.

"No, no," Robert said, waving his hand dismissively. "I mean, that was pretty disturbing, and if I were Elmira, I would be especially worried." He turned and faced Edgar. "Who do you think did that? Was it…?" His voice trailed off.

"I don't know how it could be anyone else. Not since Elmira was targeted."

Robert nodded in silence and then asked, "How did your father react to all of this?"

"He wasn't happy. It's obvious the sheriff thinks it's a prank we pulled on Elmira. I don't think my father necessarily believes that, but I can tell he thinks it's possible."

"Did you tell him about you getting knocked out in the crypt?"

Edgar shook his head. "They wouldn't believe me, and telling that part of the story would make me seem like more of a liar."

Robert pointed to Edgar's head. "How did you explain that?"

Edgar touched the discolored spot and scar on his forehead. "I told him I bumped my head going into our cellar at Moldavia. I've done that before; there's a low beam over the bottom step. Fortunately, my mother was out yesterday so my story is plausible."

"I have to say, if I were in your father's shoes, I'd likely think of it as a prank we pulled too."

"He's given me a list of chores to do at the warehouse. Today, for example, he wants me to be there for a delivery and inspect something that came in for one of his customers. He could easily do it himself but I think he wants to keep me busy and out of trouble. 'Idle hands' and all that. I'm on my way there now." He smiled and touched Robert's arm. "Why don't you come with me?"

Robert returned a small smile, but said, "I think I'd best stay––"

"Edgar. I thought I heard your voice." The comment was so faint Edgar almost didn't hear it.

He nearly gasped when he saw the figure standing in the doorway. The woman who leaned against the doorframe had little resemblance to the beautiful woman he had seen only weeks before. Her face was so thin she appeared to have aged a decade. The dark circles around her eyes made it seem they had sunken into her skull. Her face was pale, and she wrapped her arms around herself as if she were in pain.

"Hello, Mrs. Stannard. It's good to see you."

"It's always good to see you, Edgar." She smiled and Edgar saw a hint of her former beauty. "I thought I would come out and visit but I'm afraid I overestimated my strength. I'm so tired. I'd best lie down. Please forgive me." Her smile faded, and she turned and disappeared slowly into the house.

Robert looked out into the yard. "She's...um...as you can see, she's not well."

"What's wrong, Robert?"

"Doctor Tarr described it as melancholia and prescribed laudanum, but I don't think he knows any more than we do."

"I'm sorry. Your mother is, well, so special; I hate for her to suffer."

"That's why I need to stay here."

Edgar nodded again. "Of course. If I can help, please let me know."

"Maybe a visit when she feels up to it. She really likes you, Edgar."

"I like her too. It's almost like I was given two mothers to replace the one I lost."

"I'll tell her that. It will lift her spirits."

Edgar embraced his friend and left the porch with Morella following close behind. They turned on Pearl Street and his step quickened as he approached Elmira's house until he came to the gate leading into the front garden. He scanned the darkened windows and his face brightened as he saw the front door open and Elmira come out.

"I'll just be a minute, Mama!" she called over her shoulder. Her brows were drawn down to a point above her eyes as she hurried down her steps and toward the gate. Edgar saw the still silhouette in the doorway remained.

"Hello, Edgar," she said. Her face softened as she saw Morella at Edgar's feet. She gave Edgar a small smile not much bigger than Robert's had been. She reached up and lightly touched the discolored spot on his head. "That's quite a bruise." She grinned. "At least now maybe we can tell you apart from your twin."

Edgar smiled back, but then he grew serious. "How are you?" He looked at her so intensely, she glanced away for a second before answering.

"I'm fine. My parents aren't happy, especially my father, as you can imagine." She turned back to face him. "If the grave had been one for a prominent citizen, I think the sheriff might have thrown you in jail, Edgar."

Edgar's eyes widened. "They really think I did that? The teeth too?"

Elmira nodded. "You're lucky your father is the richest man in town."

"He's not––" Edgar let her statement go. "I suppose that's why the sheriff hasn't come to talk to me. Still, you'd think a grave robbery with a missing corpse would warrant more investigation."

"It's better for him, too, if the community thinks it was only a foolish prank." They looked at each other for a moment and Elmira took a deep breath. "It's probably best if you don't come here for a while." Edgar's face showed his disappointment. His heart lifted though, when she grinned. "But maybe there's a way for us to still see each other. I'll leave you something here at the gate when I'm able to leave the house. A sign of some sort. If you see it, you'll know I've gone to the graveyard."

Edgar nodded. "I'd like that! What should I look for?"

"Elmira!"

Elmira rolled her eyes at her mother's call.

"I have to go. Keep a watch out. I'll see you soon."

She turned and made her way back across the yard and up the steps into the shadows of the porch. She turned and gave Edgar a small wave which he returned before moving on.

And the angels, all pallid and wan,

   Uprising, unveiling, affirm

   That the play is the tragedy, 'Man,'

   And its hero, the Conqueror Worm.

Edgar looked up from the verses he had just written and set his journal aside. He sat in his favorite spot when allowed rare moments of leisure in his father's store, a wide ledge inside the tall front window which ran the width of John Allan & Company. From there he could see the full gamut of Richmond citizens who passed by his father's business on their daily chores. A few saw him and acknowledged his nod and smile, but others deigned not to respond. To Edgar, it seemed they might have even cast disapproving looks at him before acting as though they had not seen him at all.

You are reading too much into this.

Morella lay on her side, sunning herself in the window as her tail twitched occasionally.

"Not according to Elmira and Robert. I'm lucky I'm not in jail."

Two men on the other side of the street caught Edgar's eye. One lay his hand on the other's forearm, and both looked eastward up the street. Edgar leaned closer to the window and followed their gaze to see a horse pulling a wagon toward him. Other citizens had stopped to look as well. A woman talked with her mouth close to her companion's ear, and Edgar saw she pointed to John Allan's business. When the wagon had pulled in front of the shop, it stopped, and Edgar saw the driver was likely the man making the delivery his father had asked him to meet. In the back of the wagon sat a long oblong box. Edgar set his writing journal aside, exited the shop, and approached the man in the driver's seat.

"You Mr. Allan's boy?" the man asked. His mouth was lost in the thick, wiry beard that flowed down his chest.

"I'm Edgar. This must be the delivery for Mr. Cornelius Wyatt."

The driver nodded. "I suppose you want this around back?"

"Please," Edgar said, pointing to the side of the building. "There's an alley––"

"Been here before," the man said curtly as he shook the reins, making the wagon jerk into movement again. Edgar shrugged and went back into the shop and made his way into the large, open portion of the building at the back where he unhitched the rope to raise the large back door that allowed delivery wagons and carriages easier access to their storage area. Because of the warehouse's proximity to the alehouse behind his father's business, Mr. Allan insisted the large door be kept closed as much as possible in spite of the gloom it caused. He feared the less respectable clientele of Swan's Tavern might wander inside the warehouse to idly pass the time of day, or even worse, pass out from their overindulgence.

When the wagoneer stopped with his load, he hopped down and motioned for Edgar to join him at the back of the wagon. He let the back panel down and nimbly jumped up onto the bed and pushed the oblong box so half of it extended over the edge.

"Think you can safely carry your half?" the surly man asked.

"That depends," Edgar said. "How heavy is it?"

"Two of us loaded it. You look a bit scrawny, though. I don't want to be blamed for the damage you caused."

"I'll be fine," Edgar said, frowning. He gripped the end that hung over the back and walked it back as the driver skillfully took the other end in hand and together, they carried it into the warehouse. They placed the box on two sawhorses Mr. Allan had apparently set out for that purpose in anticipation of this delivery. Without a word of acknowledgement to Edgar, the driver hopped up onto the driver's seat, took the reins in hand and with a click of his tongue and a flick of the reins was moving again.

"Wait," Edgar called. "My father wanted me to check for damages as soon as it got here."

"You'd best do that then," the man said, turning the wagon back the way he had come. "I got it here safe and sound. The rest is on you."

"But––!" Edgar's protest fell on deaf ears.

Seems like a nice man.

Edgar frowned at Morella, who squinted into the sunlight, and then made his way to the rope to lower the door. Once the door was down, the large space was much darker. Two small windows on either side of the door allowed some light in, as did the open door to the office side of the business, but Edgar lit several lanterns and set them on crates near the box as he prepared to open it for inspection. Morella jumped onto a stack of crates from which she could better see the newly delivered box.

What do you suppose is in it?

"My father didn't say. His instructions were to make sure it was undamaged before his client shows up to pick it up."

An oblong box. You know what it looks like.

Edgar felt familiar phantom fingers running up his spine and declined to answer. He gathered a crowbar and hammer from where they hung with other tools on a side wall and wedged the flat end of the bar between the top and the sides. When he had nearly worked his way around the box, he heard footsteps coming from the other side of the building.

"Hello?"

"Coming," Edgar called back as he moved quickly through the doorway that separated the two halves of the business. A clean-shaven man with curly brown hair settling over his ears and above his eyes waited near his father's desk. "You must be Mr. Wyatt," Edgar said, extending his hand. "I'm Edgar, Mr. Allan's son."

"Cornelius Wyatt," the man said, accepting Edgar's welcome. "I understand you have a delivery for me?"

"It just came in. I was about to inspect it. Would you care to join me?"

Mr. Wyatt followed Edgar into the warehouse. Looking up into the rafters, he said, "There's more space here than I thought."

"There are living quarters above the office area, but my father has yet to make a second floor on this side," Edgar explained as he, too, looked upward. "He plans to enclose it one day, but for now it feels rather like a barn." He moved back to the oblong box and picked up the crowbar and hammer. "Shall I?"

"Please." The man's eyes shone in the dim light of the lanterns, his excitement so obvious Edgar felt another chill. With only a few strokes the lid was free. Wyatt gripped one end of the lid while Edgar took the other and they set it to the side against a wall. As Edgar stood, a shadow crossed the entire warehouse as if a huge dark cloud had crossed in front of the sun, throwing the area into even deeper gloom. The lanterns were an absolute necessity for Edgar to make his inspection. When Edgar looked back inside the oblong box, he thought his heart might have stopped. Wyatt, in contrast, was clearly delighted.

Lying in a bed of dirt was a body.

It was long dead, and its clothing, apparently once a long dress of plain black cloth, indicated a female. Bones and decaying flesh showed through worn holes in the fabric where rodents might have feasted. The corpse's skull still bore a few strands of long, gray hair, and patches of wafer-thin skin curled up from the ghastly face, so thin that Mr. Wyatt's excited breathing as he hovered over the body caused them to flutter. Dried, wrinkled skin covering the sunken eyes made Edgar recall sketches he had seen of mummies rather than the skeletons he saw on many of his beloved tombstones.

Inexplicably, Wyatt dashed out of the warehouse into the shop area of the business leaving Edgar alone in the gloom with the corpse. Morella no longer sat on the stack of crates and was nowhere to be seen. Edgar's heart raced and he backed slowly away from the oblong box until his back contacted a stack of crates. As quickly as he had left, Wyatt was back, but Edgar saw he held an odd contraption, something unlike anything Edgar had ever seen before.

Mounted on a wooden base was a composite of wires, coils and magnets, with one small gear connected by a thin band to a larger gear with a handle. Wyatt moved a stack of empty crates next to the oblong box and set his machine on it near the corpse's waist. To Edgar's horror, he lifted the corpse's left hand and attached one wire from the device to its rotted middle finger, and then repeated the process with a second wire on the middle finger of the right hand. Wyatt then turned the handle which produced a number of small sparks, and Edgar detected a pungent, coppery odor he could not identify.

Wyatt's glee as he worked was unnerving. Edgar could see sweat forming on the man's brow and upper lip, but his client's excitement only grew the more he cranked the device. As repulsed as he was by the decayed corpse, Edgar couldn't keep himself from staring at it. It seemed the body jerked at times, although Edgar dismissed that movement at first as being an illusion of Wyatt's brisk cranking motion. But then he looked more closely at the dead thing's eyes––the wrinkled skin seemed to be twitching, as if the deceased were trying to open its eyes.

That can't be! Her eyes would have decayed years ago, he thought.

As if that were her cue, the corpse's eyelids flew back to reveal gray orbs without a hint of iris or pupil. Her bony hands appeared to shrink, but then Edgar realized the corpse was slowly clenching her hands into fists. The wires attached to her fingers fell away, but that did not stop them from moving. Wyatt stopped cranking the handle and looked at her with an expression of reverent adoration. When she had successfully closed her hands, she worked as diligently to stretch the fingers out again. She then raised her arms to grip the sides of the oblong box and began to raise herself to a sitting position. Edgar tried to retreat further backwards, but he had already backed himself against a wall of crates. Wyatt continued to gape at her with rapturous joy.

"Welcome," Wyatt said almost breathlessly.

The corpse turned her head toward Wyatt. She did not blink nor did she appear to be breathing. Edgar felt his blood rush down to his feet and his head felt light.

Deep slow breaths, Edgar.

Edgar realized Morella crouched on a crate next to the stack he was leaning against. Grateful for her presence, he closed his eyes and drew in a big breath through his mouth and released it through his nose. He repeated that process two more times and opened his eyes. The corpse stared at him.

"Do you know who you are, my dear?" Wyatt asked.

She seemed at first to ignore the question, continuing instead to look at Edgar. The dried lips, little more than thin folds of flesh that looked like strips of dried fruit, parted slightly. Edgar watched, horrified as a black slug slid out and ran its tip over her lips, but then he realized it was actually her tongue, and that the dead woman was attempting to moisten her lips. When Edgar saw the corpse had no teeth, his scalp tingled and goosebumps formed down his neck and arms.

"Ed...gar." Each syllable came slowly, tortuous for the corpse to form, and yet her desiccated lips curled into a toothless smile. The dry, parched voice caused Edgar's stomach to spasm. "You know me...do you...not?"

Edgar could not speak; he shook his head.

"Do you not...recognize...your own...mother?" The words came a bit more quickly the more she spoke, although they still sounded dry and scratched, like patches of dirty wool yanked from a sheep farmer's carder. Flashes of another image, another woman, flickered within the skull-like visage for fractions of a second, an image that looked like the portrait Edgar had seen of his birth mother.

"Or am I...another...mother?" A second image flashed so quickly over the deathly visage Edgar couldn't tell whether he recognized it or not. Once he thought he saw Francis Allan, but then it also looked like Robert's mother, Jane.

"I am...every woman...you have loved...or will ever love...Edgar."

A succession of female faces including Elmira's flickered with the corpse's as she tilted back her head and cackled. Wyatt joined his laugh to hers until abruptly she stopped and collapsed, leaning over until her head sat on her bony thighs.

Edgar turned to look at Wyatt. The madman only smiled at him, the grin growing wider and wider; his curly hair straightened and darkened, and the hairline drew back higher onto his forehead. His nose grew smaller and the eyes darker and closer together until Edgar realized he was looking once again into the devilish, smiling face of his eerie echo.

"The life has gone out of our guest it seems," he said, his head tilted into the unnatural pose that frightened Edgar so much. "But that can be remedied." Dark Edgar reached into the oblong box and from under the corpse's dress he pulled two objects, each made of a thin wooden bar about a foot in length with two smaller bars fastened across them on one half. Edgar had seen a puppeteer use such props in a traveling show the previous summer. The doppelgänger winked once at Edgar and then in a feat no circus acrobat could have matched, completed a series of nimble leaps and somersaults from one stack of crates to another which ultimately landed him in the rafters of the warehouse. He squatted on a beam directly over the oblong box with his arms out before him.

He made a dramatic gesture with his right hand, and the corpse sat up again in its box. Standing, he raised both arms dramatically and the corpse stood in its box with its head drooping on its chest. A flip of his wrist and the corpse's head looked up at Edgar with its dull eyes staring and its toothless mouth gaping. Edgar's phantom twin crept nimbly along the beam as he gazed down at his life-sized puppet while miming the action of pulling invisible strings. As he did so, the corpse climbed out of the box to stand facing Edgar. Despite the absence of any visible strings or wires, the corpse performed as any marionette might at the hands of a masterful puppeteer.

The dead woman bowed slightly at the waist and curtsied, an action all the more horrifying in its grotesque mimicry of a live, young woman. It straightened and stepped stiffly toward Edgar which finally caused him to snap out of his paralysis and to step slowly away from the oblong box. Edgar kept his eyes on the approaching corpse, but his double's shadow swept the room as he leapt from one rafter to another. The corpse below made a corresponding leap with its arms out wide and landed on top of Edgar, knocking him to the ground.

Edgar pushed the corpse away from himself easily enough as it weighed little more than a dried cornstalk, and rushed for the dimly lit doorway that led to the shop and his father's office. Bursting wild-eyed into the brighter room, he was barely able to keep himself from running into his father, who stood wide-eyed before him.

"Edgar! What on earth is the matter with you?"

Edgar's father was not alone. Beside him stood Cornelius Wyatt. Edgar stood speechless and looked from one man to the other as he tried to make sense of the surreal sequence of events. He knew an attempt to explain the experience with his double was futile, but he had to say something.

"I thought, I thought I heard a disturbance in here." He paused to control his breathing. "I wasn't expecting you. I thought maybe an intruder..." Mr. Allan still frowned, but to Edgar's relief, he did not press Edgar for further explanation.

"This is Mr. Wyatt," Edgar's father said. "The owner of the delivery we expected today." He turned to Edgar with a look of obvious embarrassment. "And this, Mr. Wyatt, is my well-meaning but sometimes over-imaginative son, Edgar." The gentleman with Mr. Allan looked identical to the man Edgar had met previously, before his transformation into Dark Edgar, but he showed no sign of recognition as he offered his hand to Edgar in what appeared to be a genuine show of cordiality.

It's not him.

Edgar looked down to see Morella was at his feet. *Not Mr. Wyatt, or not my double?* he thought.

Not your double.

Edgar offered a small, nervous smile as he shook Mr. Wyatt's hand, but threw a quick backward glance over his shoulder toward the warehouse, fearful the animated corpse might burst upon them at any second. Sensing Edgar's discomfort, Mr. Allan rejected any further attempt at polite small talk, including an explanation of why he was there with Mr. Wyatt when he had arranged for Edgar to handle the reception of the delivery. Instead, he addressed his primary concern directly.

"Was the delivery made, Edgar? Was there a problem?"

When Edgar failed to answer quickly but only looked helplessly toward the warehouse, Mr. Allan took a deep breath and then in an exasperated tone nodded to Mr. Wyatt with an arm extended to the rear doorway. "If you'll follow me." He stepped briskly into the warehouse. Mr. Wyatt gave Edgar a quick worried glance and followed Edgar's father, and Edgar reluctantly fell in behind him.

To Edgar's amazement, the oblong box was sealed. The lid was secured as tightly as if Edgar had never removed it. Edgar looked up to the rafters and was relieved to see no sign of his double. Both Mr. Wyatt and Mr. Allan also seemed a bit relieved upon seeing the box sitting apparently unharmed on the sawhorses. Edgar's father's face relaxed as he looked at his son. "I see you haven't had time to check the contents." Edgar looked at his father silently, searching desperately for what he should say. "Mr. Wyatt, if you don't have any objections, we can open the crate and perform an inspection now. Then we can help you load it onto your wagon and you can be on your way."

"That would be fine, yes," Mr. Wyatt said.

Edgar's father fetched the same crowbar and hammer Edgar had used earlier. When the lid had been loosened, Mr. Allan gestured for Edgar to grab one end of the lid, and together they lifted it and set it aside. Edgar's heart raced as he worried what his father would think when he saw the corpse. Edgar held his breath and looked inside.

A grandfather clock carved of a rich dark mahogany nearly filled the inside of the oblong box. Sawdust and straw packed tightly around the timepiece had effectively preserved its beauty and kept it intact.

"It seems to have survived the voyage from Germany and the last leg of the trip to Richmond quite well," Mr. Allan said. Mr. Wyatt beamed as he gazed at his valuable new possession.

Bra-a-ack!

A raven flew above their heads causing all three to duck as it crossed the warehouse in a low flight and then came to a stop on the same rafter where Edgar had first watched his dark twin perch.

"How the devil did that damn bird get in here?" Mr. Allan exclaimed. "Edgar, raise the door so it can escape." Edgar quickly unhitched the rope on the far wall and within a minute refreshing sunlight poured into the space.

Mr. Wyatt smiled and, for a second, Edgar feared that he would transform again. But then Edgar realized Wyatt's pleasure was simply the joy one has upon an anticipated event coming to fruition. He wasn't bothered in the least by the raven's presence; in fact, he seemed amused by it.

"Perhaps this bird is a good omen," he said. "You could keep it on as a mascot."

Bra-a-ack! "Nevermore!"

Morella rubbed against Edgar's leg.

My sentiments exactly.

7

"He is, as you say, a remarkable horse—a prodigious horse! Although as you very justly observe, of a suspicious and untractable character; let him be mine…perhaps a rider like Frederick of Metzengerstein may tame even the devil from the stables of Berlifitzing."

from "Metzengerstein"

Finally, he saw it.

For two weeks Edgar had walked by the Royster home nearly every day regardless of his destination hoping Elmira had left a sign indicating her willingness to see him. He didn't know what he was looking for exactly but, when he saw it, there was no mistaking it had been left intentionally for him. The small, stuffed black cat propped up against the fence near the gate was missing its left eye. Edgar smiled as he pictured Elmira vandalizing one of her childhood toys for his sake.

I suppose I should be honored, but it does seem a bit ominous.

Edgar stroked Morella's back as he stooped to pick up the toy.

"We should hurry. There's no telling how long she's been there, or how long she can stay."

Morella had no problem keeping up with Edgar in spite of his hurried pace. She stopped occasionally to sniff at wild flowers or bits of offal along the road, giving equal attention to each before running to catch up with her human companion. Edgar's heart sank when Elmira wasn't at the gate to the cemetery, but his fears were allayed quickly once they arrived at what Edgar now thought of as "Morella's stone" and he saw Elmira sitting there. Her smile matched Edgar's when they saw each other and she took Edgar's hand in her own as he sat beside her on the memorial rock.

"I was so afraid you wouldn't come by my house today," she said.

"Father's kept me very busy lately and, on the rare days I couldn't check for you, I was afraid I had missed your sign."

"I know. It's been so hard to watch you from my window and not be able to speak to you."

They sat quietly for a moment, enjoying the chance to be together. Edgar broke the silence first.

"Have you had other signs of him since--"

"No." She cut him off before he had to mention the specifics of the grisly teeth left on her porch. "I think that may have been more for your benefit than mine. And you? Have you had any other contact with him?"

Edgar told her of the encounter he had in his father's warehouse. Elmira's hand flew to her mouth when Edgar told her of how his double had made the corpse/puppet jump on him.

"And then, he was gone?" she asked.

"As if he had never been there."

"And this man--Mr. Wyatt?"

Edgar nodded.

"He didn't show any sign of having seen your twin?"

"No. I don't think he would have. Somehow Dark Edgar can appear as anyone he wishes, and that person will have no knowledge they have been impersonated. As when he appeared to you as me. And to my father." Edgar felt the shudder that ran through Elmira's body and then he saw she was studying him carefully.

"What if he impersonates you again?" She reached up and touched Edgar's forehead. "I can barely make out where your wound was. And who's to say he wouldn't bear that mark too?"

"I promise. I'm me," he said, squeezing her hand, "The real Edgar."

She smiled weakly. "I believe you. Oh, Edgar. It's just all so frightening."

I can tell the difference.

Morella jumped up on the stone and rubbed against Elmira's elbow.

"I don't think you'll ever see Morella with him," Edgar said. "Or if you did, you'd probably be able to tell that something's not right. She would let you know." Elmira stroked Morella's head and ran her hand down the cat's back.

"Thank goodness for you, girl," Elmira said. Morella purred and settled herself on Elmira's lap much to Elmira's delight. "How is Robert? Have you seen him lately?"

Edgar shook his head. "I don't think he's well. I can't ever get him to leave the house. When we talk, he's not the same. He's so worried about his mother."

"Do you know what's wrong with her?"

"No one seems to know. And the medicines the doctor gives her seem to make things worse. Robert says she spends most of her time sleeping."

"I know that must make you sad too. Robert's your good friend." Elmira smiled. "Although I don't know how you can stand him sometimes. He's so silly." Morella lifted her head to look at Edgar.

I told you she's a smart girl.

Edgar smiled and petted the cat. "He is that." Edgar's smile melted and he picked an acorn up from the stone beside him and tossed it out onto the grass. "Or at least, he used to be." Elmira looked at him and frowned, but then her expression suddenly brightened.

"Father says a traveling company arrived last night and is setting up a carnival on the fairgrounds. He said he heard they have animals from faraway lands and all kinds of exhibits. I think there's even a magician. You should convince Robert to go; it would be good for him."

Edgar tilted his head as he considered that news. "He would like that. And so would I." He turned to face Elmira. "And what about you? Will your parents let you go?"

"Oh, yes." Edgar perked up but, sensing his excitement, she quickly added, "They may insist I stay with them." Edgar's shoulders fell, but he nodded. "But I might see you there. And perhaps they'll be in such good spirits they'll let me have a few minutes with my friends."

"I'll do my best to refrain from digging up any more corpses," Edgar said. They both laughed, and then sat silently for a moment enjoying each other's company with the sound of the birds chirping and the rustle of the branches swaying gently in the summer breeze. Eventually Elmira broke the spell.

"This has been so nice, but I'm going to have to go home, Edgar. I don't want my mother to be angry with me. Especially if we might have a chance of being together tonight."

Edgar nodded and smiled. "You won't mind being with Robert, if he comes along?"

"I'll suffer through it," she said, smiling at him in a way that made Edgar's heart race. As she shifted her weight to slide off the stone, Morella stood and jumped down to the ground.

"I can walk you at least part of the way home," Edgar said. "Then I'll go to Robert's house and see if I can talk him into leaving his house after dinner for a little fun."

"That sounds perfect." Edgar noticed her smile seemed mischievous, as if she were planning something, and then grabbing the lapels of his vest, she pulled herself to him, raised up on her toes and kissed him quickly on the lips. Before he could say anything, she stepped quickly toward the entrance of the graveyard.

If you're going to walk with her, you better get moving.

Grinning broadly, Edgar jogged a few steps to catch up with her and Morella followed behind, her tail raised as straight as a ship's mast.

It wasn't the first time Edgar and Robert had seen a traveling show in Richmond, but the one spread out before them with its torches and lanterns blazing in the dim light of the setting sun looked like a village had magically appeared. Nine large tents arranged in three rows formed a square with pathways running between them strewn with straw that in effect served as small streets. The three tents in the interior had all their walls rolled up so their wares and activities were viewable from every side, while the other six along the exterior were accessible only from one side.

Robert and Edgar both stood in amazement at the edge of the fairground as they stared at the visual extravaganza. As usual, Morella had accompanied Edgar on his trek to Robert's and then on to the carnival. She rubbed against Edgar's leg as he surveyed the bustling scene. Edgar wondered if she might be frightened by all the strange smells and sounds, but her ears were perked up and she held her tail high. Clearly, she, too, was enjoying herself.

The makeshift streets were already bustling with excited townspeople and vendors calling out to sell their wares. To the left of the exhibitions and entertainers, Robert, whose face was glowing with excitement, noticed a much larger tent with a gated pen next to it that contained what appeared to be ponies in the fading light. A swarthy man with a full, thick mustache covering his top lip and hanging down to his jawline nodded at them as they approached.

"Edgar!" Robert exclaimed, gripping his companion by the arm and pointing into the pen. "Is that...? It is! It's a zebra!" In addition to the zebra, in other sections of the pen there were three llamas, a donkey, something close to the size of a boar Edgar could not identify, and several small ponies for children to ride.

No tigers? No lions? Ah, well, I suppose that's for the best. Might have been interesting to see some distant relatives, though. Edgar looked down and smiled.

The nearest side of the large tent was rolled up so the boys could see makeshift stalls partitioned off with ropes and stakes in which several horses were quartered. Off to one side, away from the others, one horse shook its head which caught Robert's attention.

"Oh, that stallion's a beauty!" He turned to the man who had watched them since they had arrived. "Could we take a closer look at that one?" Edgar chuckled to himself, amused that of all the exotic animals available, Robert was enthralled by a horse. But then again, his friend's love of horses was no secret to anyone who knew him.

"Yes, but please, no too close," the man said in imperfect English. "He is the Baron's. No touch or frighten." Edgar and Robert followed the worker into the tent where Robert gazed admiringly up at the black stallion. The beast stood over fifteen hands high at the withers.

It looked at the boys with what Robert interpreted as pride but what Edgar regarded as disdain. The lantern light reflected in its eyes made it look as if fire burned within them. Morella hopped onto a bale of hay at a good distance from the horse's stall.

That is no ordinary horse.

"The Baron's, you said?" Edgar asked of the attendant.

"Baron von Metzengerstein. Owner of carnival. He was Prussian officer and very––"

"Omar!"

The attendant's eyes grew wide and his mouth dropped as a tall man strode briskly into the tent. The figure's posture and bearing commanded respect, leading Edgar to believe they were in the presence of the Baron himself. He wore a black leather jacket with gold buttons tailored to hug his athletic form. A crisp white shirt underneath bore a high collar and ruffles that protruded from the sleeves of the jacket. His pants were a deep red, and tucked into knee-high black leather boots. His hair was as dark as his beard but was pulled back and oiled so that it shone in the lantern light.

"You boys must leave. I'm sorry. Omar should not have allowed you entry."

"It's my fault," Robert said. "I couldn't help asking. He's such a beautiful horse!" The Baron's face softened somewhat.

"Yes, my Teufel is a remarkable beast. From the Prussian cavalry. He has seen more than his share of death and fears nothing. There is not another like him the world over." He looked at both of the boys with narrowed eyes before speaking again, and then with a forced smile directed his next question at Edgar, which made Edgar extremely uncomfortable. "I am Baron von Metzengerstein. You are enjoying my carnival, yes?"

Morella stirred, both ears perked and single eye wide as she looked on from her perch on the hay. *Careful, Edgar.*

"We only just arrived, but it looks...wonderful," Edgar answered. "Like nothing we've seen before."

"Yes, we're really excited to see the performers and exhibits," Robert added, anxious to ease the tension they had caused.

The Baron nodded. "Enjoy yourselves. But for now, I must ask you to leave our modest stable."

Edgar and Robert nodded and headed quickly out of the large tent. Morella jumped down and followed. When they were out of sight, they heard a loud slap followed by the Baron's angry voice.

"Imbecile! I've told you never to let anyone near Teufel!"

"I'm sorry, sir. I just--"

Another sound of flesh hitting flesh was followed by the thud of a body collapsing.

"I want no excuses. The next time you disobey me..." What else the Baron had to say was lost as Edgar and Robert put more distance between themselves and the Baron's discipline.

"Well, off to a fine start, eh, Edgar?" Edgar said nothing but continued on toward the orange lights illuminating the carnival village. "I'm only teasing," Robert continued. "I'm glad you asked me to come." He stopped to survey the scene before them. "Where should we begin?"

There were choices since there was no one specified entrance. The lanterns and torches made the gaily decorated village look enchanted. Several craftsmen displaying their wares of pottery, basketry, and jewelry shared the tent in the center of the first row, and prospective buyers could approach their tables from all sides. The boys ambled down the greenway to their left, hardly knowing where to look with so many diversions. To the left, an artist worked on a sketch of a young woman who sat with an embarrassed smile while the man who obviously had commissioned the work stood watching. To the right, a man wearing a turban threw knives at a target at the other end of his tent. He wore a loose-fitting white shirt which showed most of his chest over multi-striped trousers tucked into soft, brown boots. The shirt flowed down nearly to his knees and was closed at the waist by a red sash. A bandana which matched the sash covered his head, but his long hair hung down past his shoulders, as did both halves of his flowing mustache. Seeing he had garnered Robert's attention, he called out.

"You know a good weapon, when you see one, no, my young friend?" He pulled the knives he had thrown from the wooden board and walked back to the boys, extending the handles to Robert. "Go ahead, examine them!" Robert took one of the blades with a pattern that came alive when held at the right angle. The handle was smooth and fit Robert's hand perfectly while the curved hilt did not bite into his finger. Robert ran the flesh of his thumb across the blade to test it. "I see you are quite knowledgeable about fine metalwork. It is an excellent blade, is it not?"

"Very nice," Robert agreed. "I'll have to think about it. I have much else to see here as my friend and I just arrived."

"This knife may be gone before you return," the bladesman warned. "If you buy it now, I will include this sheath with the purchase at no extra charge." He pulled a black leather sheath which would easily slide onto a belt from under the black felt-covered table on which other fine blades were displayed.

"How can you turn down such a fine deal?"

Robert and Edgar turned to identify the owner of the feminine voice that had urged Robert. Elmira grinned mischievously, and Edgar's smile nearly split his face.

"Beauty and intelligence," the bladesman said, nodding his thanks to her. The young trio stepped away from the knife display, and the carnie turned his attention to a man in a low-crowned hat who was inspecting another set of knives.

Edgar looked up and down the midway and asked, "Where are your parents?"

"They're here. As I had hoped they got caught up in the spirit of the carnival and said I could explore a bit on my own. They're so giddy you'd think they were younger than us. It's almost like Father is courting my mother all over again."

"Oh, that's a spectacle I can do without," Robert said.

"Oh, Robert!" Elmira scolded. "I think it's sweet. Don't you, Edgar?"

Honesty is not always the best policy. Edgar looked down at his feline companion who sat primly out of the main pathway and then back up to Elmira.

"A carnival brings out the child in everyone, I suppose," he said.

Well played, sir. I'm impressed.

Elmira turned to Robert. "How is your mother?" She had dropped her tone of playful banter. Robert cast his eyes down to his feet before looking up again with a smile carved onto his face.

"She's better, I think."

Elmira didn't say a word but continued to look at Robert as she nodded and looked into his eyes, sensing the unspoken truth. Edgar noted how Robert's face softened, comforted by so little. Edgar marveled at how she could convey so much without saying a word.

She's a special person, that one is. Morella's tone conveyed no hint of her usual sarcasm or playfulness.

"Well, who wants to have their fortunes told?" Elmira gripped each of the boys by the elbow, skillfully drafting them as her official escorts, and pulled them back into the stream of excited citizens who seemed all too eager to part with their hard-earned coins. "I've been waiting until I had two brave companions before approaching the witch-woman's tent, but I can't wait to visit her."

Elmira whisked the boys past a tent where a bearded strong man with long curling hair grunted as he bent an iron bar to a cheering crowd. He wore an outfit made of animal skins which showed the powerful muscles along his arms, torso, and legs, and on top of his head a well-preserved lion's head missing only its lower jaw sat with its light brown pelt spilling down the performer's broad back. The sign on a tripod proclaimed, "Hercules, the Strongest Man on Earth." Robert slowed to watch, but Elmira jerked his arm nearly causing him to trip.

"Hey, I'd like to see that!" he objected.

"We can come back later. The fortune teller might be gone!" Elmira hurried the boys along, turning after a tent in which a barker called out to them to try their luck with a ring toss game. They turned down an improvised alley between two other rows of tents, Elmira clearly knowing exactly where she needed to go. Morella trotted along beside them, mindful of the feet of other unwary carnival-goers.

Finally, they stopped in front of a tent with a sign reading "Madame Sofia, Diviner of the Past, Present, and Future." Instead of rolling up an entire side of the tent as other carnies did to make their wares more visible, only a single flap served as an entrance to the fortune teller's den, but it was down which blocked any view of its interior. "Oh, drat!" Elmira released her hold on the boy's arms and stomped her foot. "As I feared. She's――"

"Shh!" Edgar held one finger up. He spoke in a low voice, "Someone's in there."

"Karl, no! I can't!" A woman's voice muffled by the thick canvas wall of the tent and the noise of the carnival but still audible.

"No one travels for free, Sofia." The deep Prussian accent Edgar recognized. He looked at Robert.

"The Baron," Robert whispered. Edgar nodded.

Elmira frowned at both of them in turns, questioning them silently. Edgar held one finger up again and turned his head to hear the conversation in the tent more clearly. All three held their breath as they listened.

"I will pay you everything soon. You know the hardships I've faced."

"Yes, I know, Sofia. And I'm not heartless." There was a pause and then he continued in a different tone. "Far from it." Elmira's eyes widened and then narrowed quickly as she realized the implication.

"Baron, no."

"Don't resist, my dear." Another pause. "You are so beautiful."

"Please, don't."

Elmira gripped the flap of the tent and threw it back and entered.

"Madame Sofia?" she called in a loud, cheerful voice. Morella darted into the tent as Edgar looked first at Robert and then entered behind her. Robert rolled his eyes and followed.

The Baron turned to the entrance of the tent, his scowl like a gargoyle's at the interruption.

"Oh, I'm sorry," Elmira continued. "We wanted our fortunes told. Is this a bad time?" Her expression was one of exaggerated innocence. The woman in the dark hood and flowing garments stared at her, clearly startled but also relieved.

The Baron's eyes narrowed even further as he recognized Edgar and Robert. "You again."

Elmira continued to play her part. "Oh, you've met my companions?" She held out her hand. "I'm Marie. Marie Kunstler. And you are...?"

Baron Metzengerstein stood quiet, appraising the brazen young girl who stood before him. "I'm impressed." A slow smile crept over his face. Elmira let her hand slowly fall to her side, and her own smile faltered as he continued to look at her. He stepped closer and raised a hand to Elmira's face, and gently caressed her cheek. "Such a lovely child," he said, his voice hardly more than a whisper. Elmira trembled slightly at his touch, but continued to look steadily into his eyes, her lips pressed tightly together.

"Baron! No!" The fortune teller's dark eyes flashed. Metzengerstein's hand dropped to his side and he turned to Madame Sofia. "We will finish our business later, Sofia." He turned back to Elmira. "I certainly hope you enjoy the carnival. I look forward to seeing you again." He stepped toward the tent flap and stopped as the boys blocked his way. Robert stepped to his left to allow the Baron to pass. Edgar stood still, staring defiantly at the carnival owner.

Edgar. Let him pass. He is capable of more than you can imagine.

Edgar glanced at Morella who crouched at Elmira's feet, her ears back and her tail twitching. He looked back at the Baron and then moved to stand beside Robert, glaring as he did so.

"You boys tread on dangerous ground," he said. He punched the word *boys*. "I advise you not to let our paths cross again." He glared at them both as his words hung, suspended it seemed, on the clouds of incense that permeated the air, and then briskly exited the tent.

No one spoke for a moment. The sounds of the carnival seemed distant as the fortune teller looked at each of her visitors and assessed the situation. She finally spoke first to Elmira.

"Thank you. You are a brave girl."

"Sometimes a foolish one, my mother says. I often act before I think." Everyone smiled along with Elmira, grateful for the break in the tension.

"Your mother is not wrong. But you have good friends," Madame Sofia said. She swept her gaze over Robert, Edgar, and then over to Morella who had jumped up onto a large chest."

Elmira smiled. "Indeed, I do." Once again, her face changed as she addressed a serious situation. "I hope we didn't make matters worse for you. It seems that man is..." she faltered for the right words to say.

"He is problematic." The fortune teller's English was perfect. Her accent in no way impeded her ability to communicate; in fact, it served as an asset, making her speech more resonant, more fluid than native English speakers. "But you did not come here to hear my problems. I think perhaps you'd like your fortunes told?"

She gestured to the tasseled cushions lying about the carpeted floor. The three friends looked at each other for signs of what each wanted to do. Robert looked as if he would be happy to leave, but Edgar looked to Elmira for his cue.

"That is what we came for, yes," Elmira said.

Rather than sitting in the high-backed chair behind a table draped with black cloth on which a crystal sphere sat, the fortune teller took her place on one of the cushions and the three young friends followed suit. The richly colored arabesque carpets covering the walls muffled the noise of the crowds outside.

"You don't need..." Robert gestured toward the ball on the table.

"The crystal is but a prop," Madame Sofia said with a smile. "Most people would be disappointed if I did not have one. But I don't need it for my craft."

Edgar could not help but note how exotically beautiful the fortune teller was. It was no mystery that even the owner of the carnival would be taken with her. Her hair fell in raven waves around her shoulders in spite of the gray hood covering her head. Her eyes were dark, as was her complexion, yet Edgar could not determine what country or culture she might have claimed. She wore bangles of gold and silver, some set with turquoise and other stones, which jingled when she moved. Her hands were perhaps her most striking feature, with long, tapered fingers decorated with many rings, her nails painted a deep red.

"Can you really tell the future?" Robert asked.

"Would I tell you if I couldn't?" Madame Sofia's grin erased any possible sting her words might have had. "I am able to see certain things that are to come," she said, the teasing gone from her words. "I see what the spirits allow me to see. Often, I have no control. But I see things from the past, and things ongoing as well." She looked sadly at Robert. "There is suffering in your family now, I fear," she said. Robert said nothing. "Your mother is not well." Robert nodded. "But the doctors cannot treat her."

"Will she get better?"

The fortune teller looked intently at Robert. "I must be honest. I do not see improvement." Robert's gaze fell to his lap. The fortune teller reached over and gripped Robert's hand. "But you have much to look forward to. You will have many good times. A rewarding life awaits you." Madame Sophia turned her head to look at the other two friends. "There is so much sadness in this group." Her eyes settled on Edgar. "You have already lost a mother."

Edgar felt his skin crawl. Morella hopped down from the chest and crawled into his lap. The fortune teller smiled at that activity, and then added, "But she is with you." Edgar looked at Madame Sophia with a confused look. "It is not important that you understand how. You are dealing with very special circumstances. Potentially dangerous circumstances. But know that your mother knows this, that she loves you, and that she is with you." Edgar's eyes watered and, without thinking, he stroked Morella's head and back. The cat's purring filled the tent. "But I cannot lie. There is much hardship ahead for you, Edgar. So much death."

"You know my name?"

Sophia smiled. "I heard your mother call you this." The friends looked at each other, confirmation of the fortune teller's abilities if they had doubted before. Sophia turned to Elmira. "And now you. NOT Marie, I might add." The friends laughed. "You were the one who wanted to be here, correct?"

"Yes, I made them come."

"I'm grateful you did."

"Will you be safe from...him?"

Sophia nodded. "I will be fine." Elmira's doubt showed on her face. "You are a kind girl. But don't worry. I'm not lying. I will be fine. The Baron will not be a threat to me for long." Elmira nodded.

"But what about me? What do you see for me?"

Sophia looked at her and took her hands in her own. "You will have a good life but, like many, it will have its share of sadness." She looked at Edgar but continued to hold Elmira's hand. "Things may not go as you hope they will." She turned back to Elmira. "But do not give up hope. The two of you are meant for each other."

Robert grinned broadly as his two friends blushed. "Are those wedding bells, I hear?"

The fortune teller's smile faded for a second, but then her face brightened. "We don't always get what we want in the way we want it." She released Elmira's hands and turned to Edgar. "And we may not always see the results of our efforts. You will be greatly respected in your chosen field, but there will be much heartache before that." Edgar's eyes narrowed. "Try to enjoy the moments of happiness that come. Don't waste them by immersing yourself in the sorrow that must also come. Embrace and celebrate the joy that is given as it is given."

"Well, this is not what I expected at all," Robert said. "I feel like I've been to church!"

"What do we owe you for all of this?" Edgar asked.

"You owe me nothing. You were sent here, and I am grateful for that."

The group rose from their cushions and made their way to the exit, including Morella. They took turns shaking Madame Sophia's hand and thanking her.

"Be well, my friends," the fortune teller said as they exited the tent. "And take care."

Once out on the midway, Elmira slapped her hand to her head and said, "Edgar! We forgot to ask her the most important thing!"

They turned and Edgar threw back the flap to the tent, but when they stepped back inside, the fortune teller was not there.

"Now what do we do?" Robert asked.

"We've done what I wanted," Elmira said. "Edgar, what do you think?"

"Robert and I haven't seen what's on the other midway. Let's turn to the right past this tent."

As they left the fortune teller's tent and joined the larger path, the spirit of the carnival returned to them once again with the chatter from the vendors and the laughter of customers who were trying, and mostly failing, at games of chance. A barker called out for Robert and Edgar to "impress the little lady" with their prowess at archery. He stood at a table with a bow in his hand, holding it out to Edgar. Behind him stood a target in front of a stack of baled hay about fifty feet away. Lanterns hung at intervals down the lane toward the target. Edgar shook his head and the trio walked on.

They passed booths with more crafted items for sale: pipes, clay vases, and artistically shaped brooms made of twisted wood. The female barker in front of one tent caught Robert's attention. A woman with long blond hair cascading down her back wearing a costume of snakeskin that left little to the imagination encouraged people to pet the huge boa constrictor draped over her body. She held the snake up high above her head with one hand and the snake's body wrapped itself once around her torso while the rest of it stretched out onto the ground. A glimpse past the partially open flap showed a dimly lit tent which was filled with huge cages of writhing snakes. They slithered over dead trees positioned to create a semblance of their natural habitat.

"There are more snakes inside. For a single coin you can see for yourself." She looked at Robert. "Show your friends what you're made of, sir. Are you a man or a mouse?"

Call him Squeaky.

"Um, maybe later," Robert said. Edgar and Morella grinned and the trio moved on.

When they had passed the last tent on that makeshift avenue and arrived back at what Edgar considered the front of the carnival, Edgar noticed the crowd had gathered as if in anticipation of an event. "What's happening?" Robert asked a portly man who was perspiring profusely in the warm summer air.

"Time for the carny parade!" the man answered, mopping his forehead with a handkerchief.

Edgar scooped Morella up and placed her on his shoulders where she settled once getting a good grip. Edgar worked his way through the crowd so he could look down the lane that ran away from them back toward the point in which they had entered the carnival. People were lined up along the sides of the avenues, having been corralled and instructed by the carnival workers of the parade route to do so. A cheer went up in the vicinity of where the makeshift stable was, where Edgar and Robert had first encountered Baron Metzengerstein. Sure enough, Edgar saw the Baron himself riding on his magnificent black stallion.

Teufel, which means "Devil" in German.

The Baron looked regal in his black and gold jacket, his crimson trousers, and black boots. But now he also wore a black, wide-brimmed leather hat. The crown was low and tapered at the top, and encircled with a gold band which held a long, curved red feather extending further even than the brim. He wore the hat at a rakish angle, which accentuated his image as a handsome heroic warrior.

Behind him came the llamas, the ponies, two donkeys, and finally the zebra. Some children, squealing with joy, had been allowed to ride the ponies, while painted clowns in rainbow-striped costumes rode the donkeys. Behind them, to the crowd's obvious delight, came the small zebra on which rode a swarthy man no larger than a child. He wore a garment made of a tanned hide which reached barely above his knees and left one shoulder bare. A headdress of bright blue, red, orange, and yellow feathers which stood two feet into the air was secured on his head by a band decorated with beads and cowrie shells. No one rode the llamas; handlers walked slowly beside them along with other clowns who teased and joked with the crowd.

The Baron smiled and waved at the crowd as he passed. When he came near Edgar's group, they stepped back and tried to disappear into the shadows between the tents, but the Baron made eye contact with each of them, staring at them intently without breaking his smile.

Bra-a-ack!

Seemingly out of nowhere, a black streak flashed across the Baron's path. A thin stream of blood trickled down his cheek.

Bra-a-ack!

The crowd gasped as the large black bird darted again across the Baron's path. The black sky hid it from view once it made its pass, but it made repeated strikes at the Baron who cursed and struck out with his fist to no avail. When the raven struck at Teufel's head, the horse reared up, and the crowd scattered, seeking safety between the tents. Again and again the raven struck the horse which neighed and whirled on its back legs, unable to tell where the next strike might be. The Baron held the reins with one hand while he struck out at the raven with the other. As the mighty horse careened into the front of a tent, the baron hit a lantern which exploded over his head. Burning oil covered both horse and rider, igniting the Baron's costume and singing the horse's flesh.

The Baron fought to regain control of the stallion, but it was mad with pain and terror. It crashed into more torches spilling even more oil over the tent walls, its own body, and the Baron's legs. The tent ignited quickly and Teufel, blind with terror, ran into the burning tent. People screamed and ran in all directions; some ran away from the flames while others ran toward them, thick blankets in hand to smother the flames. The trio of friends stayed in place off the midway, unable to make themselves look away from the site where the Baron and his horse had disappeared into the fire.

Suddenly a fireball exploded from the tent. It was the Baron, who somehow still sat astride his horse, totally engulfed in flames. Edgar saw that his hat and most of his clothes had been burned from his body. His mouth gaped open in a silent scream, and the remaining flesh ran like melting wax. His eyes were gone, and although he still held the reins, his hands were mostly bones with only smoking tendons remaining in places.

Teufel, also, was little more than a corpse on fire. The horse galloped down the midway with its mane and tail in flames, and then galloped across the back road and up the other midway to arrive once again at its starting point. From there it repeated its initial route until it came to the burning tent, completing a grotesque parody of the parade route.

Inexplicably the horse re-entered the heart of the inferno. People were too shocked to act. Even the carnival workers stood in amazement. Someone, realizing the other tents were likely to catch fire as well, shouted orders to form a bucket brigade from the nearby James River to save the other tents. The heat was so intense there was no thought given to the idea of attempting a rescue of the Baron.

Edgar held tight to Morella as he and Elmira watched Robert join in the line of men who threw water only on the adjacent tents since there was no hope of extinguishing the tent that had originally caught fire. Workers also threw blankets soaked in water on the tents in hopes of saving them. The owners of the other exhibits beat the embers that landed on or near their property.

Their efforts proved fruitful. When the last flames were gone, the surrounding tents had suffered some damage, but the vendors had saved most of their goods, and no additional lives or livestock were lost. The area where the Baron and his horse had burned was nothing but glowing embers and ash. Not a single recognizable item was left. Not a bone, stirrup, or button. Nothing.

"Do you think we should see if Madame Sophia is safe?" Elmira asked.

Edgar shook his head. "She said she would be fine."

Elmira nodded. "It's like she knew. She said she had nothing to worry about from the Baron."

"Elmira!" Running down the midway were Elmira's parents. "Thank goodness, you're safe!" her mother said, taking her daughter into her arms. Mr. Royster wrapped them both in his arms. When they allowed Elmira the opportunity to break free from their embrace, Elmira said, "I wasn't ever really in danger. Edgar made sure I was safe."

"I didn't--"

"He pulled me to safety between those tents over there," Elmira said, interrupting Edgar. "If he hadn't, we might have been trampled by the crowd."

Mrs. Royster smiled at Edgar, but Elmira's father seemed less impressed.

"I see Robert Stannard aided the rescue effort." They all turned to see Robert was making his way toward them. Mr. Stannard then looked at Edgar who still held Morella, and shook his head.

Don't mind him. The man screams at spiders in the privy. I've heard him.

Suddenly Robert stopped in his tracks. Edgar saw he looked at several people who stood pointing at the sky. Edgar looked to where they pointed. A massive cloud of smoke glowed with pulsing orange light, illuminated from the flames and lanterns below. Murmurs of astonishment rippled through the crowd. The shape of the cloud was undeniable.

A giant horse and rider appeared to gallop across the firmament.

8

from "The Tell-Tale Heart"

As Edgar approached the porch at Moldavia after working at the warehouse for most of the day, he thought it odd to see his mother sitting in one of the wicker chairs on the porch in the heat of the afternoon. When Francis saw Edgar coming up the walk with Morella in tow as usual, she rose and went to stand beside the top step where she gripped the porch railing as she greeted him. Her smile did not reach her eyes.

"Hello, Mother? Are you well? You seem upset."

"I have something to tell you, Edgar. Why don't we sit here on the porch?" Not waiting for an answer, she led Edgar back to where she had been sitting. Edgar sat next to her, perching on the edge of the cushion. Morella, sensing something was wrong, rubbed against his leg.

"You know Jane Stannard has not been well for some time now." Edgar nodded. "I'm afraid she's finally lost her battle." Edgar felt the blow like a hammer to the chest.

"What...when...how did it happen?"

"Mr. Stannard found her. Apparently, she died in her sleep during the night." Edgar stared at his hands. He fought the tears threatening to run down his cheeks. "I know you cared a great deal for her, Edgar. She was a wonderful woman." Edgar nodded again. "I know she loved you too. She told me so more than once."

"I told Robert she was like having a second mother." He smiled at Francis. "Although, I guess it was more like a third mother." His voice broke as he said "mother," and Morella rubbed against him again. Edgar took a deep breath and rubbed his eyes and pinched the bridge of his nose as he worked to control his emotions. Francis reached over and squeezed his hand and then wiped a tear from her own eye with her free hand.

"It's all right to grieve, Edgar."

That broke the dam and the tears flowed down his face. When he felt he could speak, he asked, "How is Robert?"

"I'm sure he's very upset. I imagine he would like to see you if you feel up to visiting him."

"Yes. Of course," Edgar said, wiping his eyes again. "Once I'm sure I won't be making it worse for him."

"Maybe he needs someone who can share his grief. Don't feel that holding onto your emotions is what makes you strong." Edgar looked at his mother and nodded yet again. "I have some gingerbread made with the molasses we got from the Ellisons you can take for his family. There will be guests coming and they'll need to have something to offer them."

"Mother, they have a cook."

"I know, but you can't have too much at a time like this."

"I'll clean up a bit first. I worked up quite a sweat in the warehouse today."

"Of course," his mother said. "I don't imagine you'll have to worry about interrupting their dinner tonight."

Edgar rose and leaned over to hug Francis. "Thank you for being *my* mother," he said softly in her ear. He straightened and went into the house, holding the door for the cat to enter first. Francis watched him go, listening to his footsteps on the stairs with a heart almost as heavy as his.

"This was a good idea. I needed to get away from the house for a while." Robert found the sound and sight of the water breaking over the rocks on the James River soothing. Unsure of what would be best to say, Edgar chose to say nothing. He watched Morella who sat like a statue except for her twitching tail as she, in turn, watched the birds darting in and out of the trees along the shoreline.

"There will be a service on Saturday," Robert said, finally breaking the silence. Most of our family is here in Richmond, but my father asked if you might be able to help us with something." Edgar turned to his friend, open to hear what the Stannards needed of him. "You know of one of my mother's brothers who lives here. Uncle Julius."

The one who killed the cat. Morella did not break her gaze away from her birdwatching.

"The one with a drinking problem, as I recall," Edgar said.

"Yes, that's the one. But I have another uncle who lives several hours south of here in Petersburg. He is a widower and lives alone. His health is poor now, but he and my mother were very close, especially in their youth, and they used to visit often. We know he'd like to come for my mother's funeral, but he cannot make the trip himself. I would go to Petersburg and bring him back here, but my father..." Grief swallowed the rest making it impossible for Robert to continue.

"Would you like for me to get him?" The look on Robert's face spoke volumes. "My father is away. Again." Edgar paused to look out across the water. "But I'm sure my mother would want me to do this. I can take our wagon and--"

"Father said you could take our brougham and one of our horses," Robert said after clearing his throat. "That way if it should rain on the way Uncle Rob would stay dry."

"Uncle Rob?"

"Yes." Robert returned Edgar's smile. "That's right, I am named for him. As I said, he and Mother were very close. He and Aunt Catherine never had children, so after she died a few years ago, he has lived alone. He insisted he was fine, and when he was in good health, we saw him often. But now, with Mother...well, I'm afraid it's been quite a while since we've seen him."

"I assume he doesn't know of your mother's passing?"

Robert took a deep breath and looked at Edgar anxiously. "No. I realize I'm asking a lot of you, Edgar. My father will have a letter for you to give to him that explains what's happened." He paused and took Edgar by the arm. "But if you'd rather not?"

"I'm glad I can help," Edgar said. "Should I prepare to leave tomorrow then?"

"If you could. Uncle Rob will need some help preparing for the trip, but you can stay with him overnight. He has plenty of room. Too many rooms, to be honest. Ask the housekeeper."

"I should probably get home to prepare for the trip," Edgar said.

"I should be getting back too," Robert said. "I'm sure there's a houseful of people paying their condolences and Father, well, he can use all the help I can offer."

Both boys rose and dusted the dirt from the seat of their trousers. Morella followed closely as they made their way up from the bank of the river and onto Front Street before parting ways on Main.

Edgar gave the horse a pat on its rump and climbed back up onto the driver's seat of the Stannards' brougham carriage. Morella crouched on all fours on the folded blanket Edgar had placed so she could sit with him on the trip. He knew the horse likely needed to rest after its frightening experience, and Edgar could have used rest as well after chasing the horse for two hours in unfamiliar terrain, but he still had at least two more hours to travel before reaching Petersburg.

I was afraid you and the horse were lost.

"I was for a while."

Was it the raven?

"Yes. It came out of nowhere, as at the carnival when it attacked Teufel. It struck at the horse's head. I should have kept hold of the harness while the horse was drinking, but everything seemed fine. Before I knew it, the raven was attacking and the horse was running."

It would have bolted regardless. You did well to catch it and find your way back here.

Edgar nodded. "I don't know what I would have done if I had lost Mr. Stannard's horse. But now we'll be even later getting to Robert's uncle's farm."

It will still be daylight when we arrive.

They rode in silence for a while, and then Edgar asked, "Why do you think that happened?"

You're asking why the raven attacked this time?

Edgar considered her question. "Yes, but more importantly, why is it in my life at all?"

I can't answer either of those.

"Why don't you know? It cannot be a coincidence that you entered my life at the same time this other Edgar appears. Or that he has a raven companion as I have you."

I agree. Morella looked straight ahead at the road rather than at Edgar.

"Then why did both of these things happen?

I cannot say.

"You cannot, or you will not?"

Morella remained silent. Edgar frowned at her and then returned his gaze to the road. The muscle on his jaw stood out clearly.

They rode on in silence again until they reached the outskirts of Petersburg.

Edgar pulled the carriage up to the hitching bar that ran along the front of the farmhouse. They had passed the old tobacco barn where he could stable the horse and secure the carriage on their way up the dirt drive leading to the house, which was exactly as Robert had described. According to Robert, there were other barns where the farmers who rented the land from Robert's uncle would store their harvest.

"I should go in and meet Mr. Craig first," Edgar said. "I'll see to putting the carriage away after I've met him and explained the situation. You'd best stay outside for now."

That's wise. I may investigate the grounds a bit, including the barn. There might be some tasty bits hiding about.

Edgar smiled and stroked the cat's head. "I don't mean to be angry. I just don't understand any of this."

Of course. Life is full of mysteries under the best of circumstances. Sometimes they have answers; mostly they do not.

Morella watched Edgar climb down from the seat of the carriage and make his way to the front door. He stopped once he had reached the top step; the two-story farmhouse was in good repair. Edgar recalled then of Robert telling him how he had helped his father replace rotting boards and give the structure a new coat of paint the previous summer.

Edgar used the brass knocker on the front door to rap loudly three times. He waited for at least a full minute, and then, hearing nothing from inside, knocked three times again. A thin white curtain over the glass in the door obscured his view from being able to see much of the interior, but he could tell there was a hallway and stairs in the center of the house with rooms off to either side. Finally, a figure emerged from the shadows, a man Edgar was certain, who shuffled as he made his way to the door.

"Who is it?" The gruff voice sounded hoarse, as if he rarely spoke.

"Edgar Poe, sir. I'm a friend of the Stannards in Richmond. Your sister, Jane Craig Stannard?"

A gnarled hand pulled the curtain aside and Edgar drew a sharp, quick breath. Robert had told him his uncle was not in good health, but Edgar was not prepared for what he saw. A few long strands of gray hair hung loosely from the old man's scalp not quite to his jawline, and his pale deeply-wrinkled face was liberally sprinkled with brown age spots. His mouth hung open exposing a mouth of less than a dozen teeth in various states of decay. Although all of those features were disturbing, what took Edgar's breath was the old man's singular pale blue eye. An image from Edgar's nightmare adventure at the Tamerlane mansion flashed into his mind, an old man, terrified, peering at Edgar with a film-covered eye like Robert's uncle's as he clutched his bedclothes to his chest.

Mr. Craig tilted his head as he peered inquisitively at his visitor. His right eye was normal, dark brown, so dark as to be nearly black. But the other eye, his left, the one higher up and closer to Edgar due to the tilt of the old man's head, was covered in a thin film. The iris itself had lost most of its original color so the entire eye took on a light bluish-gray cast, the film allowing only the slightest hint of the iris and pupil under it.

"What about my sister?"

"I...I'm afraid I have bad news, Mr. Craig. Edgar reached into his jacket and withdrew an envelope. "I have a letter from Mr. Stannard which explains why I'm here." More than anything, Edgar wanted to drop the letter on the stoop, climb back into the carriage, and start his journey home. Instead, he called through the door again. "May I come in?" The door opened and Robert's uncle stood back and motioned for Edgar to enter. Morella remained out of the old man's sight on the porch.

Edgar was surprised to see Mr. Craig dressed in what Edgar took to be his finest clothes. He wore a dark, charcoal suit with a frock coat that hung down to his knees and a black vest over a white shirt with a wide, emerald green puff cravat. The stickpin in the tie appeared to be a diamond.

Edgar handed the letter to Robert's uncle and stood awkwardly in the entryway, looking at his surroundings as Mr. Craig read. The dining table in the room to the right was set neatly for a party of four; it and the china cabinet standing against the far wall were tidy and dust-free. The sitting room opposite the dining room held two upholstered chairs and a settee, all of which were also clean and well-tended. The wallpaper in both rooms was in good repair and devoid of spider webs, a fact Edgar found surprising given Mr. Craig's status as a widower.

Edgar noted as Robert's uncle read further into the letter that the old man was profoundly affected by the news of his sister's death. "Would you like to sit down?" Edgar asked softly, motioning to a chair in the sitting room as if he were the host. Mr. Craig allowed Edgar to guide him to a padded rocking chair while he took one of the upholstered chairs next to it. Robert's uncle looked up from the letter and stared absently across the room. Eventually he turned to Edgar, and with narrowed eyes asked in a voice confirming his confusion, "Robert?" Edgar found it difficult not to stare at the blue eye despite how unnerving it was.

"No, sir, I'm Edgar. A friend of Robert's. That is, of a friend of Jane's son, Robert." The old man still seemed confused. "Robert and his father asked if I would come here to Petersburg and bring you to Richmond for your sister's funeral. I think Mr. Stannard mentioned that in the letter?" Robert's uncle looked at the letter again, but Edgar was unsure if what he had said registered with the old man. "Would you like to go to your sister's funeral?" Edgar asked.

The old man nodded. "Yes. Yes, I would. And you will take me?"

"Yes. The Stannards gave me a carriage to transport you and anything you want to take with you to Richmond. I can help you prepare if you'd like, and we can leave in the morning."

The old man nodded again. Edgar thought he seemed to be gathering his wits again. "We have a room for you to stay in tonight," he said. Edgar wondered what he meant by "we." "My wife should have dinner ready soon." Edgar felt a tingle crawl up his spine. Robert had said his aunt had died several years before. Robert's uncle then shook his head slowly from side to side and lifted a hand to his forehead. "I'm sorry. Please forgive me. I'm not thinking straight. My wife...she passed some time ago. Mrs. Ryan, yes, *Mrs. Ryan* comes every day to clean and prepare meals." Mr. Craig accentuated the name of the housekeeper as if trying to lodge it more firmly in his mind. "She's left for the day. She likes to be home before sundown, but she always cooks too much. I can share what she left for me this evening."

Feeling only slightly relieved, Edgar nodded. "Thank you. That will be fine. I need to see to the horse and put the carriage away, and then if you'd like I can help you pack any things you'd like to take to Richmond."

"That's not necessary. I can do that. But first I'll warm up our supper."

Edgar smiled politely and stood to go outside. Robert's uncle stayed seated and returned his gaze to the letter. Edgar hesitated, but then walked to the door and out onto the porch. He saw Morella waited for him on one of the rails. She followed Edgar down the steps and hopped back up onto her blanket as she watched Edgar unhitch the horse and join her on the driver's seat. As they drove the carriage to the tobacco barn, Edgar said, "I didn't ask Mr. Craig for permission about you staying inside the house, and I don't think I intend to, but I'd like to have your company just the same.

I can stay out of sight.

Edgar found he was obviously not the only one to use the barn as a stable as he found it well-stocked with feed for horses, most of which was unspoiled. The dying light from the setting sun cast most of the barn in shadows, but he found a bucket in one of the corners and took it to the pump he had noticed near the house. Once horse and carriage were safely secured and cared for, he turned to Morella.

"Should I look for food for you? Mr. Craig said he would share the meal his housekeeper had left for him with me, but I don't know what it will be."

I've dined already, thank you.

"One less rodent on the Craig estate?" he asked, smiling as they started toward the house.

One serves as one can.

Edgar lifted his bag out of the carriage and started back to the farmhouse. When they had reached the open doorway, he saw lanterns burned already in many of the rooms. He called loudly to announce his arrival so as not to startle his host. "Mr. Craig? I'm back." No response. He called again. "Mr. Craig?" Receiving no answer again, he looked at Morella.

I hear someone upstairs.

Edgar walked slowly up the steps and called out again. "Mr. Craig?"

"Up here, my boy. Seeing to your room, as I said."

At the top of the stairs Edgar had a choice of several rooms from which to choose as he searched for the old man; there was a closed door to his left, and a hallway with two closed doors on each side and an open door at the end. Morella moved without hesitation to the right and paused at the open door, careful to stay in the shadows. Edgar followed her and saw Mr. Craig was sitting in a wicker rocker. The old man smiled widely, a grin that belied a sense of sanity, an effect made worse by the light from the lantern which threw long shadows on the wall, and much worse, illuminated the film of his pale eye.

"A moment to catch my breath. My wife has everything in ship-shape order, as I thought, but I wanted to make sure there was a bed ready for you."

Edgar flinched at the second mention of Mr. Craig's wife, but nodded and gave a small smile in return. He set his bag on the floor beside the four-poster bed and said, "You mentioned your housekeeper had left a meal for you. Is there anything I can do to help? Divide up the portions? Pour us each a glass of water?"

A look of amused confusion crossed the old man's face. "My boy, we've already eaten." Edgar frowned. "Cornbread, salted ham, apple-sauce, and greens. Surely you haven't forgotten already?" Edgar didn't know what to say.

"Of course. Perhaps just the water then," he said.

"I'm sorry if the portions weren't what you're accustomed to. Had I known to expect you...Well, help yourself to the water. You know where to find it." He pushed himself up from the rocker, and took a small step or two to steady himself. "I normally retire soon after sundown, so I'll leave you the run of the house. Please make yourself at home."

"Thank you," Edgar replied. "I can help you with any of your preparations for the trip in the morning. We can take food for a mid-day meal on our way, but the journey shouldn't take more than five hours at the most."

Mr. Craig nodded and waved his hand in a gesture of friendly dismissal, but the way he paused and grinned, especially the way it seemed he focused his unseeing eye directly at Edgar made Edgar's skin crawl.

Edgar left the room and Morella slipped out of the shadows to trot beside him. Once they were downstairs, Edgar waited until he heard the master bedroom door open and then close behind his host. Wall lanterns lit the way down the hall to what Edgar assumed was the kitchen.

"Very strange." He spoke barely above a whisper so that his voice would not carry upstairs. "This could prove to be an interesting night."

And a long one.

When they got to the kitchen, they saw a small table against one interior wall where Edgar assumed Mr. Craig likely took most if not all of his meals. The dining room might not have been used for years. But to Edgar's astonishment, two plates sat on the table with two empty glasses. The plates showed crumbs of cornbread, with smears of grease and oil and remnants of green vegetable and fat. A greasy fork sat on each of the plates.

"Someone appears to have shared a meal with him," Edgar said.

Or gone to great lengths to make it appear so.

Edgar's senses reeled. He pulled a chair out and sat down to steel himself, but a movement at the window drew his attention. An all-too-familiar face leered obscenely at him. When it disappeared as quickly as it had appeared, he took a second to collect himself, and then jumped up, rushed to the back door and stepped out onto the small back stoop. Morella followed and together they looked into the darkness behind the tree line marking the woods which began only a few yards from the house.

"Edgar." A soft whisper, followed by a familiar laugh which trailed off so that only a chorus of chirping cicadas remained.

That's him.

"He was at the window. I'm sure of it."

And acted as Mr. Craig's dinner guest, as well?

"Most likely."

Another muffled voice broke Edgar's concentration on the woods; this one came from inside the house. Edgar stepped back into the kitchen and paused to listen. It was a male voice, not the familiar husky voice which often haunted him, but one likely to be their host's.

"Who is he talking to?"

There is only one voice.

Edgar closed and locked the back door and they moved up the hall to the front of the house where they could listen from the bottom of the stairs. It appeared quite obvious by his cadence and phrasing, the old man was talking to someone, but it was a one-sided conversation. He paused long enough for someone else to reply but, in those lapses, Edgar heard only silence.

"I wonder if Robert's family knows the extent of his uncle's dementia."

It may be a recent development. Perhaps the housekeeper can tell you more in the morning.

"I suppose there's nothing to do now but to go to bed ourselves. I should be tired enough to fall asleep within minutes, but something tells me this will be a long night." Edgar gathered the dishes from the table and set them in the sink, and then searched the cabinets for a glass or cup. Finding one that matched the two glasses used in the meal he had not enjoyed, as well as a small saucer for Morella, he filled them both with water from the large pitcher on the table and set the saucer on the floor. When they had both finished drinking, they made their way back down the hall.

Morella sat on the bottom step as she watched Edgar lock the front door and extinguish all the lanterns but one which he used to light his way upstairs. When he got to the top, he paused to listen again to the monologue within the old man's room.

"Remember the year you got the doll with the blue dress and the golden curls?" A pause. "Mother and Father had me hide it from you so you wouldn't see it until Christmas morning." Another pause, and then a laugh. "Well, what else are big brothers for? To scare their little sisters, of course."

Edgar moved down the hall and into his room. As a lantern already burned there, he extinguished the one he carried and put it to the side.

"All we can do now is wait out the night, I suppose."

Because the night held so many uncertainties, Edgar did not change into his bed clothes but simply removed his boots, vest and tie. Once he had shut the door, he pulled a box of matches from his pocket and set it beside the lantern, but paused as he prepared to blow out the flame.

Too many ghosties hiding in the dark?

"It might be wise to keep it burning."

I see better in the dark than in bright light.

"Bully for you. The lamp stays on."

Edgar stretched out on the bed and let out a long sigh. Morella jumped up on the bed and curled up beside him, gently kneading the thick comfort on which they lay as she purred softly. After a few seconds, a long, rumbling growl from Edgar's empty stomach filled the room. The purring stopped and Morella's ears flared back before resuming their normal upright position.

"My apologies."

Should have had a mouse. There are plenty.

"No thanks."

Might give you night vision.

"And cat breath."

No need to be rude. You're not exuding rose scent yourself.

"I'd like to get some sleep if possible."

Understood. I'll be as quiet as a...I'll be quiet.

"Who's there?"

The cry woke Edgar from a sound sleep. As he struggled to clear his head and clarify where he was, he noted Morella stood still at the foot of the bed, staring at the door.

"Did you hear a shout?" Edgar whispered.

It came from the old man's room.

"Were there other noises before that?"

Some mumbling, like what we heard before. But nothing like the shout.

Edgar sat up and turned so that his feet nearly touched the floor. He listened with his head tilted, but there was no other sound. "Perhaps I should check on him."

You'll get no more sleep if you don't.

Edgar reached for the lamp and moved quickly and quietly to the door. It squeaked as he opened it, but in his stockinged feet, the only audible noise as he and Morella made their way down the hallway was the creaking of old floorboards. He stopped outside Mr. Craig's room where a faint light flickered through the crack at the bottom of the door and listened. He turned and looked at Morella with raised eyebrows.

Nothing.

Edgar listened for another moment and then rapped a knuckle softly on the door. At first there was no sound, but then they heard the old man's voice speak out, not quite as frantic as before.

"I say, who's there?"

Edgar opened the door to see Mr. Craig sitting up in bed, still fully dressed. A lantern like the one Edgar held sat on a bedside table and as before, the light made the old man's blind, pale eye shine horribly.

"You, again!" he exclaimed.

"I don't mean to disturb you, but I wanted to make sure you were all right. I heard a cry earlier."

"Why are you torturing me?"

Edgar frowned. "I don't know what you mean."

"Why do you keep spying on me? Sneaking into my room while I'm sleeping?"

"I heard you cry out and wanted to check on you. This is the first time I've been in this room."

"Oh, no, you've been sticking your head in before I had the light on. I saw you!"

"Mr. Craig, I really don't know what you're talking about. Perhaps you were dreaming?"

"It was no dream! I heard you opening the door, ever so slowly. You thought you were being sly, but I saw you in the dark. I know it was you. And you've done it several times. The first times I pretended to be asleep, but no more! No more!"

"Mr. Craig, I assure you this is the first time I've opened your door. I care only about your well-being. I promise I have no interest in harming you. I want to help get you to your family in Richmond for your sister's funeral. I'm sure the news of her loss is disturbing to you, affecting your sleep and your dreams. Such a shock would disturb anyone." Edgar paused as he looked at the terrified old man. "What can I do to put you at ease?" Robert's uncle did not answer but sat on the bed trembling. Edgar's heart went out to the old man in spite of his frightening appearance. "Perhaps you'd feel safer if you locked the door? Do you have a key?" Although he didn't answer, Edgar noted that Mr. Craig looked to the drawer of the same bedside table on which the lantern sat.

"I'll leave you now, and you can lock the door behind me," Edgar said. "I promise I won't disturb you again until the sun is up and it's time for us to prepare for our trip."

Edgar waited, and then taking Mr. Craig's silence as acceptance, he nodded at the old man, withdrew, and closed the door. Morella followed Edgar back to their room where Edgar paused inside the doorway to listen. He heard the old man's footsteps approach the bedroom door followed by the click of the lock. Leaving his own door open and his lantern burning on the side table beside his bed, Edgar sat on the edge of the bed.

"What do you make of all that?" he asked Morella softly.

Probably more hallucinations.

"But he seems so definite. Might it have been...?"

That's also possible. We can't rule that out. But either way, there's not much you can do about it.

"If it is the other Edgar, what do you think he wants?"

Unknown. But if he wanted to harm you, he certainly could have done so before now.

Edgar pondered that thought. "Why do you suppose Mr. Craig is dressed so formally? He looks ready for church. And why is he still wearing every stitch?"

Morella stared at Edgar, taking him in from head to toe. Edgar looked down at his own clothes.

"Oh...well...yes, point taken." He shook his head. "It's all so strange. I can't help but wonder how all of this might have played out differently had Robert been the one to fetch his uncle instead of me. *If* it would have played out differently."

An interesting idea. Not particularly helpful, but interesting.

"I suppose the only thing that would actually help me would be if I could get a few hours of restful sleep so I can get Mr. Craig safely transported to Richmond."

Agreed.

Edgar stretched out on the bed again as Morella, too, settled as before. Edgar felt he was too wound up to fall asleep but, within minutes, exhaustion overcame him and he was quietly snoring.

And then he dreamed.

That damned eye!

Being careful not to wake the cat, he slipped off the bed and crept down the hallway holding the lantern before him, but the metal shade covered it so that only a small spot shining through a hole in the shade illuminated his way. In his other hand he grasped one of the thick pillows from his bed. He stopped near the top of the stairs at the old man's room and put his ear against the door. Hearing nothing, he tucked the pillow under one arm, set the lantern down with the tiny spot of light shining away from the room, and turned the doorknob, very slowly, so slowly it didn't make the slightest sound.

Unlocked!

He stepped so slowly, so carefully into the room that not even a single floorboard creaked.

He must be asleep if I'm to do it. And then I'll be rid--no, the WORLD will be rid of that damned eye!

He reached back to grip the handle of the lantern, slowly, oh so slowly, careful not to let it fall back and clink against the metal shade. He didn't make a sound as he brought the lantern to his chest, turning the hole toward his body so the single beam of light would not shine on his prey until precisely the right moment.

Suddenly he heard the rustling of fabric.

He's awake!

He froze, determined to keep his presence secret.

I mustn't lose this chance.

It seemed that hours passed.

Thump-THUMP! Thump-THUMP! Thump-THUMP!

A faint rhythmic beat sounded far off in the distance, as if someone a mile away beat on a large kettle drum. The vision of the eye, *that damned pale eye,* tortured him as he stood like a statue, his muscles aching to the point that he might scream. He tried to think of other things, of other sensations to keep his body from betraying him. Even the pillow under his arm seemed too heavy to bear.

Thump-THUMP! Thump-THUMP! Thump-THUMP!

The drumming sound was louder.

He focused on the warmth of the lantern against his chest. He counted the ticks of the clock on the wall, each tick marking the small pendulum's trek back and forth in the darkness, and he noted how it clicked in time with the drum which continued to get louder.

But most of all, he thought about the eye itself.

That horrid, looming eye! That thing of evil!

Finally, the old man's breathing turned into a rhythmic snore. Slowly he moved the lantern so he held it away from his body and out before him. The small circle of light shone now on the wall to his right. The old man was but a lump of darkness, shadow turned substance, blended indistinguishably from the bed on which he lay. Ever so gently he turned the shade on the lantern, so carefully it made not a single sound as the spot of light traveled over the figure on the bed toward the old man's face. Once he was sure the old man was asleep, he could pounce with the pillow and with but a brief struggle, the eye would be shut forever.

THUMP-THUMP! THUMP-THUMP! THUMP-THUMP!

But the pounding beat continues, so loud now that surely the old man can hear it!

Slowly he turned the lantern, moving the light closer, closer. The drumming was so loud he was sure it shook the bed. He moved the light closer; it was on the old man's chest, his chin, his eye––

The wrinkled eyelid flew open and the horribly illuminated eye shone in the darkness, cold and unblinking as a dead fish's eye. The old man was awake.

The beating stopped.

Edgar's eyes flew open. His heart raced and he realized Morella was looking at him from the rocking chair. He drew himself up to a sitting position and rubbed his face. He saw with relief that the room was illuminated by more than the lantern. It was dawn at last.

You seemed to have a restless night.

Edgar rubbed his eyes. "Bad dreams." He yawned. "Any other sounds from our host down the hall?"

I heard some mumbling at first, then all was quiet.

"I could use a trip to the privy." Edgar said as he pulled on his boots. Then I'll see how Mr. Craig is this morning. Hopefully his housekeeper will bring enough breakfast for us to share." He put out the lantern on the bedside and slipped the matchbox back into his pocket.

Morella followed Edgar out of the bedroom and paused with him as he listened at the old man's door.

"Nothing. I'll let him sleep a bit longer."

Edgar went down the stairs without attempting to be quiet, hoping his footsteps might rouse Mr. Craig. Morella scurried off across the yard toward the tobacco barn as Edgar found his way to the outhouse. When he was finished, he went to the barn where he got more water and feed for the horse.

Being out of the farmhouse and back outside in the sunshine again provided such relief, Edgar almost forgot how hungry he was. The mundane tasks of preparing the horse and carriage were a welcome distraction. When the horse had finished eating, Edgar hitched it up to the carriage and drove it back to the hitching rail at the front of the house for easier loading. He saw Morella waited for him on the same porch rail where she had waited upon his first arrival and meeting with Mr. Craig. As he was in the process of securing the horse, he saw a woman approaching the house on foot whose bright red hair fought to escape from the gray kerchief she wore. As she got closer, Edgar could see she was frowning.

The housekeeper, no doubt.

"Wondering with good reason who I am and what I'm doing here."

Edgar crossed in front of the horse and walked toward the woman. "Mrs. Ryan, I believe?" he asked, smiling to put her at ease.

"Yes," she answered, the uncertainty still evident in her eyes and tone.

"I'm Edgar Poe, a friend of the Stannards, Jane Stannard. Mr. Craig's sister. The family sent me on sad business, I'm afraid. Mrs. Stannard passed away, and the family asked me to deliver the news to Mr. Craig and to transport him back to Richmond for the funeral."

Mrs. Ryan's look softened, but she still appeared somewhat dismayed. Still frowning, she said, "I'm afraid I have bad news for you too." She looked down at her hands briefly and Edgar shifted his weight and looked intently at her to continue. "Mr. Craig died night before last. I came over to clean up a bit and to see to his things. I believe the sheriff was still looking into how to contact family, but now I suppose that will be up to you."

Edgar looked at her in disbelief. "But that's impossible. We...I just spent the night with him here last night."

"Last night?"

"Yes, I arrived late yesterday, shortly before sunset, and told Mr. Craig about the loss of his sister. He invited me to share the food he said you had left for him for supper, and we agreed I would help him prepare to go to Richmond; we would leave before noon. He was still sleeping when I came out to prepare the carriage. I was about to see if he had awakened yet."

"Mr. Poe, is it?" Edgar nodded. "I found Mr. Craig in his bed when I arrived here yesterday. The body was cold. They took it away around 2:00 in the afternoon. I don't know who you saw, but it wasn't Mr. Craig."

"But he's––never mind. Let's go see." Edgar moved toward the house and Mrs. Ryan came behind shaking her head. She followed him inside, then up the stairs, and waited with him, a frown on her face, while Edgar knocked on the bedroom door.

"Mr. Craig? Are you awake? It's time to get ready for our trip to Richmond." Mrs. Ryan looked at Edgar skeptically. She reached past him and grabbed the doorknob.

"It's loc--." The door opened and they looked into a room where a bare mattress lay on the bed frame.

"I stripped the bed yesterday before I left," she said. She leaned back on her heels as she looked at Edgar with her arms folded across her chest.

"But I don't understand. He shared the meal."

"You ate with him?" Mrs. Ryan's doubt was unmistakable.

"Well, no. He offered, but..." Edgar flailed as he tried to think how to explain it. "Cornbread, greens, applesauce and ham, he said. There were dirty dishes..."

"That is what I had planned to prepare for him," Mrs. Ryan said, her eyebrows raised in surprise. "But as I told you, there was no need. He was dead when I found him. "She paused as she watched the confusion grow on Edgar's face. "I don't know who prepared the meal you mentioned," she paused and peered at Edgar with narrowed eyes. "If there *was* a meal." Edgar felt his face grow warm. "Mr. Poe, I assure you, Mr. Craig was not here last night."

Edgar closed his eyes and took a breath. Not knowing what else to say, he turned and went downstairs. The front door was still open and he saw Morella waited on the porch. He stepped outside while Mrs. Ryan walked back to the kitchen. After a moment or two, she joined Edgar on the porch.

"I see the dishes. Somebody did eat a meal as you described. But that wasn't you? And...a friend?"

Edgar shook his head. "No, I didn't eat it. But wait! There are pictures in the sitting room. I didn't look at them before but maybe..." He went back inside and turned left into the sitting room. Mrs. Ryan followed him. Displayed on a bookshelf among other painted portraits sat a framed portrait of a man and a woman. Edgar picked it up and showed it to Mrs. Ryan.

"Is this Mr. Craig and his wife?"

"Yes, it would have been made at least ten years ago, but that's them."

The man in the picture had more hair and was definitely in better health, but Edgar knew it was the same man. "That suit," Edgar said. "That's what he was wearing yesterday. Including the green tie and the diamond stick pin."

"That's his best suit. He only wore it on very special occasions. I gave it to the mortician myself."

Edgar sank into the chair he had sat in the day before and remembered how he had waited for Mr. Craig to read the letter from Mr. Stannard. "The letter!" He patted his jacket and felt something in the inside pocket. He reached inside and pulled out the unopened letter addressed to Robert's uncle in Mr. Stannard's handwriting. Edgar stared at the envelope in disbelief.

"How...?"

"I don't know what to tell you," Mrs. Ryan said. "Maybe somebody pretending to be him? For what reason I can't say, but––Mr. Poe, you don't look well. Maybe you should step outside for some air?"

Edgar walked out onto the porch where Morella waited. He sat down on the edge of the porch with his feet on the next step. Morella hopped down from the rail and rubbed against his side.

It was him, Edgar. You're not imagining things.

Bra-a-ack!

A raven swooped across the yard and landed on the lowest bough of the elm tree that grew a short distance from the dirt drive. The horse blew a blast of air out its nostrils and shuffled its feet nervously.

Bra-a-ack!

"That bird was around here all afternoon yesterday," Mrs. Ryan said. She walked back into the house and Edgar could still hear her talking as she walked into the kitchen. "About drove me crazy." Morella rubbed against Edgar's arm and looked up at him.

Maybe that's the goal.

9

"To be buried while alive is, beyond question, the most terrific of these extremes which has ever fallen to the lot of mere mortality."

from "The Premature Burial"

"Hello?

Robert stood in the open doorway of the customer entrance to John Allan & Company. Elmira pushed him gently from behind.

"He said we should go in even if no one was here," she said. "He mentioned he might have to step out, but that he wouldn't be long."

In spite of his doubts, Robert entered the shop area of the business and Elmira followed, closing the door behind her. "It still seems strange he would leave it unlocked. It's certainly not something his father would approve of, and Edgar's not exactly comfortable with his father as it is." Running his hand over the top of a rosewood cabinet, he turned and asked, "What exactly is it that Edgar said he needed me for?"

"He didn't say. Only that he could use your help." Elmira turned to view the bookshelves, statuary, and furniture all arranged in rows with comfortable aisles for walking and viewing the stock merchandise.

"I've never been in here before. I didn't realize Mr. Allan sold things. I thought he just bought expensive things from exotic places for other people. A sort of buying agent."

"He does both," Robert said. "And he wants Edgar to go into business with him one day."

"Not a bad business." Elmira eyed the paintings on the walls as she worked her way to the back. "And yet what Edgar really wants to do is to study the arts. He wants to be a writer."

Robert snorted. "I wish him well with that. His father would box his ears if he heard Edgar voice such a thing. He'd be a fool to toss all this aside."

Elmira shrugged. "He needs to follow his heart if he wants to be happy." Noticing the door on the back wall that led to the larger portion of the building where more items were held, she said, "Maybe he's working in the back." Robert followed her into the large, open warehouse but nearly ran into her when she stopped suddenly. Sitting on a pair of supports was an ornately carved ebony coffin with elaborate silver handles and trim work. Robert stepped around Elmira to examine the casket more closely while Elmira remained where she had stopped.

"It's beautiful!" he said as he rapped three times in rapid succession on the lid. "The craftsmanship is––" Three unmistakable slow, muffled thumps responded from the interior of the coffin. Robert backed away slowly, wide-eyed and gaping. As he and Elmira watched, the lid gradually opened. Elmira could not keep herself from giggling as a very solemn-faced Edgar rose to a sitting position from where he had been reclining in the satin-lined coffin.

"Damn you!" Robert cried but his smile belied any true anger at his friend. "And you too!" he said to Elmira. "Did the two of you lure me down here just to play this prank or do you really need my help?"

"I thought you might like to see this," Edgar said. "It's one of a kind. Or the only coffin I've ever heard of like this." He pulled on a lever on the interior wall of the casket which made a loud click. "It has a release should the deceased happen to change its mind about internment." Edgar slipped the lever back into its original place and then crawled out of the coffin to stand beside his friends.

"Why on earth would anyone require such a thing?" Robert said.

"My father has a client with a very rare physical condition called catalepsy. He says it is possible for him to suffer a seizure that renders him unconscious and completely immobile. The body can turn rigid which overall resembles death. This poor fellow lives with the fear that he will suffer one of these attacks and his loved ones might have him buried alive."

"How dreadful!" Elmira exclaimed. But then a smile crept across her face and she asked in a low voice, "I wonder how many funerals have actually been held for living people?"

"You're as demented as he is," Robert said, gesturing at Edgar and grinning despite his mock outrage. "You two deserve each other. I don't know why I keep company with such ghouls." Elmira and Edgar smiled at each other, each of them appreciating Robert's notable effort to resume his old joking ways despite his mother's recent passing even if it was forced.

"Apparently the fear of premature burial is more common than you might think," Edgar said. "An undertaker my father does business with said that on more than one occasion he's been asked to make a contrivance so that a client who has been mistakenly taken for dead can pull a cable from within the coffin to ring a bell hung above the grave to alert any mourners above ground to come to his rescue."

"Edgar! What's all this?"

The three friends grew as stiff as if they had suffered a cataleptic attack themselves. Robert and Elmira looked at each other wide-eyed as Edgar turned to address his father.

"Um, I thought my friends might like to see this unique feature on Mr. Whittaker's coffin," Edgar explained. "It's something not many people would ever hear of, much less--"

"The dignity and privacy of our customers is sacrosanct, Edgar. Putting their personal treasures on exhibit like a barker at a sideshow is a serious offense, to them and to me."

Edgar's cheeks blazed crimson, and his friends shuffled in place and stole quick glances at each other. "I'm sorry, Father. I didn't think--"

"That's it exactly! You didn't *think*! I don't know how many times I have to tell you our customer's needs always come first. If you could use that imagination of yours to have some empathy for others, to think of what their needs might be instead of dreaming of fantastical worlds and ethereal beings you might become a good businessman. But the day that might happen seems a long time coming."

Edgar raised his head as if to speak, but then re-considered and remained quiet. Elmira spoke instead.

"Please forgive us, Mr. Allan. I can assure you we had no intention of disabusing any of your client's property. I am to blame as much as anyone, for I encouraged Edgar to show us this coffin once I had heard of its ingenious escape latch." Mr. Allan frowned, but as her tone was calm and respectful, he allowed her to continue. "And may I say, sir, your son is one of the kindest, most empathetic people I've ever known." She shot a glance at Edgar. "I'm proud to know him." She looked back at Mr. Allan and added, "You've obviously raised him well."

"Yes, I'm sure that in your--What? Fifteen, sixteen years of life?--you have experienced the full range of humanity." It was Elmira's turn to blush but there were sparks in her eyes. Edgar was relieved to see her remain quiet. Robert found the tools hanging on the wall to be suddenly of great interest.

Mr. Allan's gaze took in both of Edgar's friends as he addressed them along with Edgar. "It's probably best if both of you return to your homes as I'm expecting a client from Fredericksburg this afternoon. Edgar, you can see if your mother has some use for you at Moldavia as I certainly have none for you here."

The three friends exchanged glances and then moved in single file to exit the warehouse and then the shop. Once outside, Elmira gripped Edgar's arm.

"I am so sorry, Edgar. I'm afraid this is all my fault."

"No, he's right. I shouldn't have made light of the coffin. But thank you." As they started their walk home, Edgar looked at Elmira and smiled. "That was very nice...what you said."

She smiled and said, "It's true, though. I think you are very special."

"The kindest of *all* the people you know in your *infinite* travels about the globe in your many years of life," Robert said. Elmira responded by making a face at him, to which he grinned and added, "Sorry. Only teasing."

Edgar turned to Elmira. "I'm sorry my father said that."

"Aren't we just the sorriest, saddest lot?" Robert said. "Well, what should we do now that your father has kicked us out of the warehouse?"

"I suppose I should check on my mother since he mentioned it," Edgar said.

"Perhaps we could at least take the long way home?" Elmira asked. "Enjoy a walk through the cemetery before going our separate ways?" She turned her head to Robert. "Or perhaps you'd rather walk elsewhere since..."

"I have the entire afternoon since Elmira had convinced me I would be needed at the warehouse," Robert said. "And I'd actually enjoy stopping by her grave."

"The long way then," Edgar agreed.

Once they passed the graveyard gates, Elmira hooked Edgar's arm with her arm and smiled at him, and then took Robert's in the other, giving herself two official escorts as they strolled the shady paths. When they got to Jane Stannard's newly covered grave, they stood silently for a moment. The grave looked raw since the grass had barely begun to grow over it, but the tombstone was expertly carved and there were fresh flowers lying on the dry, packed earth that Edgar assumed Mr. Stannard had placed there. Robert wasn't the only one to wipe a tear from his cheek.

"Would you like a moment alone?" Edgar asked. Robert nodded and, after giving his friend a pat on the back, Edgar and Elmira resumed their way along the cemetery path.

When they came to Morella's favorite resting place in the graveyard, they found her stretched out on the stone basking in the sun.

"There she is!" Elmira cried. "I thought it was odd when she wasn't at the warehouse."

"I couldn't find her when it was time for me to leave." Edgar said. They stopped and leaned against the stone as Morella lifted her head and blinked her one eye at them as she yawned.

That warehouse is not among my favorite places.

"You didn't tell me much about what happened when you went to Petersburg. What did happen there? At the funeral you said Robert's uncle had died, but it seemed like much more occurred than that."

Smart girl.

"I couldn't really talk about it there, but I thought I met Mr. Craig. We talked, and he even offered to share his meal with me."

"But then he died?" Edgar looked at Elmira before answering.

Tell her. Robert doesn't need to know, but you don't need to keep everything to yourself.

"He died the night before I got there."

Elmira frowned. "But...how could that be?"

Edgar shook his head. "My point exactly. I don't know."

"Was he a ghost?"

"Maybe. I know Dark Edgar was around that night too."

"He might have been posing as Robert's uncle?"

Edgar shrugged. "I don't know. Maybe. But somehow, I don't think so."

Elmira took Edgar's hand. "That would have been terrifying,"

"It was. He was so strange. That night I heard him in his room talking to her. I thought he was a bit addled because he was old. And the news about his sister might have made him more confused. But now I wonder if maybe he was seeing her all along."

"Then you might have spent the entire evening and night with a ghost?"

"I think I did."

I think so, too.

Elmira shivered. Edgar thought about telling her about the dream he had, how he had imagined he was about to murder the old man.

Perhaps that's one to keep to yourself.

"Should we check on Robert?" he asked.

Elmira nodded and pushed away from the stone. They met Robert on the path and the three continued their circuit of the cemetery. They walked along the wooded edge of the property until they came to a mound of dirt beside an empty grave.

"I'm surprised they haven't filled that back in," Robert said.

"They still haven't found the body," Edgar answered.

"What do you think happened to it?" Elmira asked. "Do they really think they're going to find it?"

"I imagine so," Edgar said. "Otherwise, they would have filled it." They stared at the site for a moment, until Edgar spoke again. "I wonder what they did with the coffin."

"Probably at the mortuary," Robert said. "Or maybe at the coroner's." He turned to Elmira. "What did you ever do with those teeth?"

Elmira shivered again. "Ugh! Those nasty things. I don't know. Father threw them out, I imagine. Or gave them to the sheriff. I don't care as long as they're gone. What kind of person could dig up a body and then pull out its teeth?"

"Apparently someone like Edgar," Robert said. When Edgar and Elmira both whirled their heads to glare at him, he quickly added, "Not Edgar. Someone *like* Edgar. You know, Edgar's double."

"If it was him," Edgar said, "I hope there weren't any witnesses. I've enough problems with public opinion as it is."

"And you're not faring so well at home either." This time Elmira punched him. "Ow!" Why do you two keep hitting me?"

"Because you keep being an idiot!"

I love this girl so much.

"I only meant that Edgar's father––"

"I know what you mean," Edgar said. "And you're right."

When Edgar arrived at Moldavia, his heart skipped a bit as he saw Francis Allan sitting on the porch. The last time he found her there was when she relayed the news of Jane Stannard's death; he wondered what other tragic news might be in store. Francis gripped a bunched handkerchief in her lap and her eyes were red, but she quickly brushed a tear from her cheek and attempted a smile. Edgar noted that she tucked a paper into her sleeve as he ascended the steps.

"What's wrong?" he asked, sitting in the other wicker chair. Morella leapt up onto the rail, her accustomed spot.

"I'm fine. Edgar. Just getting some fresh air. How are you?"

Edgar didn't respond immediately as he studied her. Rather than pressing her, he decided to follow her lead. "I'm...disappointed. And embarrassed."

"Oh? What about?"

"I invited my friends to the warehouse to see a casket Father had purchased for a client. It has a latch that can be released from the inside in case someone is buried accidentally and needs to escape. Father wasn't happy I had brought them in to see it."

"He is very protective about his customers and their property," Francis said.

Edgar nodded and looked down at his hands. "I shouldn't have brought them in, I suppose, even though I thought it was harmless." He looked up. "I still do. But that wasn't really what bothered me. Father insulted me in front of my friends. A familiar chorus––that I am too much of a dreamer. And that because I lack empathy for our customers, I'll never be a successful businessman."

"You know that's not true, Edgar."

"No, I don't know that. But to be honest, I don't care if I'm not a good businessman. I want to write."

"I know you do. But it's hard for your father to accept that. He wants you to take over the business someday."

"Well, he may need another son for that."

Francis twitched, almost as if she had been pinched. Edgar noted the movement. "What?" he asked.

"Nothing," Francis said, looking at her own hands.

"It's something. Tell me." He spoke gently, but still Francis shook her head and continued to avoid looking at him. "What is it that you're hiding?" Francis' right hand went involuntarily to her other forearm. Edgar held out his hand to her. "Please, let me see it." Francis looked into Edgar's eyes for a moment and then slid the paper out of her sleeve and handed it to her son. Edgar unfolded it and began to read the feminine handwriting.

His frown deepened the more he read. Francis dabbed at her eyes with the handkerchief. When he was finished, he folded the letter back as it was and handed it to her.

"Do I understand this correctly? There's another woman?"

"Another family." Edgar's eyes widened.

"Another…?" The word hung in the air between them. They sat quietly for several minutes.

"What…how long has this been going on?"

Francis shook her head. "For a good while, I'd say."

"Does he know that you know?"

Francis nodded. Edgar didn't know what to say.

"I'm sorry," he said finally. "You don't deserve this."

"One thing I've learned is that life doesn't always give you what you deserve." She wiped her eyes again and then straightened her shoulders. "But we press on, living the best that we can."

"Playing the cards we're dealt," Edgar said. Francis nodded again.

"He's not a bad man, Edgar. I know he loves me. He has been very good to me. Very generous."

Edgar's face grew sullen. "Having another wife is not being good to you. Having other children is not being good to either of us."

"Edgar, please. Do not say anything to him about this." Edgar looked up at her in disbelief. "No, Edgar. Please. Promise me."

Edgar said nothing.

It's her decision, Edgar.

"Edgar, I'm begging you."

Edgar drew in a deep breath. "I don't know how long I can remain silent but, for your sake, I'll try."

Francis gave her son a weak smile. "That's all I can ask."

Go to her.

Edgar stood and stepped over to her chair. He leaned over, embraced her, and kissed her cheek before he straightened. "Do you need anything?" he asked as he held her hand.

Francis shook her head as she wiped her eyes.

"I need to go for a walk." She squeezed his hand before letting it go, and Morella jumped down onto the porch with a solid thump and followed Edgar to the road.

Edgar needed to be alone, and the one place he was sure he wouldn't run into his friends was back at the cemetery since they had all left there hardly an hour before. When Edgar came to the crypt, he was surprised to see both the iron gate and the wooden door standing open. Morella brushed against his leg as he surveyed it from the path.

Careful, Edgar. You don't have a good personal history with this place.

"Agreed. Perhaps it's best to keep on walking."

Good choice.

Edgar turned away from the crypt and followed the path leading to Jane Stannard's grave. As it came into view, he wished he had something to lay on the soil. He thought of his sketch and the poem Robert had teased him about, and realized that, like Francis a short time before, he could use a handkerchief.

"Edgar Poe?"

Edgar turned to see a young man––a boy actually–– one a little younger than himself, nervously wringing his hands.

"Yes, I'm Edgar."

"My name is William. William Wilson. My father is John Allan."

"John...Allan?"

"Yes. Your father too."

Seeing one of his father's bastard children so soon after only just learning of his father's other secret family was another blow for which Edgar was not prepared. He stared at the boy not knowing how to respond.

"I think there's something here you may want to see."

The boy turned and started walking before Edgar had thought of a response.

Beware, Edgar. This doesn't feel right.

Edgar nodded, but followed the boy. "I have to know."

When William walked right to the open crypt and entered it without stopping, Edgar felt the familiar tingle up his spine.

Don't do it.

"I've got to see what he means. He's only a boy. And I'll be on my guard. But you should stay out here."

Edgar walked very slowly into the crypt both out of caution and because it took a moment for his eyes to adjust to the gloom. Toward the back he saw a box, in fact, a familiar coffin. The coffin from the disturbed grave. But this time it was not empty.

Edgar drew closer to see what lay within it. By her dress he could see it had been a woman, a very thin woman, little more than a skeleton, so reminiscent of the hideous marionette in the warehouse. Her jaw hung open and Edgar saw she was missing her teeth. Edgar's heart beat wildly and his vision blurred.

Is she moving?

Edgar felt his knees give as everything around him began to twirl. The corpse seemed to shift, its bony hands reaching out to grip the sides of the coffin just as it had in the warehouse. A mad, cackling laugh, one with which he was too familiar, echoed in the crypt followed by a sharp crack to his head with a flash of blinding light.

Edgar awakened to darkness, a darkness like he had only experienced in the cellar below the apothecary's shop when he had been sealed up in the wall of the dungeon-like cell. The air was stale and smelled of earth and mold. He lay on something hard and sharp which painfully poked his back, legs, and arms. When he reached out to push himself to a sitting position, he realized he was confined by wood on either side. Panicked, he threw his arms up only to find that there, too, his movement was constricted by a wood panel above him.

The coffin.

He was in the coffin.

Edgar screamed and pounded on the lid of the coffin.

"Let me out! Please! Let me out! Somebody, help me! Please! Let me out!

He pounded and pounded until he had to stop to catch his breath. He had never been so scared in his life. Claustrophobic terror consumed him so that his whole body squirmed in a futile attempt to break out of his confinement. He struck out with his fists and kicked until exhaustion finally wore him out.

As dirt sifted down through the cracks, his terror increased with the realization that the coffin was no longer in the crypt. It was back in its grave. He was buried under the earth in a grave with a corpse.

"Morella, where are you! Help me! Get help! Get someone who can get me out!"

He pounded the lid with both fists in desperation. Dirt fell onto his face and into his mouth; he turned his head to the side only to realize his cheek pressed against the cheek of the toothless corpse.

He screamed again, but got no answer.

Robert sat on the steps of his porch with his back against a column while Elmira rocked in the Bentwood rocker above him.

"Do you think Edgar's father will ever let him go to school to study the arts and literature as he wants?" Elmira asked.

"I don't know," Robert answered. "I can't really imagine he would. And I don't see why Edgar can't see that he's got a very good future just waiting for him to accept it. Mr. Allan's business is successful and Edgar is an only child, so one day he will inherit Moldavia, one of the best properties, if not *the* best, in Richmond."

"But none of that matters if you're not happy."

"I think I could find a way to be happy in that situation. If Edgar would agree to work the business with his father, he could also write. I'm not sure I see the problem."

"But Edgar might be miserable as a businessman. At least as his father's kind of businessman. He's talked about publishing a magazine that showcases the nation's best writers."

"And, of course, he would be among those writers." Robert laughed.

"Oh, don't be mean. Edgar is a wonderful writer. I think one day he will be a great writer."

"I'm just teasing. He is a good writer. I've told him so many times. But I think he shouldn't put all his eggs in one basket. You should be giving him the same advice. That is, if you don't want a poor, starving artist as a husband."

Elmira's cheeks turned bright red. "Who said anything about a husband?"

"Well, if you haven't noticed, Edgar is quite smitten with you. And you don't seem like you're horrified by the idea."

Elmira smiled in spite of herself. "You're awful, Robert Stannard! And if you ever manage to find a girl who'll marry--"

"Yeeeowww!"

Robert pushed away from the column and Elmira leaned forward in her chair to see the origin of the screeching noise. Morella ran up onto the steps and then back out into the yard, all while howling pitifully.

"I've never seen her do that before!" Robert said. "Is she hurt? Or sick?"

"Where's Edgar? I've never seen her without him." Morella ran away from them for about twenty feet, and then stopped to look back at them. They both stood to see her better. She ran another ten feet, and then turned around again.

"She wants us to follow her," Elmira said as she hurried down the steps. Robert joined her and together they followed the cat down the street. Morella, satisfied the humans were following her, led them to the cemetery and to the site of the desecrated grave where she began to scratch the dirt with her front paws.

Robert turned to Elmira. "How did it get filled in?" he asked, even though he knew she had no answer. Elmira knelt on the bare patch of earth and turned an ear to the ground. "What are you––"

"Shhh! I hear something. Listen!"

Morella paced back and forth along the edge of the grave.

Edgar, help is here.

Robert knelt beside her and mirrored her posture. "I don't hear––"

"Hush! Just listen."

After a moment, Robert turned his face toward Elmira. "Is that crying?"

"We've got to get shovels! Quickly!"

"We've got some at my house," Robert said.

"That will take too long. There must be some here in the graveyard. Do you know where there might be a storage shed on the grounds?"

"Yes, I think so."

They both stood and Elmira ran behind Robert following a path to a small, wooden building situated off the paths of the graveyard. When Robert tried the handle, he found it unlocked. Inside were various tools, including several shovels. Elmira grabbed one with a pointed edge while Robert got a flat-edged shovel. They dashed out of the shed without bothering to close the door.

Elmira immediately began to dig. Robert hesitated, and said, "Are you sure we should––?"

"Dig, Robert! We've got to get him out!"

"But we can't be sure——"

"Dig!"

Robert waited a moment longer, the doubt etched on his face, but then joined Elmira in digging. The soil was so loose they made quick progress in moving it from the grave, but within minutes blisters had formed on both of the youths' hands. Elmira's skirts kept getting in her way, and her shoes did not make it easy for her to drive her shovel into the dirt, but she worked with such a fierce intensity the pile of dirt she removed was larger than Robert's.

Robert stopped digging. "I hear him." Elmira paused and she, too, heard the muffled yet unmistakable sounds of thumping and human cries.

"Edgar! Can you hear me?"

The cries stopped briefly, then they heard a faint response, though Edgar's anguish was clear.

"Elmira? Is that you?"

"Yes. Robert's with me. We're going to get you out."

The two resumed digging even more frantically than before.

The solid thump of Elmira's blade striking wood caused her to stop momentarily and exchange hopeful looks with Robert. Fortunately, the grave was shallower than the six-feet they had feared. Robert's shovel with its flat-edged head proved more effective at moving dirt from the top of the coffin, but Elmira continued to pitch her smaller loads of dirt up and out of the grave. When nearly all of the dirt had been removed, they faced the challenge of how to open the coffin.

"I could smash the lid with my shovel," Robert said.

Elmira shook her head. "I'm afraid you'd hurt Edgar. We need to see if Edgar can push it from the inside. The nails may be loosened from his pounding."

"Edgar, can you hear me?" Elmira called.

"I hear you."

"Edgar, we need to get the lid to open," Elmira called. "We're going to climb out of the grave and get our weight off the coffin, then we'll see if you can push the lid open. The nails may be loose enough for you to do that."

As the edge of the grave only came to Robert's chest, he had no problem pulling himself out. He knelt down and gripped Elmira's forearm as she gripped his, and he pulled her out onto the grass.

"Edgar! Push on the lid now," she called.

Robert and Elmira could hear Edgar strain as he pushed. They could hear the boards creak but the lid did not move.

"Pound on it again, Edgar," Robert called. "And use your legs too."

Elmira and Robert looked at each other and grimaced as Edgar frantically pushed and pounded at the lid. The pounding stopped, and they heard only his heavy breathing.

"Can you see any light at all around the edges?" Robert called. Instead of an answer, they heard more pounding, and the side of the coffin furthest from them moved up a bit. Obviously, Edgar had noticed the lid give as well, for his pounding then resumed even stronger.

"Put your weight on my legs," Robert said to Elmira. He lay on his belly and reached down into the grave, stretching toward the edge of the coffin lid. When it popped up far enough for him to grab it, he pulled hard as Edgar pushed from below. Suddenly the lid popped free, standing on its side and revealing a nearly exhausted but extremely relieved friend. Robert pushed himself up and away from the grave as Edgar pulled himself to a sitting position. Robert knelt beside the grave again and reached down to grip one of Edgar's outreached arms as Elmira reached down beside him to grip the other. Then Robert saw what else was in the coffin with Edgar.

"Edgar," Robert said. "In the coffin. There with you..."

Edgar struggled to sit up.

"Oh, Edgar!" Elmira said, still gripping his arm. "Hurry, Robert. We've got to get him out of there. Let's help him to stand first. Then we can pull him out. Ready, Edgar?" Edgar nodded. "Ok, now!"

Once they had Edgar standing, they were able to get him out of the grave with one additional pull, and all three of them collapsed onto the grass. Morella rubbed her face on Edgar's upturned cheek as he lay on his back, and he could hear her purring. Elmira moved to kneel beside Edgar and brushed his hair from his forehead, the tears making tracks though the dirt on her cheeks. Robert sat up, drawing one leg up so he could drape an arm over his knee, and grinned broadly at his friend.

"Maybe you should order one of those fancy coffins with the inside latch."

In spite of his exhaustion, Edgar smiled faintly.

"He needs water," Elmira said.

"I imagine we all do," Robert said, patting Edgar's shoulder before rising to his feet. "There's a well near the storage shed. I'm sure there's a bucket too." He looked back at his friends and grinned. "Don't go anywhere."

Elmira continued to stroke Edgar's hair. His breathing had become more regular, and color was returning to his face. Morella crouched near his head still purring loudly.

"Your cat saved your life," Elmira said.

It was a group effort.

"Edgar, who did this?"

Edgar shook his head. "There was a boy..." Edgar stopped and swallowed. His voice was hoarse and, when he spoke again, it was barely above a whisper. "He said his name was William Wilson."

"A boy buried you?" Elmira frowned.

Edgar slowly pulled himself to a sitting position. "I don't think he was a boy."

"Ah. Our dark friend, then."

"I don't know how it could be anyone else."

"What will you tell the authorities?"

"Whatever I tell them, they won't believe me."

Elmira nodded and pointed to the grave. "They'll believe you did this. That you desecrated the grave, stole the body, took its teeth, and then put it back here."

"It would be the only logical conclusion to make."

"We have to fill it back in."

"They'll still think it was me."

Elmira peered at the grave with steel-eyed resolve, her jaw set firm. "Then we need to get rid of the body and the coffin. Leave the grave open and empty as it was today before we came upon it. Before you were buried in it."

"Bury the body someplace else?" Edgar shook his head. "She doesn't deserve that."

"She doesn't," Elmira agreed. "No one does. But Edgar, wherever we move her, it won't be worse than here. She has no family to visit her or mourn her." Edgar still looked doubtful. "We can do it respectfully. More so than when she was laid to rest here."

"Where would we bury her?"

"Didn't Robert mention a relative with land?

Edgar, she's right. Listen to her.

Edgar stroked Morella's head. At the sound of footsteps on the path they both jumped but were quickly relieved to see Robert coming with a bucket of water. He knelt beside them and they saw he had also found a clay cup. Robert dipped the cup into the bucket and handed it to Edgar. He passed it to Elmira and after she had taken her fill, she gave it back to Edgar. As Edgar drank again, she turned to Robert.

"We have a problem, but we also have a plan."

"I don't know how you two talked me into this. I don't know what the penalty is for grave robbing, but I'm sure it's enough to ruin my life." Robert rubbed his hands together to remove what dirt he could. The half-moon shining in the clear sky provided enough light for them to work without the use of a lantern. Although the horse was accustomed to pulling the wagon, it had never done so in the dead of night, and it was clearly anxious about being in the woods.

"We're not grave *robbers*," Elmira said as she stroked the nose of Edgar's horse to calm it. "We're grave *movers*."

"I'm not sure the sheriff would appreciate the distinction. Nor would my uncle." Robert raised an eyebrow as he noticed Edgar leaning against the wagon while staring at the ground. "Are you all right, Edgar? Do you need to sit for a while?"

Elmira had been looking at Edgar, too. She knew he had to be exhausted, but his reticence worried her. He was quieter than usual, and seemed not to follow their conversation. "You shouldn't really even be out here with us," she said. "I can't imagine how you are still on your feet after what you went through."

Edgar straightened and waved his hand dismissively. "I'm really fine. You two are the ones who should be tired; you did all the labor."

"Yes! While you napped in your coffin!" Robert quipped.

Elmira shuddered. "Not *his* coffin! And not alone!"

"I'd rather not think about that part of it," Edgar said. "The sooner she's back in the earth, the better."

"Are we ready then?" Robert asked.

Edgar nodded and climbed up into the back of the wagon and pushed the coffin toward the edge while Robert pulled it. Elmira also went to the back and helped steady the coffin as it tottered on the edge while Edgar jumped down to hold the other half. They then carried it off the trail and set it near the north side of the hole they had dug, positioned so they could slide it feet first into the newly made grave. Morella watched their efforts from her seat on the driver's bench of the wagon.

"I hope we dug deep enough," Robert said. "This was a lot harder than in the cemetery."

"It's not quite as deep as the grave was, but I think it's deep enough," Edgar replied. "Here we can cover it up with leaves and branches so it will be practically invisible." He looked at Robert. "Shall we?" Robert moved to the end of the coffin where Edgar stood, and together they pushed the coffin until it settled into the hole. They each grabbed one of the shovels they had left sticking up from the mound of dirt they had made digging the grave and started to fill it back in.

"I can't remember when I've worked so hard," Robert said. "Even my blisters have blisters. But at least I have gloves this time."

Elmira nodded in sympathy. "I had a time explaining my raw hands and ruined clothes to my mother."

Edgar stopped his labor long enough to look at her and ask, "What *did* you say?"

"I told her while I was on my walk, I saw Widow Morrissey hoeing her garden and I felt so sorry for her, I offered to help. Mother wasn't thrilled I hadn't changed clothes first, but she couldn't scold me too much for an act of charity." For a moment, the only sounds were the shovels sinking into the mound and the dirt hitting the coffin. "What about you, Robert? Did you have a problem explaining your dirty clothes to your father?"

Robert continued working without looking at his friends as he answered. "Father hasn't been particularly attentive to much of anything these days."

Robert struggles, too. It's hard losing a mother. But they are truly never gone, Edgar.

Edgar looked from Morella to Robert, and then to Elmira, who offered Robert a sad, small smile.

"I'm so sorry, Robert," she said.

They worked on in silence until the grave was filled. When they had finished raking some of the forest debris over the grave and smoothing the surface to blend it into the contour of the woods, Elmira said, "I think someone should say a few words for this poor woman. Pay our respects." She looked at Edgar. He laid his shovel down alongside Robert's and the three friends positioned themselves around the site, looking solemnly down at the grave with their hands clasped before them.

Edgar cleared his throat. "Although we never knew the woman who lies here, we return her body to the earth with the hope she has found peace. Her life, without doubt, was filled with many challenges. No marker was left to tell us of her life, of whom she loved, or whom she might have left behind. We regret her body's final resting place still does not offer any memorial other than this simple stone." Edgar stepped over to the large flat rock they had found and placed it amidst the leaves and twigs covering the new grave. "Our hope is that by returning her body to the earth here, far from where her first internment was disturbed, her soul might take comfort in this final resting place."

Bra-a-ack!

"Nevermore!"

All three jumped at the raucous cry, and the horse whinnied and moved restlessly in its traces. Morella shifted on the driver's seat with her ears flared back, but she did not jump down. A low-hanging pine bough settled back into place from where the raven had launched itself and swooped over their heads. They could hear its wings flapping as it continued to croak its mocking cry and caught only a glimpse of moonlight reflected on its dark feathers as it circled above them once before flying off into the night.

"Edgar?" Elmira asked quietly. "Is he here?"

He's not here. But he wants you to know he's watching.

Edgar remained still but, like the others, peered intently into the darkness around them. "I think it was just the bird. But we should all go home as quickly as possible."

They moved almost as one toward the wagon, but then a sudden breeze stirred the leaves all about them. Elmira stopped suddenly and gasped. She did not speak but stared into the woods. Edgar and Robert turned to see what had caught her gaze. In spite of the constant breeze, a pale patch of mist had formed about thirty feet from where they stood. As it glided toward them, the trio could see it was gradually taking a human form.

The manifestation stopped short of becoming fully corporal; it was nearly drained of all color, transparent, almost like a fluid sculpture made of pale blue ice. Although the strong breeze continued to move the branches all around them, it had no effect on the approaching figure. Long hair hung down loosely over her shoulders framing a face that would have been considered quite pretty had it not been so thin. A long dress hugged her slender torso, the same one worn by the corpse/marionette in the warehouse but likely as it had been when it was new. She stopped about ten feet from them. Her sad eyes searched those of each of the three friends and, as she reached out to them, Edgar felt his heart ache for her. She moved her lips, but they could not hear what she said.

"We cannot hear you," Edgar said, and he brought a finger to his ear and shook his head in case she could not hear them either. The apparition nodded, and then brought her hands together in front of her chest, palms touching. She bowed her head once to them.

She's thanking you.

The spectral woman then shifted the position of her hands so they gripped each other and she tried again to speak, as much with her pleading eyes as with her lips. She spoke only one word, very slowly, and it was clear she spoke mainly to Edgar.

Beware.

She did not walk away, but faded from view as the breeze lessened until all was still and there was no sign of her.

No one moved or spoke until Edgar finally broke the silence. "I think she appreciated what we did."

Elmira gripped Edgar's hands. "Yes, but she also wanted to warn us. Especially you, Edgar."

Robert gathered the shovels and put them in the back of the wagon, then climbed into the driver's seat. "I'll drive us to your stable, Edgar." Edgar climbed into the back and then offered a hand to help Elmira in beside him. Before snapping the reins to get the wagon moving, Robert turned back to his friends.

"Edgar, what do you think this...person...this demon...or whatever it is wants? Why did he dig up her grave and then bury you with her?"

"I think he wants to take my place."

10

"Edgar, are you alright?" Elmira's tone clearly indicated she didn't think so.

"I'm fine. Merely a bit of a headache." Edgar leaned against the side of the stone memorial and idly poked the ground with the tip of his new walking stick. He had made the cane himself and taken to carrying it with him on his walks since his attack in the cemetery. He told his parents and his friends it was a new hobby, and that he thought he might be able to sell more like it, but in truth he felt safer, stronger even, when he carried it. With his free hand he drummed his fingers on the stone while scanning the cemetery with narrowed eyes. Morella stepped back and forth in front of Edgar, rubbing her black coat against Edgar's shins with each pass.

"Mother says there have been more cases of Yellow Fever reported this week," Elmira said as she looked thoughtfully at Edgar. "You need to be careful."

"Careful indeed. And about more than Yellow Fever," Robert said. "I know it's been a few weeks, but I don't know if I would *ever* set foot in this cemetery again if I were you. I'm not too keen on being here myself. Even with a stick like that." He pointed at Edgar's cane. "It is probably smart to carry something like that to defend yourself should you meet up with your evil friend again."

"This seems to be one of his favorite places," Elmira agreed.

"I'd like to meet him," Edgar said firmly, stabbing the ground with the hickory cane. "I'm tired of being his prey. It's time I became the hunter."

"But you don't even know what he is," Robert said.

For once the boy makes sense.

"It doesn't matter. I'm ready to be done with it all."

"But how do you fight an enemy you can't even see?" Elmira's frown deepened. "Especially when he can appear as anyone. Even one of us."

Bra-a-ack!

"That damn bird again!" Edgar stood with his jaw set, ready to strike the raven out of the air. Robert picked up a rock and threw it at the bird, but it was already flying away from the branch where it had been watching them. Morella leaped up onto the stone beside Edgar.

I'd like to make a meal of him.

Edgar smiled grimly and ran his hand from the top of her head down her back and gripped the hickory cane tighter and then sat down on the large granite marker.

"Do you think it reports back to him?" Elmira asked.

"Maybe it *is* him," Robert offered.

Edgar remained silent, staring into the woods where the raven had flown. Elmira and Robert both looked at Edgar with even greater concern. After a moment, Robert clapped his hands once and grinned broadly.

"I think we all need a diversion," he announced. "I, for one, plan to see the act at the Valdemar Hotel tonight. There's a performer who claims, "You Won't Believe Your Eyes!""

"The mesmerist?" Edgar asked. Robert nodded. "I've seen the posters."

"Supposedly he can heal people, too," Robert added. "Draw their illnesses from their bodies using something called animal magnetism. I've read about it. But this is purely for entertainment. I'm interested in seeing what happens when he puts someone in a trance."

"Like making someone bark like a dog or think they're French?" Edgar shook his head and grinned at his friend.

"Or maybe bark in French if it's a poodle," Robert said, laughing at his own joke as his friends rolled their eyes.

"That doesn't sound like fun to me," Elmira said. "You two can go if you want. I'm sure my parents wouldn't let me go anyway."

"So how about it, Edgar? Care to go with me?"

"It sounds interesting. But I have to admit I'm feeling...off. Very tired."

"I don't think you look well at all, Edgar." Elmira said. She felt his cheek with the back of her hand the way Francis Allan had checked him for fever when he was little. "You're warm too. You really should be careful."

"A nap would be wonderful."

"It's probably nothing. Go home, rest up, and then I'll look for you at the hotel, Edgar. They're setting up chairs in the ballroom, making it into an auditorium with a stage and everything."

"We'll see," Edgar said. "Hopefully."

"I know all I've said so far seems like a fantasy from a fairy tale, " said Professor Gordon Pym. "But soon I will show you something much more exciting than fantasy." The performer's pointed beard and sweeping mustache, each half of which, oiled and curving outward like the tusks of a boar, reminded Edgar of an image he'd once seen of Mephistopheles. "I'll need a volunteer from the audience to assist me in a demonstration of the powers of mesmerism." He pointed to an attractive young woman who gasped and shook her head. She turned to her female companions for support, but they only giggled and encouraged her to stand. "Yes, thank you. You'll do nicely," the mesmerist said, extending his hand to assist her as she finally succumbed and climbed the three steps to join him on the stage. "I need an intelligent subject for this to work, and you clearly fit the bill." She smiled modestly as he led her to a high-backed, elaborately upholstered chair that likely had been used in a play as a throne. Off to the side, a white-haired musician with equally white whiskers sat with bow in hand, poised to draw it across the strings of the cello which he held between his legs.

What am I doing here? Edgar looked about the hall feeling only mildly confused. Part of him felt he was exactly where he was supposed to be even though he had no idea of how or when he had arrived there. Although he had never been inside the Hotel Valdemar, he also wondered how such a facility as this auditorium could possibly be contained within its walls. It was larger even than any ballroom he had imagined from his reading, and the stage was much grander than the temporary arrangement Robert had mentioned earlier.

And where is Robert? Edgar thought as he scanned the crowd. *Morella, are you here?*

No sign of either companion.

"Relax and listen very closely to what I say," the performer said to the woman who had been persuaded to volunteer." You need not fear I will harm you..." the mesmerist swept an arm to take in the scope of the auditorium, "...for there are far too many witnesses." The young woman smiled and laughed along with the crowd. "But seriously," Professor Pym continued. "I want you to close your eyes and listen only to the sound of my voice." The volunteer dutifully complied, and the mesmerist nodded to the cellist who then drew his bow slowly across one string resulting in a single, low note that resonated in the hall. That note blended seamlessly into the next one of a different pitch without suggesting any melody or tune. The effect on the crowd was remarkable; the laughter and whispers ceased. Only the droning sound of the cello and the mesmerist's voice could be heard in the entire hall.

"I'm going to take your hand, and remind you that you will hear my voice only. You can respond when I ask you a question. What, my dear, is your first name?"

"Mary," she said without opening her eyes.

"Are you comfortable, Mary?"

"Yes."

"You are getting very sleepy, Mary. As I count backwards from 10 to 0, you will get sleepier and sleepier. By the time I get to 0, you will be in a very comfortable state, and you will be able to perform amazing tasks at my request. But be assured, I will not harm you. Do you understand?"

"Yes."

"Ten...nine...eight..." The cellist continued to play a series of long, sad notes as the mesmerist counted backwards aloud. When he reached 5, Mr. Pym nodded to the musician again and the cellist pulled his bow away from the strings, stood, and exited the stage with his instrument. The professor's voice as he counted down to 0 could still be heard by everyone in the auditorium despite the fact that he spoke at a volume intended only for his subject who sat to his right within three feet of his voice.

"Now," the mesmerist said once he had completed his countdown, "you should be in a deep state of high suggestibility. You may open your eyes." Mary opened her eyes and sat calmly without expression, looking vacantly out into the crowd. "You will be able to perform some surprising feats, but nothing will frighten or embarrass you. I repeat, you will hear only the sound of my voice." Pym touched her left hand. "Do you feel my hand on yours?"

"Yes."

The professor removed his hand. "Your hand is getting very heavy. It is as heavy as a blacksmith's anvil. If you tried to lift it, you would find it impossible." A titter of amusement rippled through the crowd. "Go ahead, Mary, try to raise your hand."

Mary shifted in her chair, obviously trying to raise her left hand but, in spite of how she struggled, she could not lift it from the arm of the chair. She reached across her body with her right hand and gripped her left arm, apparently pulling with all her might, but her left hand seemed as if it were glued to the chair. The laughter from the audience did not faze her in the least. She simply continued to try unsuccessfully to lift her hand.

"All right, Mary, you may stop." Mary visibly relaxed. "In fact, now your hand is getting lighter, and lighter. So light now that you can't keep it on the chair." Mary's hand slowly floated up from the arm of the chair until it hung suspended above her head. "It's so light, it's lifting you up, Mary." Mary stood, lifting her heels from the floor and walking on tiptoe as if her hand were indeed pulling her up. "And your body is as light as a feather too. You're like a dandelion seed caught on a light summer breeze." The young woman glided gracefully across the stage like a dancer. "That's it, Mary. The breeze is carrying you around the stage in a circle." Mary circled the stage in quick, sure steps, pulled by her suspended hand as the audience laughter grew louder. Mary was not distracted by the laughter at all.

"The breeze is getting stronger. It's moving you faster, still in a circle." Mary's walk turned into a run. "It's a tornado, now Mary. You're caught up in a tornado!" Mary twirled madly about in a tight circle, her hand still held high over her head as she whirled faster and faster.

"It's getting weaker now, Mary. The tornado is giving out." Mary's spinning slowed. "It's become only a breeze. One final circle and it will gently let you down, back into your chair." Mary trotted gracefully around the stage and then sat exactly as Pym had said she would with her hand still held high. "When I touch your hand, its natural weight will return and your hand will feel normal again." The mesmerist reached over and touched her left hand which dropped instantly into her lap. A collective gasp from the audience followed by applause did nothing to change Mary's placid demeanor.

Professor Pym bowed slightly and stepped to the edge of the stage to address the audience. "I know what many of you are thinking. Some of you suspect Mary is an accomplice. That she is merely acting as if she's in a trance. But let me demonstrate to you that she is without a doubt under my power, a power that supersedes even her own nervous system." The white-haired assistant now re-entered the stage and approached the mesmerist. He made a quick, short bow and then presented Pym with a needle that appeared to be approximately a foot long and then exited.

"I need another volunteer at this time," the mesmerist said to the crowd, "one who can act as witness and authenticate what I'm doing. This person will be under no danger." Pym pointed to a man in formal attire with thick white sideburns whose stately posture and manner suggested that he might be a judge or a city official. "Would you stand, sir?" The man stood, smiling but also clearly a bit uncomfortable to have been chosen." And would you tell us your name, please?"

"Dr. Nathaniel Harrison," he said.

"*Doctor* Harrison! Interesting! And would you be a medical doctor, by chance?"

"Yes, that's correct."

"Splendid. That will be perfect. Can anyone else here verify that this gentleman is indeed who he claims to be and that he is a doctor?"

Several hands went up and many heads nodded.

"Would you join us on stage, please, Dr. Harrison?"

The doctor did so. Pym held the long needle up for the crowd to see.

"This, ladies and gentleman, is an upholstery needle. It is used to sew heavy fabrics when making furniture." He turned and handed it to the doctor. "Dr. Harrison, can you attest to the fact that this is a real needle, not a prop, and that it is indeed very sharp?"

Harrison inspected the needle and touched the tip of his finger to its point. "I can, sir. This is, in fact, a genuine needle as you described."

"Thank you, sir. Please observe carefully what I do now. I will ask you to verify there was no trickery involved in this next activity."

Pym addressed the audience once again. "This next demonstration may make some of you very uncomfortable. I assure you Mary will feel no pain and will not be harmed whatsoever." He walked back to stand beside Mary, who remained sitting still, staring out into the audience.

"Mary, can you hear me?"

"Yes, I can."

"Are you comfortable?"

"Yes."

"I want you to know you will not be harmed in the next portion of our demonstration, and that you will feel absolutely no pain. Do you understand?"

"Yes."

The mesmerist held the needle in front of her face with his right hand. "I am going to pass this needle through your left hand, the one that felt so light a moment ago. And yet, you will feel no pain, and you will not be harmed. You will not even bleed. Do you understand?"

"Yes."

"Raise your hand in front of you, please, and allow me to manipulate it freely." Mary offered her hand to Professor Pym. "Doctor Harrison, please observe carefully." While holding her hand lightly, the mesmerist moved to stand directly behind Mary. He then shifted his grip so that he held Mary's left wrist with his left hand and held it up above her head for everyone to see. Grasping it more firmly, he took the needle and brought the point to her palm. The sound of people squirming in their seats and several soft gasps rippled through the auditorium. Slowly he pushed the needle, holding her left hand tightly in his left, until the needle appeared through the back of Mary's hand. Pym continued to push the needle until at least five inches of it had passed through. Pym let go of her hand and stepped back as Mary continued to hold her hand up, sitting as calm and expressionless as before. Not a drop of blood ran down her arm.

"Doctor, would you examine Mary's hand, please, and verify that the needle did indeed penetrate and pass through her hand?"

The doctor, seemingly astonished, took her hand gently and turned it as he inspected it. Satisfied, he released her and took a step backwards. "It is as you said, the needle did penetrate her hand without causing any bleeding."

"Thank you, sir, you may return to your seat." As the doctor left the stage, Pym addressed the audience again. "As you can see, Mary has not experienced any discomfort from this experiment. By placing her in the trance state, I was able to override her body's natural inclinations, overriding functions such as nerve sensitivity and bleeding, purely through my suggestion. But it was Mary, herself, who actually blocked the pain and prevented any hemorrhaging. Can you begin to imagine the implications this has for healing?" Again, murmurs could be heard in the crowd. Professor Pym's tone changed and he smiled broadly. "But I'm sure Mary would appreciate it if we removed the needle." Pym stepped back to his place behind Mary and in one swift motion, much quicker than he had acted in piercing Mary's hand, he withdrew the needle from her hand. "You may drop your hand now, Mary."

As Mary resumed her normal posture, Pym moved so that he stood beside her. "Now, Mary, I am going to take you out of the trance. You will remember the event, but have no embarrassment or discomfort from this experiment. As I count back to ten, you will become more awake, in fact, you will be more invigorated, feel happier, and literally be healthier than you've ever been before." With that, he counted from one to ten. When he reached ten, Mary smiled and looked from him to the audience who clapped enthusiastically.

"Thank you, Mary. You may return to your seat. Your cooperation is greatly appreciated, for it literally set the stage for a truly remarkable event."

As Mary returned to her seat, beaming at her friends, Edgar saw two ushers wearing white, hooded robes go to the lanterns on each of the walls lining the sides of the hall, and turn down the wicks so the lighting in the room was greatly reduced. The white-whiskered musician whom Edgar assumed must also serve as Pym's general assistant appeared once again on stage. He and Professor Pym pushed the chair in which Mary had been sitting out of sight, and the mesmerist returned to center stage where he was illuminated by footlights encased with metal shields angled to throw light upward, dramatically lighting his person. The effect served to cast his face in eerie shadows and added an aura of menace that had been absent to that point.

"And now, ladies and gentleman, you are going to witness something never seen by anyone before! Not in the entirety of human history. It was necessary for you to experience firsthand the demonstration which preceded this one so you could see there was no trickery involved." He paused and took a breath; to Edgar he seemed genuinely excited about what was about to happen.

"Until this moment, we have had no physical proof of man's immortal soul. Many of the world's religions have told us life continues even after the physical body ceases to exist. But that has been a matter of faith." He took a few steps closer to the audience, allowing the suspense to build. He held up one finger, and smiled. "Until now."

"What if I told you, my friends, that tonight, you will witness the transition of the human soul, at the very moment in which it passes from 'this mortal coil,' as Shakespeare put it, into the eternal?" A murmur rippled through the audience like a wave. "What if we could suspend the process of dying long enough to ask someone who finds himself *in articulo mortis,* literally at their moment of death, to describe what they see, what they experience? Might it be possible for us to get a glimpse, through their eyes, of what we might expect?" Pym drew a breath, and in the slight tremble of his voice as he spoke again, it was obvious he was truly excited. "Might we find proof, right here in this hall, *of our own immortality*?"

The room was so quiet everyone could hear the rustle of Pym's clothing as he moved before them. He took a moment to gather himself, even pulling a handkerchief from his pocket to wipe his brow. "Ladies and gentlemen, I will now share with you the steps I have taken for this grand experiment. A very dear friend of mine, one whom I have known for many years, one who has studied the physical and mystical arts with me in a shared desire to learn the secrets of the universe, fell prey to a very deadly disease within the past year. My friend, Dr. Heinrich Kempelen, graciously agreed, in the name of science and metaphysics, to allow us all to witness something very special." Pym had been pacing back and forth across the stage as he talked but, at this point, he stopped to face the crowd. His excitement was obvious, but with the shadows thrown from the footlights, his excitement might easily have been taken for madness.

"Seven months ago," Pym continued, "I received word that the moment of Dr. Kempelen's death was imminent. I went to his home and commenced the plan we had agreed upon, for me to induce the trance state as you witnessed with our earlier volunteer, but for this purpose." Pym drew a breath, and spoke in a voice barely above a whisper but, the audience sat so still, so quietly, that not a word was lost. "In that state, I commanded him *not to die*." The mesmerist then stood in the tomb-like silence of the hall, staring at the audience, allowing the full impact of his words to sink in.

"Since that time, Heinrich has not spoken. He has received no sustenance of any kind and yet his body has not decayed. He remains as he was seven months ago, the night I induced the trance. His heart beats at most only once every few minutes, and his breath is practically undetectable. Only the movement of his eyes beneath his lids suggests that he hears my voice. He has been unable to speak while in the trance." Pym paused to clear his throat, and then took a few steps to the side with his hands clasped behind his back, appearing to gather his thoughts of what to say next. He then stopped, turned to the audience, and gestured, wagging one finger at them as he smiled, intimating that he was about to say something special.

"I am going to release him from the trance tonight, with all of you as witnesses, so that, before he releases his last breath, he might share with us what he saw and experienced in these last seven months. His testimony, I believe, will be an account of what we all might expect after the end of our physical time on this earth. *Proof that we all are indeed immortal.*"

At that point, Pym walked into the wings and briefly out of sight until, with his whiskered assistant, he returned, rolling a bed onto the stage. Within it lay an extremely frail figure. The head of the bed was elevated with the foot positioned toward the audience so the man's thin frame was propped up for all to see. His skin was so thin and pale as to give him a corpse-like appearance. The disease had wasted him horribly. His eyes were closed as in a deep sleep, but he seemed to be in no emotional distress. Pym's assistant exited as the mesmerist moved to stand beside the bed.

"Heinrich, can you hear me?"

Although Pym spoke softly, his voice carried in the hall. Edgar could see the old man's eyes did move under the lids, but what appeared to disturb Pym was the movement of Dr. Kempelen's lips.

"Are you attempting to speak, Heinrich?" Everyone could see when the dried lips parted. Although the voice was weak and thin, like the scratching of a rusty knife dragged across a metal plate, all could hear his plaintive cry.

"Let...me...die."

Pym frowned. "What do you see, my friend?"

"Let...me...die."

Professor Pym's eyes grew wide. "I will bring you out of the trance now. As I count to 10, you will gain more clarity of what has happened for the last seven months. "One...two...three..."

Kempelen's eyes opened slowly. They were nearly devoid of color, and reminded Edgar of Robert's uncle's loathsome pale blue eye.

"Four...five...you are waking, Heinrich. You are leaving the trance."

"Let...me...DIE!"

"Six...seven...eight..." The old man's eyes darted back and forth, unseeing, but panicked.

"What did you see, Heinrich? Did you see the afterlife?"

"PLEASE! LET...ME...DIE!

"Nine...TEN!"

Kempelen's mouth was wide open, displaying his blackened tongue, and his eyes stretched wide. What little color had been in the irises of his eyes drained away before the eyeballs themselves melted and ran as the skin covering the skull shrank and withered. The thin frame of his body collapsed upon itself as the bones crumbled into dust, and the bedclothes turned dark from thin streams of putrescent fluids formed by the disintegrating organs. Pym backed slowly away from the bed, his own eyes wide at the horror he had created. Moans of disgust and cries of fear issued from the audience along with fits of deep, painful coughing.

Suddenly all was dark and silent.

Tick.....tock.....tick.....tock.....

A horrifying yet familiar sense washed over Edgar, a feeling that paralyzed him--the feeling that he was back in the coffin. He could see nothing; all was pitch black. He heard but one noise, the slow, methodical ticking of a clock.

As suddenly as the darkness had descended, light returned, a sickly yellow light, and Edgar realized he was still sitting in the auditorium. The lanterns on the walls burned brighter, but they cast the eerie yellow light. The man who sat next to Edgar leaned against him, and when Edgar pushed him away, he fell to the floor. Edgar saw then that all of the other people in the hall either slumped in their chairs or lay on the floor where they had collapsed. Many looked outward with unblinking eyes, and everyone's skin seemed jaundiced, possibly as an effect of the lantern light. No one moved. All was deathly quiet except for the ticking of a clock which was nowhere to be seen.

Tick.....tock.....tick.....tock.....

Movement on the stage diverted Edgar's attention. Professor Pym lay crumpled in a heap where he had been standing. A figure in a long, black hooded robe stood on the opposite side of Kempelen's bed. The robed figure wore a yellow, featureless mask which conveyed no sense of emotion. Edgar found that blankness more disturbing than if it had been monstrous and, once again, a similar image from his waking nightmare at Tamerlane mansion superimposed itself on what he saw before him.

The robed figure descended the steps from the stage and walked up the center aisle of the auditorium. When it got to the double doors that presumably led into the rest of the hotel, it turned and looked directly at Edgar before exiting through the doors.

"Am I dreaming or is this real?" Edgar asked aloud.

Yes.

"Morella? Is that you?"

Yes, I am with you.

The cat's presence gave Edgar immense comfort despite his confusion about where he was and how he had gotten there. "Where? I don't see you."

Nevertheless, I am with you.

Edgar knew he had no other choice but to follow.

Tick.....tock.....tick.....tock.....

11

Tick.....tock.....tick.....tock.....

The sound of the unseen grandfather clock's slow pendulum was so loud Edgar felt there was nowhere in the Valdemar Hotel where it could not be heard.

Edgar pushed through the doors where he had seen the robed figure leave the auditorium and found himself in a wide hallway also bathed in yellow light which gradually gained an orange tint the further the hall went. It shone through a series of gothic windows with mono-chromatic panes of yellow or orange glass lining the left side of the hall. Whether the gold in the diamond-patterned carpet turned to orange or whether that was only an effect caused by the change of stained-glass Edgar couldn't tell but, regardless, it added to the illusion that the hallway ran an impossible length given the appearance of the hotel as Edgar remembered it.

The doors on the right side of the hall stood open which allowed Edgar to see the various activities happening within the hotel rooms as he passed. Revelers dressed in costume, many in robes or togas of classical times with half-masks, simple gold or silver bands that merely surrounded their eyes in a token attempt to conceal their identities. The inebriated guests spilled wine out of elaborate goblets as they laughed loudly, darting in and out of the hotel rooms like pollinating bees. Their gaiety diminished only momentarily as they parted to allow the solemn, black-robed figure to pass as he strode slowly down the center of the amber hall.

A woman whose skin was painted green with snakes writhing in her tousled black hair locked eyes with Edgar briefly. The pupils within her yellow irises were black vertical slits, and when she threw back her head and laughed, Edgar saw she had reptilian fangs to complete her Medusian appearance. She brushed past Edgar to embrace a bare-chested man with goat-like horns whose fur-covered legs ended in cloven hooves. In general, the guests either paid Edgar no mind or acted as though they couldn't see him, so Edgar was able to move among them without interference.

Tick.....tock.....tick.....tock.....

Above all the noise of laughter and chatting, the ticking of the clock remained audible. Morella's voice overrode the din of the celebrants in Edgar's mind.

What is your plan, Edgar?

Who can plan in a dream? Things simply happen. For now, I'm following the one in the robe.

Sounds like a good way to never wake up.

Do you have a suggestion?

Be aware. And think before you act.

When Edgar looked into the first room, he saw more guests costumed similarly to those in the hall, but these sat in chairs and couches in a space that resembled a darkened parlor in a private home. One area of the room was lit more brightly and, in that spot, a young man and woman spoke and postured as though they were performing in a play. Unlike the drunken partygoers, they were not costumed but dressed as Edgar would have expected of any guests who called on his parents or walked the streets of Richmond. The woman was remarkably beautiful with hair that fell to her shoulders in a cascade of light brown curls, and the dark-haired man opposite her presented a striking figure with his dark hair and mustache, full sideburns, and high forehead. The actress stopped mid-line in her delivery to look where Edgar stood in the doorway, and stared. Edgar's heart skipped a beat as he recognized her face from a portrait he kept in a locket that had belonged to his father, the image of Elizabeth Poe.

It's an illusion, Edgar.

How do you know?

I just do. Trust me.

"Edgar?"

The actress took a step toward the door with her arms reaching out toward him. Edgar moved to enter the room when Morella's urgent plea stopped him.

Don't go in there, Edgar!

Almost as if she had heard Morella's voice as well, Edgar's mother froze. She stopped. Her smile fell and her arms dropped to her side. Her eyes seemed to grow larger as the tissue surrounding them shrank and withdrew, and then they disappeared altogether leaving only dark sockets; the skin tightened over the bones of her cheeks and brow making it seem as though her face was drawing in upon itself. The glossy hair turned flat, its curl unwinding so the locks hung limply about a grinning skull before falling to the floor. Her performing partner had suffered a similar transformation, for he, too, was but a standing corpse who, because of his grinning skull, seemed to be mocking Edgar. The other guests turned to see what had interrupted the performance and Edgar saw that many of them had changed, as well. The simple half-masks had fallen into the laps of those who had worn them, for they no longer had ears on which the masks could hang. Mixed among the guests were skeletons who gaped at Edgar from their seats or where they stood about the room.

"Will you leave me, Edgar, when I have only just found you again?" Edgar's heart ached, but the dead thing gaping at him was no longer recognizable as his mother.

That's not her, Edgar. And you're losing the object of your quest.

Edgar forced himself to turn away from the room. As Morella had said, the robed figure was further down the hall. He would lose him if he didn't follow.

It's best if you don't look in the rooms.

Edgar found that hard advice to take. He avoided looking into the next room but when he passed by the orange window opposite the third room, he heard the British accent of a familiar male voice.

"Before we begin our lesson today, I think we might take a moment to note that one among you is celebrating his birthday today." While the parlor in which he had seen his parents perform was odd to find in a hotel, the room into which he looked next made his mind reel. "Shall we all––" The white-haired gentleman speaking stopped to look at Edgar, who stared from the doorway. The dozen or so boys who sat at desks with their backs to Edgar in the sun-lit space didn't move. The scene playing out before him he well remembered, his eighth birthday at the Manor House School near London. "Yes? What is it, young man?"

"Reverend...Bransby." Edgar said, a statement rather than a question. As had happened in the other room, the schoolmaster's stately countenance and body changed horrifically into something that belonged in the grave. Simultaneously, in one fluid motion, the boys turned in their seats to face the doorway. He did not recognize any of them, and for that he was grateful. But two of the boys gaping at him were obviously dead.

Edgar turned away from the schoolroom scene and hurried down the hall. The black-robed figure was barely visible at the end where the orange light blended into a green glow cast by the furthest emerald windows. Edgar could tell that rather than stopping in a dead end, the hall turned to the right. What lay beyond that turn Edgar dared not imagine, but he knew he didn't want to lose the robed figure.

Tick.....tock.....tick.....tock.....

He tried not to look into the rooms he passed, but he couldn't resist a quick glimpse into the next one. He recognized it as being his bedroom above the warehouse when he had lived there with John and Francis Allan before John had inherited his fortune and built Moldavia. He hurried on, feeling only the slightest contact as he brushed shoulders with more robed guests whose eyes flickered like flames behind their half-masks in the orange glow. A bearded man in classic armor that might have served Achilles well at ancient Troy stepped out of the last room in the hall, and Edgar noted with a chill that the dark eyes within the red-crested helmet were focused on him.

"Your Helen awaits," he said with a nod of his head. He then moved past Edgar into the hall to engage with other guests.

Don't look, Edgar. Don't torture yourself.

Edgar could not resist. Within the room Jane Stannard stood next to a table in a kitchen Edgar knew very well, having shared an informal meal there with his good friend many times.

"Edgar, how is my Robert? Does he miss me terribly?" She appeared as beautiful as she ever had even though deep sadness welled in her eyes. "Look after him, Edgar. Please don't let him fall into the darkness that engulfed me." Edgar knew what would happen next, but he could not look away. Like the others, she began to change. The dark circles grew under her eyes and her face became drawn, reminding Edgar of how she had looked before her death. Edgar turned and fled before a ghastly *post mortem* image of her would be forever locked in his memory.

Looking into the green light at the end of the hall, Edgar saw no sign of the figure he pursued, but he assumed the specter must have turned to follow the course of the hall. As Edgar neared the point at which the hall turned, he saw the orange pattern in the carpet had changed to green as well, corresponding with the colored tint of the windows. This change, like the light from the windows, was gradual. There was no clear line of demarcation between the different colored sections.

Tick.....tock.....tick.....tock.....

Halfway down the hall, Edgar saw the black-robed figure moving through new crowds of revelers who wore costumes much darker than those in the amber hall although they were more contemporary. A caped gentleman in fine clothes tipped his top hat and grinned at Edgar as he passed, baring fangs as he did so. Two men in work clothes and heavy boots with dirt-smudged faces stage-whispered dialog, bragging of treasures gained through a successful grave-robbing to a pair of women in gaudy gowns cut provocatively whom Edgar assumed also played unsavory characters in the curious masquerade.

"Do not ask more of me! I have done all I can do, more than most men would do. Have you and William not been provided for?"

The voice cutting through the noise of the celebrants from the adjacent room was too familiar for Edgar not to look. The woman nursing a baby sat stone-faced as John Allan paced in front of her. A tow-headed boy of three or four played with wooden blocks on the oval rug, building a castle for crudely carved miniatures of people and animals Edgar remembered from his own childhood.

"Father?"

Move on, Edgar. These are visions; they are not real.

Mr. Allan turned at the sound of Edgar's voice. His jaw dropped and his brow furrowed in confusion as he gaped at the doorway.

Edgar! Do not interact with them!

Heeding Morella's advice, Edgar turned away from the room and stepped down the hall further into the green light. There were fewer guests along this hall, and the costumes were darker, all drab tones of gray, brown, or black. As before, many simply hid their eyes with the simplest of masks but, in the mix, some wore replicas of animal heads which covered their heads completely. Edgar found those unnatural blends of human with horse, pig, and ape more disturbing than the monstrous creatures from mythological lore that roamed the yellow hall.

Focus on your goal, Edgar.

Edgar saw the black-robed figure had moved all the way through the green-lit portion of the hall and into a darker, blue section and he quickened his pace to catch up. He managed not to look into the first room at all, but as he passed the doorway after that, its uniqueness made him stop. The room was closed, and its arched door featured its own panel of green stained glass. Edgar knew it very well; it was the door to the crypt in the graveyard even though it had no iron gate, and the stained-glass window contained only green glass rather than the multi-colored panes he remembered. He gripped the familiar latch to enter, but froze with Morella's warning.

Don't do it.

He drew his hand back, but somehow his surroundings had changed. He already stood within the crypt even though he had not opened the door to enter; apparently just the thought of entering was enough to place him inside. He fought the urge to sneeze from the dust tickling his nostrils. The details of the walls and floor were exactly as he remembered, even to the coffins in the walls.

Yet one coffin was open.

Close your eyes, Edgar. Take a deep breath.

Tick.....tock.....tick.....tock.....

Edgar did as Morella instructed, and when he opened his eyes, he stood once again in the green-lit hall before a closed hotel room door that resembled all the others. The crypt, if it had ever been there, was gone. Masked guests in dark costumes milled about the hall, but the robed figure was not in sight. Reasoning that the hall must take another turn, he hurried toward the blue-lit portion but, before he had left the green, the scene within another room stopped him in his tracks.

It was his bedroom in Moldavia, and Francis Allan sat by the bed, her brow creased with worry. She dipped a cloth in water and wiped the forehead of the person who lay motionless in the bed. Even though he could not see past the figure of his adoptive mother to identify the face of the person she tended, he knew it was himself.

Edgar forced himself to look away from the room. A glimpse of black confirmed that the hall turned yet again. He brushed past a couple dressed all in black as mourners at a funeral, their laughter contrasting ironically with their assumed roles, who paid Edgar no mind at all for his rudeness.

When he made the turn further into the blue hall, Edgar saw something for which he was totally unprepared. There were open doorways leading into rooms as on the other halls, but the arched, blue-paned windows on the left and the open doorways on the right seemed to hang impossibly in place as if the walls, ceiling and floor had dissolved into a clear night sky filled with stars. Edgar's quarry strode on as before as if there were still a carpeted floor beneath him. Edgar felt firmness under his feet, likely the same carpet which he could no longer see, so he took a tentative step. Looking downward into an eternity of starry skies caused his stomach to lurch, so he looked only straight ahead and slowly took a few more steps toward the darkness at the end of the corridor of windows and doors.

The dim golden light pouring from the first room provided such a feeling of sanity in the disorienting vastness of the seemingly infinite hall it drew Edgar in. From the doorway he saw four young men sitting around several small desks which had been pushed together to form a makeshift table. They played cards in a large room lit by a single lantern with several beds around the perimeter. Edgar saw what appeared to be textbooks on several of the beds. A whiskey bottle sat on one corner of the table, and smoke curled in the dimly lit room from more than one cigar.

"How about you, Edgar? Are you in?" A chill ran down Edgar's back when he heard his name called.

"I fold," said the young man whom Edgar could only see from the back. "My luck's run out tonight, it seems."

Edgar knew that voice to be his own.

Tick.....tock.....tick.....tock.....

Move on, Edgar. It's but an illusion.

Edgar forced himself away from the scene. While this hall lacked any masquerading guests, he sensed movement in several places in the blue-black void. Barely discernible clouds of vapor drifted at intervals causing the stars to twinkle as they passed. When Edgar peered more closely at the nearest, he saw one had a vaguely human shape, a robed, hooded figure not unlike the one he followed, yet lacking any real material substance. Rather than walking, it flew slowly toward Edgar and he could see the stars and the light from the gothic windows and open doorways shining through it as it approached.

It took a more recognizable form as it got closer, like an ethereal human spirit. A ghost. But when Edgar looked within its hood and saw its pale, hairless face, its bat-like ears, and razor-sharp teeth bared within snarling black lips, he knew it had no human origin. Its speed increased as it grew closer, such a threat that Edgar threw his hands up before his face to shield himself from its attack, but rather than smashing into him, the specter passed quickly through him, causing only a sensation of coldness, chilling him as if a winter wind had blown not only around but through his body.

Keep going, Edgar. They can't hurt you.

"But what are they?"

It doesn't matter. Keep moving.

Edgar cautiously took a step forward, guided primarily by the arched windows on his left which glowed with a deep blue light in the dark abyss of the hall and the light escaping through the open doorways from the rooms on his right. The light from those rooms was all that gave Edgar the sense to keep moving. Each seemed a floating buoy, an island of safety to which he might cling as he drifted through the ocean of stars. And yet nothing of safety or comfort had been offered in any of the rooms so far.

Look if you must, but bear in mind these are only visions.

The next room, though dim, was brighter than the last. Several lanterns illuminated a small lecture hall in which many people, mostly women, sat in rows of chairs with their backs to the doorway in which Edgar stood. A slender man with a dark mustache and high forehead stood at a podium, reading to them.

Ah, distinctly I remember it was in the bleak December;
And each separate dying ember wrought its ghost upon the floor.
Eagerly I wished the morrow;—vainly I had sought to borrow
From my books surcease of sorrow—sorrow for the lost Lenore—
For the rare and radiant maiden whom the angels name Lenore—
Nameless here for evermore.

The lines seemed familiar to Edgar, very familiar, and yet he was certain he had never read this poem before. The speaker looked up from his reading and his eyes seemed to lock momentarily with Edgar's. A strong wave of déjà vu washed over Edgar, and the memory of seeing his double in the graveyard for the first time flashed into Edgar's mind.

It's not him.

Edgar frowned. "But...it's me."

Keep going, Edgar. Don't get distracted.

The man at the podium also frowned but, after rubbing his brow and eyes, smiled apologetically, and addressed his audience. "Forgive my lapse. As my mother used to say, 'I suppose someone just walked over my grave.'" The audience laughed politely, and the performer gave one last glance toward the doorway, squinting as if searching for an image no longer there before shaking his head and returning to his reading. Edgar felt an urge to stay, to hear more of the poem, but Morella's voice sounded again, even more urgently.

Edgar, you must keep going! This is not for you.

Tick.....tock.....tick.....tock.....

Reluctantly Edgar pulled himself from the doorway. At the far end of the star-filled tunnel, he could make out the silhouette of the hooded figure. Focusing on that, he began walking again. More vaporous clouds took human shape to either side as he went, paying him no mind as they floated by. Edgar noticed as he continued down the celestial hall that not all of the faces were demonic. They all lacked any color, but some were quite beautiful, angelic even, like the statuary in the Richmond graveyard. Two floated past Edgar with their heads together, engrossed in their conversation, snatches of which were audible to Edgar.

"Born again?" said one.

"Yes, fairest and best beloved, Una," the other answered. "Born again."

Once they were past Edgar, he heard them no more, but as he continued to the next lit doorway, another spectral couple floated by.

"This is indeed no dream!"

"Dreams are with us no more. The film of the shadow has already passed from off your eyes. Be of heart, and fear noth––"

Once he had passed them, or they had passed him, the gentle shades and their voices were lost to Edgar. When he turned and looked back down the hallway from where he had come, he saw only the doorways, windows, and stars.

Turning back, Edgar saw the dark shape of the figure he pursued standing at a black doorway at the end of the starry corridor. It had turned to face him. The featureless mask it wore glowed faintly, illuminated by the blue light provided by the arched window and the slightly brighter candlelight that issued from the last open doorway on the hall. Slowly the figure raised its hands to remove the mask, revealing the grinning face Edgar had fully expected and feared to see.

His own.

His double then turned and stepped through the dark opening that marked the end of the hall and the door closed behind him. Only one open doorway remained on his right.

"Do not look in there, Edgar. Keep going!

Edgar moved on, averting his eyes from the dim glow of the room, but the anguished voice which cried out made him stop.

"Elmira! Help me!"

Hearing his dear friend's name was too much to resist. Edgar leaned into the space and saw he looked into a hospital room. The figure within the white sheets writhed and twisted as he shouted, as though he were being tortured. When the man turned his face toward the doorway, Edgar saw it was the same man who had been reading to the crowd in the previous room, and although he called out in distress, his eyes were closed; he was fast asleep, tormented perhaps by dreams. Edgar winced as he noted that the man's face––*his* face––was gaunt and pale.

It is not real, Edgar. It is but a dream. Leave this room!

The sight was so disturbing Edgar felt it less difficult to pull himself away.

"But why did he––I––call out for Elmira?"

It doesn't matter. You need to leave this hall. Now!

Tick.....tock.....tick.....tock.....

The door at the end of the tunnel-like hall was much more discernible although it appeared as but a black rectangle in the sky. Edgar could not see a doorknob, but he reached where he knew one should be and was rewarded when his hand closed around it.

He opened the door and stepped into darkness even blacker than when he had awakened underground in the coffin. The door closed behind him with a loud thump that echoed in the darkness. There was no light from windows or doorways. No semblance of a hall at all. He turned to look back; even the dizzying infinity of the starry sky would be more comforting than the absolute darkness. But even though he had taken only a single step through the doorway, he could not find the door. He could see nothing. Panicked, he ran his hands over the hard, smooth surface of the wall, desperately searching in his blindness for a seam, a knob, a handle, something that would suggest a door.

It was as if it had never existed.

All he could feel in any direction was the smooth surface of a solid wall. Above the sound of his shuffling feet, his own desperate pounding, and his gasping breath, Edgar still heard the relentless ticking of the invisible clock. Edgar spun and leaned back against the wall. He slid slowly down into a sitting position, and a single sob burst from him like a frightened bird bolting from its cage. It echoed in the pitch-black chamber that seemed as vast and empty as a starless universe.

Tick.....tock.....tick.....tock.....

12

"It was not that I feared to look upon things horrible, but that I grew aghast lest there should be nothing to see. At length, with a wild desperation at heart, I quickly unclosed my eyes. My worst thoughts, then, were confirmed. The blackness of eternal night encompassed me."

from "The Pit and the Pendulum"

You mustn't give up, Edgar.

"Why not? If this is but a dream, why can't I just sit here until I wake up?"

You might never wake up.

That thought shook Edgar to his core. It was all he could do to keep from succumbing to a mad state of panic when he realized he was engulfed in darkness. The fear of being enclosed again as he was in the coffin was overwhelming. Sitting there in the darkness with his back against the wall wasn't a choice. It was all he felt he could do. Morella had allowed Edgar some time to gather himself as he sat with his head upon his updrawn knees before speaking, but there was no mistaking the urgency in her tone.

"If you mean I might die, that doesn't seem like the worst option anymore."

You cannot die here, Edgar. You must find a way out. If you give up, the part of you that exists in your waking world, the world you want to return to, will die. And this becomes your eternity. Your afterlife.

"Are you saying I am doomed to this dreamworld whenever I die? That *this* is what I must face?"

Not necessarily. Much in your life can change and, with those changes, this world changes, too.

"Everything depends on what I do here?"

Much does. The only thing for certain is, if you do nothing, you continue here with no hope of changing it.

Edgar sat in silence for several moments. Near silence, for he could still hear the ticking of the grandfather clock echoing in the great empty space.

Tick.....tock.....tick.....tock.....

Finally, he rubbed his face and said, "I suppose then we'd better find a way out of here." He pushed himself up from the floor while keeping his back against the wall and steadied himself. "If this is another hall, I should be able to get to the end of it. I don't suppose you can tell me more about where I am?"

I see only what you see.

Edgar nodded even though there was no one there to see. "Well, I guess I'd best find out what's here." He splayed his arms out in front of him and moved them about as if playing a game of Blind Man's Bluff while taking small, shuffling steps.

When Edgar had taken about twenty baby steps, he felt the floor change. There was nothing supporting his weight under the toes of his right foot. He pitched forward and pinwheeled his arms as he fought to regain his balance but, failing to do so, fell backward onto the hard, stone floor. The impact of the stone on the heels of his hands as he caught himself sent pain flashing up his forearms. Taking a deep breath, Edgar shifted until he was on all fours and, using his hands, he felt along the floor as he crept toward the spot where he had lost his balance.

His left hand detected the absence of the stone first. He lowered his body closer to the floor and leaned forward, sliding his right hand until it also no longer felt the floor in front of him.

"There's a drop-off!"

Cooler air wafted over Edgar's face, drying the perspiration and ruffling his hair as he felt along the edge of the apparent cliff.

"Hello!"

Edgar expected no reply, but the echo confirmed it would be a long way to the bottom if he were to fall over the edge. He scooted to the right for several feet, and then did the same to the left, feeling along the edge all the while in an attempt to see how wide the drop-off was, but he could tell only that he was on the edge of a very wide precipice.

Perhaps it would be better to search along the wall for a door.

Edgar crawled backwards on his hands and knees very slowly, praying he would make contact with a wall and not find another pit. When his right foot finally struck a solid, immovable object, Edgar allowed himself a deep, full breath and let his taut muscles relax. With his forehead resting on his hands and his rear raised irreverently he whispered a word of thanks to whatever deity might be lurking in the darkness. He then sat up and leaned back until his back touched the wall and pushed himself again into a standing position. He took a moment to let his heartbeat slow as he leaned against the cold stonework.

Tick.....tock.....tick.....tock.....

Keeping his back to the wall, Edgar took a shoulder-width step sideways to his right, and then brought his left foot to rest beside his right. "One," he said aloud. He repeated the motion. "Two." If he didn't find a door, he might at least get an idea of the parameter of the chamber. When he had taken fifty such steps without finding any hint of a door or change in the wall, he began to doubt the value of counting.

"There's got to be another wall. This can't go on forever this way."

Morella did not answer.

"Fifty-one. Fifty-two..." At a hundred steps, Edgar stopped again and slid down the wall to sit on the cold floor. "This is useless. I'm applying logic in a dreamworld where logic doesn't exist."

Perhaps the chamber is a circle.

That possibility had never crossed his mind.

"If that's true, I have been passing by the same place, well, any number of times."

And there has been no door.

Edgar's heart sank even deeper. "No, there hasn't."

The feeling of helplessness, of hopelessness, was made even more overwhelming because of the crushing weight of being in total darkness. Edgar pulled his feet toward his body and hugged his knees so he could lay his forehead on his crossed arms.

"I'm so tired."

It might be best to rest.

The slow ticking of the clock continued, but Edgar noticed he heard something else, too. At first it sounded like a breeze gently blowing the leaves in trees in the distance. But then he recognized the sound as whispering, and his arms broke out in gooseflesh. He couldn't make out what was being said––it might have even been another language––but regardless of what the voices said, Edgar felt it offered an even greater threat.

What troubles you, Edgar?

"You don't hear them?"

Hear what?

"Those voices."

No.

"I thought you heard what I hear. And see what I see."

That has been the case, yes.

"But you don't hear voices now?"

No.

Edgar paused to listen more closely. In the incomprehensible mumbling of several different people whispering all at once, it seemed that individual voices might be getting louder. Fragments which he could begin to understand.

"True...nervous, very, very dreadfully nervous...but why will you say I'm mad?"

"There!" Edgar said. "A man. He seems very upset about being thought mad. You didn't hear that?"

I hear nothing but the ticking clock.

More voices talked, as if many people whispered and talked in a hall or auditorium. He still could not understand most of them, but occasionally something would become extremely clear.

"I had walled the monster up within the tomb!"

"Another man!" Edgar said. "Also extremely agitated. You didn't hear him either?"

I hear no voice but yours.

Morella's voice was clear and not diminished by the other voices, but the murmur continued in Edgar's head.

"Oh! Whither shall I fly? Will she not be here anon? Is she not hurrying to upbraid me for my haste? Madman! I tell you that she now stands without the door!"

"Not that one either?" Edgar asked. The male voice was so distraught, so urgent, so frantic, Edgar found it hard to believe Morella could not hear it too.

Still nothing but your voice, Edgar.

Edgar clapped his hands over his ears to block out the sounds, but the voices continued.

These voices are only in your mind, Edgar.

"But isn't everything only in my mind?"

Morella did not answer.

Edgar leaned his head back against the wall and then rubbed his face vigorously as if he might wake himself from the nightmare. When he opened his eyes again, he saw a faint glow before him, so faint he doubted at first if it was perhaps only an effect of his having pressed his hands against his eyes. Gradually it took form, and he could make out the shape of a bed, one with posts and fine, gauzy curtains.

"Do you see this?" Edgar asked aloud. The murmur of voices was still present, but it was much diminished.

No, Edgar. Whatever it is you're seeing now must be in your mind, too, like the voices.

As Edgar peered more intently at the vision, he saw movement within the bed. Someone sat up, although they were covered completely by a sheet, as if a sheet had been pulled over someone who had died. The image of the bed and its contents was so faint it held no color, illuminated as it was by a candle which sat on a small table beside the bed.

The figure in the bed turned its head toward Edgar and the sheet slipped away, revealing the person beneath it. It was a woman with blonde hair and eyes so blue Edgar could tell their color even though the ghostly figure was so faint. A voice, not hers, suddenly rang out perfectly clear.

"The greater part of the fearful night had worn away, and she who had been dead, once again stirred." Although the voice sounded mature, as though belonging to a male twice his age, Edgar knew it to be his own.

The woman shifted in the bed and stood beside it. As Edgar watched, her hair grew darker, so dark it was as black as a raven's feathers, and her eyes grew dark as well. Edgar heard his adult voice again.

"Here then at least, can I never––can I never be mistaken––that these are the full, and the black, and the wild eyes––of my lost love."

The figure changed again, and Edgar watched in disbelief as he recognized Elmira standing before him. She simply stared, unseeing, as if she were not aware of her surroundings. For her sake, Edgar hoped it was merely his own hallucination. The transformation did not stop with the likeness of Elmira, but changed again. She grew shorter, her face became rounder, and the hair turned back to lighter curls. She seemed even younger than Elmira, someone he had never seen before, but that visage lasted only a few seconds. Her features changed again, this time to an obviously older woman, not elderly, but older than the woman who had first left the bed. The hair grew darker, not as dark as before, but not fair, and she wore it differently, pulled up. Suddenly, a realization struck like a physical blow. He realized he looked upon an older version of Elmira. With that realization, the vision faded.

I sense that something's happened. You are even more troubled. What is it, Edgar?

"I...I don't know. I'm not sure. I'm seeing people."

I don't think they're real, Edgar. They can't hurt you.

"No...I don't think so either."

Another faint glow began to materialize. Like the ones previous, it was very faint and colorless, like a mist. This time a male figure formed within a corner of a room he knew well. It was his father's study in Moldavia, and it was his father who faced him.

"I should never have taken you in! You challenge me with lies of my infidelity but continue to squander the money I've generously given you! And have the audacity to request more! But hear me clearly, you shall not take advantage of my Christian charity any longer. I will no longer cast my pearls before swine."

The vision of his father faded as quickly as it had appeared. The force of the apparition's words was so strong Edgar felt as though he had been struck.

Edgar! Are you all right?

Edgar sat in the darkness, still stunned. "I...I'm..." Another cloud of mist began to form. This time it was a woman who sat in a rocking chair on a porch stroking a black cat who sat in her lap. Edgar looked at them in profile, but when the woman turned to look at him, he could tell it was Francis Allan.

"Do not let him hurt you, Edgar," she said. "You are a good, young man. Your father lashes out at you because you know his sins." She paused and smiled. "But you can rise above it, Edgar. You can do great things." She turned and looked back at a view Edgar could not see. Her features blurred and her form seemed to shift, and Edgar realized a different woman sat in the chair, but one still petting the cat. His heart caught in his throat as he recognized her from the phantom room on the orange hall where he saw her performing with his father, and from the locket.

The black cat turned its head to look at Edgar as the woman did the same. "I'm so proud of you," his mother said. Edgar's chest tightened as he noted, even as she smiled, her face was changing as the vision faded. Before it was gone Edgar was able to see that she, like the cat in her lap, lacked one eye.

Tick.....tock.....tick.....tock.....

Edgar sat in the darkness with only the sound of the ticking clock. Morella, sensing Edgar's turmoil, said nothing, but waited for Edgar to speak first.

Finally, he broke the silence. "I don't understand."

I did not see what you saw, but I can feel what you feel. I believe these visions come from you.

"Are you..." Edgar's voice broke. "Are you my mother?"

I told you your mother was always with you.

"But how--?"

It is difficult to explain.

Edgar wanted to press for more of an explanation but he sensed he should not. He sat in silence a few moments later, then asked, "What should I do now?"

I think you must leave this place as soon as you can. It is a trap.

"And how can I do that when there are no doors?"

There is but one way open to you.

Edgar frowned. "What is that?"

The pit.

"But how? Should I look for stairs along the edge? Or try to climb down the cliff?"

This is not a physical place. It calls for an act of spirit. An act of faith.

"I still don't know what you mean."

You should jump into the pit.

Edgar felt a lump in his gut. He had no response.

I cannot explain how I know this; I just feel it is right. And you will have to trust me.

Edgar nodded although he didn't know whether she sensed the movement or not, and pushed himself up from the floor. He clenched his fists and took a deep breath.

"I'm ready."

It's best if you——

Edgar broke into a run, making a straight line away from the wall. When he had taken about eight strides, he no longer felt the floor beneath his feet. He held his arms out to his sides as when he had jumped into the James River on countless summer days. He felt the wind blow his hair and his clothes as his body spun round and round in the void. He fell and fell and fell hearing only the wind in his ears.

And then he was conscious of nothing at all.

TICK.....TOCK.....TICK.....TOCK.....

The ticking was louder, but there was light.

While Edgar had seen many horrors in the nightmare of the Valdemar Hotel that had caused him to close his eyes, total darkness, he had learned, was even worse.

Edgar lay on his back strapped tightly to a hard surface by a thick leather band that crossed his chest. His arms and legs were free to move, but the band was fastened so tightly he could barely slide a finger between it and his body even when he had exhaled all of his breath.

The first thing Edgar saw in the flickering torchlight was the painting on the high arched ceiling of a grinning skeleton holding a scythe in a dark hooded robe. It peered down like a mad god at Edgar from its background of a ruined, ancient city in flames.

TICK.....TOCK.....TICK.....TOCK.....

Since Edgar's head was free to move, he could see he was in another large chamber, this one with stone walls resembling a dungeon illuminated by two torches on each of the three walls that he could see.

When he looked beyond his feet, he could see a large wooden door with massive iron hinges centered on one wall. He heard the scratching sounds of something scurrying on the stone floor and sensed movement coming toward him. Before it disappeared under the table on which he lay, he saw a glimpse of gray fur and a long pink tail.

Rusted shackles hung at intervals along two of the other walls. One set still held the bloody remains of a prisoner who had been so tortured, so mutilated, that little remained for anyone to recognize who he might have been, yet Edgar thought the tattered vest looked like one Robert had been wearing when they had last talked with Elmira in the graveyard.

Pay these visions no mind.

The sight still made him sick as he thought of his friends. It seemed to Edgar that weeks had passed since he had last seen them. Suddenly the body moved on the wall.

Edgar wanted to close his eyes against the possibility that somehow it might still be alive, but then another rat fell from the corpse onto the floor, its mouth and whiskers red from its obscene feeding.

These things aren't real.

"They seem real enough to me! If they aren't real, why do I see them? Where do they come from?"

I think they come from you.

TICK.....TOCK.....TICK.....TOCK.....

The ticking sounded much clearer in this room than it had at any other point since Edgar had first heard it in the auditorium of the Valdemar. He looked about for the clock making the noise but there was no such device to be seen from where he lay.

It's not a clock.

"What is it?"

Look up.

He hadn't seen it at first, but when he looked more closely, he detected movement below the leering face above him. Occasionally light reflected off a thin piece of metal attached to the end of a wooden pole hanging down from the middle of the portrait. Edgar saw it was swinging back and forth from the ceiling.

"A pendulum? There's a clock above me?"

It's not a clock.

"Then what––?"

Edgar realized the pendulum was not only swinging; it was descending. The pendulum bob was not simply a disc as found in most clocks dependent upon the motion of a pendulum, but a blade with a width of about three feet. If allowed to continue its descent, it would cut him in two.

Edgar gripped the band on his chest and pushed frantically, but it did not give. He could not push it down to his waist or pull it up over the swell of his chest. Panic ran over him like a bucket of ice water.

Calm yourself, Edgar, and think.

Edgar closed his eyes and forced himself to lie still while he concentrated on slowing his breathing. Once he felt somewhat in control, he opened his eyes and saw the blade was closer.

"What do you mean? That this is all coming from me?"

They are like dreams. They are of your making.

"Then why can't I wake up?"

I cannot say. You slip between worlds, much like dreaming. But you can control what happens to some degree.

WHOOSH.............................WHOOSH

The blade was much lower, only about two feet above Edgar's chest. He could hear the rush of air with each oscillation. The passage of the blade took about two seconds for it to travel from the highest point on one side of its arc to the other.

"What happens if I do nothing? If I just lie here?"

I do not know for certain. But I feel that if you believe you die here, you could really die.

"And if I believe it can't kill me?"

WHOOSH

The blade was one foot above Edgar's chest.

Like jumping into the pit.

Edgar closed his eyes. He gripped the strap and pushed with all his might, straining against the leather strap which bound him and heard it creaking.

WHOOSH

He felt something crawl across his leg.

It's trying to distract you. Concentrate.

WHOOSH

He felt the wind from the blade ruffle his hair, but ignored it as he pictured the strap breaking loose.

WHOOSH

SNAP!

Edgar felt the strap give way and rolled off the table onto the hard stone floor. He quickly got to his feet and noticed two things.

The pendulum had stopped.

The massive door stood open.

13

The doorway led into another hall.

This one had no gothic windows or doors along the side, but the crimson carpet did have the same diamond pattern. Thick candles set in simple sconces illuminated the hall without adding any additional colors.

One full-length framed mirror stood halfway down the hall. Edgar watched his reflection grow larger as he approached it. When he was within arm's reach, he lifted his arm and touched the reflection of his hand. His image in the mirror shimmered like a reflection in water, and when it settled, he was astonished to find his hand extending into absolute blackness. The darkness from which he had just come. He jerked his hand back quickly and took a step back from the mirror.

You must go through it.

"Go back there? But you said it was dangerous and that I had to leave it."

You know how to navigate the darkness now.

"I don't think I can do that again."

You can.

Edgar looked into the darkness of the mirror. In its center, he saw a small rectangle of faintly glowing blue light. He drew a breath and stepped through. The darkness was as before except for the glow in the distance, but he held out his left hand and stepped sideways to the left until he came to a wall. Feeling his way, he kept a steady pace, moving toward the light and while touching the wall in order to avoid the pit he assumed was in the center of the chamber.

When he finally reached the blue light, he saw it was another mirror. Behind his reflection he saw the starry expanse of a night sky. As before, he reached out his hand and, when the image shimmered, stepped through.

The lack of seeing any floor or walls was as disorienting as it had been before, but he could see the outline of a greenish-tinged doorway in the distance. Keeping that as his goal, Edgar walked briskly to it. As he had hoped, he saw it was another mirror. He could make out closed doors on the left side of the hallway within that mirror illuminated by blue light that came from the arched windows on his right. He reached out and touched the reflection of his hand and stepped through the shimmering image.

The hallway stretched an impossibly long way, but he walked with confidence and hope, noting as he went how the light from the windows changed to green, then orange, and finally yellow. A set of double doors awaited him at the end of the hallway and, when he pushed through them, he found himself back in the auditorium of the Valdemar Hotel. It was as he had left it, with bodies slumped or lying on the floor, their skin pallid and jaundiced. On the stage where the mesmerist had performed, Edgar's skin crawled as he saw the decomposed remains of the body Gordon Pym had unsuccessfully used in his attempt to thwart Death still dripping from the bedclothes.

Focus on your goal, Edgar.

Edgar directed his gaze to the mirror behind the bed. He climbed the steps onto the stage and stood before it. Behind his reflection was a coffin, a simple pine box with cheap lining he remembered all too well. It stood on its end, open so it appeared Edgar lay within it.

It's like the others. Only an image.

Edgar nodded, took another deep breath, and reached out while stepping into his shimmering reflection.

He found himself in a darkened bedroom where an old man sat upright in bed against the headboard with his thin, bony hand clutching at his chest. The light from the candle flickering on the nightstand beside the bed reflected in the horrible pale blue eye which made Edgar shudder.

"Is that how Robert's uncle died?" Edgar wondered aloud.

Put it from your mind, Edgar. What's done is done.

Edgar turned toward the large mirror which he knew had been there when he stayed at Mr. Craig's house in Petersburg. This time he saw a nighttime scene behind his reflection, with lanterns hanging along the booths and tents of a carnival. After stepping through, Edgar found the atmosphere especially eerie due to the lack of any sound or movement. There were no performers, no excited carnival goers, no music. He immediately saw another standing mirror at the end of the midway and made his way toward it. The smell of roasted meat and burned fabric assaulted his senses, causing his eyes to water, but he kept walking toward the mirror. In the smoking ruins of a tent that had burned, a rider and horse stood and silently watched him pass. Charred bone showed through the blackened flesh of both.

Ignoring them, Edgar reached out to his reflection in the mirror where he saw his father's warehouse dimly lit behind him. The sight of such a familiar place comforted him, and he stepped through quickly, wondering if his nightmare might soon be coming to an end. Edgar's brief sense of comfort was dashed when he saw the simple coffin sitting on two sawhorses.

Two bony hands reached up from the depths of the coffin to grasp the sides. Before the corpse could rise, Edgar turned to escape through the doorway that led to the front of his father's business. He saw yet another mirror in its place, and raced to it and felt relieved when he saw the image of Elmira's porch within its frame.

When he stepped through that mirror, he did not find anyone sitting in the familiar rocking chairs, but he did note as he felt his stomach shrink and tighten into a hardened lump, the human teeth scattered on the table between them. He turned back to the mirror that had transported him to the porch, but he saw the warehouse remained, and the corpse contained within it staggered toward him. Edgar looked frantically for a means of escape, another mirror, but he didn't see one. The corpse within the mirror continued on its way toward Edgar, its limbs and head jerking unnaturally, as if being manipulated by an amateur puppeteer's strings.

"Can it come through?" Edgar asked.

I don't know. It's best not to find out. Go into the house.

Edgar hesitated, having never been invited into the Royster home before, but the corpse in the mirror drew closer. He turned the knob of the door and stepped into the foyer of the house. He was relieved to see another standing mirror like the others situated in the narrow hallway, certainly not one placed there by the Roysters. The image behind Edgar in that mirror was dark, but Edgar did not hesitate to step through it.

He found himself in the dungeon-like basement beneath the apothecary's shop where he had been imprisoned by his double. Torches lit the way down the damp corridors and Edgar ignored the cells on either side where he remembered seeing the fleeting images of skeletons and felt the caresses of ghostly fingers in his hair. Eventually the corridor opened into a space where casks of wine, including the Amontillado he had delivered, were stored against one wall. There, too, was a standing mirror.

The image there caused a repulsion in Edgar that surpassed even that of the empty coffin. Before him in the mirror was the door to the crypt he knew so well, the crypt where he had first seen Dark Edgar.

You must go there, Edgar.

Edgar agreed. It seemed right. He took a moment to gather his resolve and noticed the walking stick he had made leaning against one of the wine casks. Edgar grabbed the cane and turned to face himself in the mirror.

"This feels like where I'm supposed to be," Edgar said.

I think you're right.

Edgar reached out and then stepped through the mirror and found himself directly in front of the crypt. He worked the latch to the crypt and stepped inside. Another mirror stood within its moldy walls, and in it Edgar's reflection. This time there was no other scene behind Edgar, only the interior of the crypt and the door through which he had entered. Edgar peered at his reflection but, unlike Edgar, his reflection grinned back.

The grin grew wider and wider, the face turning more frightful the more his reflection smiled, until Edgar saw the mad, ghoulish face he had first seen within those same walls months before.

"At last," Edgar's reflection said in his low, rasping voice.

Edgar felt the rage of all those months of fear and frustration surge within him. He released it in a scream as he raised the cane and smashed the mirror. A great rushing wind swept over and through him, so powerful it overwhelmed him, and all went dark with the sound of mad laughter fading into silence.

"You're awake."

Francis Allan cupped Edgar's face in her hand and smiled at him. "Here, take some water." Once he had pushed himself into a sitting position, she offered him the cup and watched gratefully while he drank. "You had us very worried. There have been so many cases of the fever where people––" She shook her head, pushing that thought from her mind. "Your fever broke during the night and you seem to have slept peacefully. I think you might be on the mend now."

Morella lay curled next to him on the bed, purring loudly. Edgar noticed her and smiled.

"How long have I been ill?"

"It's been nearly two days. I've been able to give you water and some broth but you haven't eaten much at all. I doubt you remember any of that."

Edgar shook his head. "No. The last thing I remember is..." he paused to think. "I was with Robert and Elmira. Robert talked of going to see a performance." He took another drink from the cup. "I thought I went too."

Francis nodded. "When you came back from being with them, you complained of feeling bad, especially of a headache. I felt your forehead and you were burning up. You went to bed then and haven't been up since."

Edgar handed his mother the cup. "I think I'm better, but I'm still so tired." He stroked Morella's head.

"Of course, you are. I do think you should eat something if you can, and you'll start to get your strength back. I'll get you something." She rose and went to the door but paused to turn back and smile at Edgar. "I'm so glad you're feeling better. You seemed so troubled. You tossed and turned. I can't imagine you rested much at all."

"I had such strange dreams," Edgar said faintly as he slid back down into his covers. He was asleep again within seconds.

Strange dreams indeed.

Edgar swept the last of the dust out the large open door, pausing for a moment to enjoy the brisk coolness signaling the beginning of fall. He returned the broom to its place against the wall and returned to the front office where his father worked at his desk. "If there's nothing else you have for me to do, I'll be on my way. I'd like to see my friends before dinnertime."

John Allan swiveled in his chair to regard Edgar. "It's good to see you back in the warehouse," he said. Edgar nodded and gave him a small smile before moving toward the customer entrance. "I was afraid I might lose my future partner."

"Others with the fever fared worse than I did," Edgar said as he reached for his coat on the hook beside his father's. "Apparently I was lucky."

"You know, Edgar, I have no complaints about how you do your work here, but I would like to see you take a bit more initiative. There's a lot to learn about running a business, and there's no better place to learn it than right here."

Edgar frowned and paused before replying, weighing whether to speak his thoughts or not. "I don't really want to learn the business. I don't mind helping you, doing my part, but running a business is not what I want to do with my life."

It was Mr. Allan's turn to frown. "And what precisely is it you want to do?"

Edgar took a deep breath as he debated whether he wanted to share such a personal thing. "I want to be a writer. But first, I want to learn as much as I can from teachers who have studied the best literature, who know the classics, and then once I've graduated, possibly create and run a respected literary journal, one in which I could publish not only my own work but those from the best writers of our time."

Edgar's father folded his arms across his chest. "And I suppose you would like for me to pay for this learning at the university."

"It's not an unreasonable request, I think," Edgar replied.

"What is unreasonable is that you would turn down the opportunity to run a very successful business, one of the most respectable in Richmond, to pursue a flight of fancy."

"But running this business is not what *I* want. I want to pursue my dream, not yours."

John Allan stood so suddenly his chair slammed back against the desk. "This is childishness, Edgar. It's time you assume an adult role, a responsible role. There is nothing more important or respectable than a man being able to support his family."

"Oh? How many families, Father? Exactly how many families should a man support?"

John Allan's eyes narrowed and he clenched his fists. Edgar returned his father's glare without flinching. When no answer seemed to be forthcoming, he slipped his coat on and left the shop.

"They should be here soon."

An interesting place to meet.

"It's where we've always met." Edgar looked over the tops of the tombstones at the ivy-covered crypt. "I don't feel there's a threat here anymore."

I no longer feel his presence, that's true.

"I wish I understood what happened. Whether it was real or not."

Everything is real in its own way. If it can be imagined, it can exist somewhere.

"Everything I dreamed was real?"

To a degree.

"Who were those voices I heard, then? And those people I saw in the dark chamber with the pit? If they were real, why couldn't you see them?"

I don't have the answers for that I'm afraid. I think some of them might be people that will exist, or might exist, but haven't yet.

Edgar shook his head.

They might even be people you create. In your writing.

"Characters created in stories can be real?"

If they can be imagined...

Edgar nodded and finished the sentence. "...they can exist somewhere."

Edgar stroked Morella's back where she lay on the stone and noted how warm her fur was in the sunlight. "I'm not sure what to make of you exactly."

What do you mean?

"Well, for one thing, where did the name come from?"

It's a character from a story. I like that name, and her spirit. Morella loved her husband so much she came back after she died to replace the woman he remarried. Love is a powerful force.

"I don't think I know that story."

You will.

"But why only the one eye?"

It made it more likely your family would take me in. And there was the history of the cat with the Stannard family.

"I see. Very clever. But why a cat? Why not a higher life form?"

I am a higher life form.

"Hello!" Robert leapt over a grave with Elmira not far behind him, but minding her step a bit more respectfully. Her smile showed she was as excited to see Edgar as Robert appeared to be. "So finally feeling strong enough to leave the house!"

"Finally," Edgar said. "I even did some work at the warehouse earlier. I get tired but I couldn't stay cooped up much longer. I hate to waste any of the time we have left." He looked at Elmira.

"It's still months before we leave for school," Robert said. "That is, if we both go." Edgar noticed Elmira's smile faded a bit although she tried not to show it.

"My father isn't too pleased with the idea but my mother has been on my side, so I feel fairly certain I'll be joining you." He took Elmira's hand. "Charlottesville isn't that far away so I'm sure we'll be home for visits frequently."

"And you'll write often," Elmira said, bouncing their hands on Edgar's leg to emphasize her point. Edgar smiled.

"You too!" He noted how beautiful she looked with the sun reflecting in her hair. She noticed he was looking at her and smiled. *She does have remarkably beautiful teeth*, Edgar thought. Morella stirred suddenly on the stone where she had been stretched out and shifted to a sitting position to look at Edgar.

"I wonder if we'll continue to have adventures like we've had this summer," Robert said. "Strange things seem to be attracted to you."

Jarred from his reverie, Edgar turned back to Robert. "I hope not. I've had enough strangeness to last a dozen lifetimes." He raised his hands in mock supplication to the sky and addressed the heavens. "O, ye gods! Spare me more encounters with spirits, demons, and doubles!"

A shadow passed over them and they heard the branches rustle in the pines behind them as the raven settled.

Bra-a-ack!

"Nevermore!"

Notes from the Author

Whenever I read a story or watch a film based on real events, I always want to know how much of it really happened, so I thought I'd share with you the facts I found most interesting from the research I incorporated into the novel. And as promised in the introduction, I thought some of you might also like to know which of Poe's stories I used as inspiration, and where exactly those points appear in the novel.

I tried to be as historically accurate as possible in regard to where Edgar lived and what his relationship was like with his adoptive parents, John and Francis Allan. It's true the Allans had only recently come into enough wealth at the point in which my story begins to have purchased one of the finest homes in Richmond. John Allan inherited a fortune from his uncle and fellow Scot, William Galt, and with that money he purchased the house known as Moldavia on the corner of Main Street and Fifth Street, not far from the James River and Shockoe Hill Cemetery. I took some liberties with my descriptions of the cemetery, modeling it instead after Riverside Cemetery, a beautiful, historic graveyard near my home in Asheville, North Carolina. I am very familiar with this particular cemetery, having given ghost tours there when I hosted Dark Ride Tours. The warehouse where Edgar worked with John Allan did have a tavern close behind it, as indicated in my story, and John Allan was not happy about it.

Edgar's relationship with his adopted father was indeed strained as is evidenced by some of the letters preserved between the two of them. John had provided Edgar with a good education as a boy, some of which occurred at various schools in England. Poe used one of these as background material for writing "William Wilson," and even used the schoolmaster of one as the model for the schoolmaster in his story. But later when Edgar wanted to go to the university, John was tight with his money. He paid Edgar's tuition, but did not give Edgar enough money for books and other living expenses. Edgar turned to gambling with his fellow students to earn more money, which likely involved drinking.

I'm going to interrupt myself here to inject a thought about Poe's reputation as an alcoholic. After reading countless articles about this, I have come to the conclusion it is most likely that Poe did have a special sensitivity to alcohol, and as a result just a small intake of wine or liquor had a much greater effect on him than most people. Most likely he did not drink very often but when he did, it was well-noted. His reputation as a gloomy drunkard (and some even suggest drug addict although I have not found credible sources to confirm that) can likely be traced back to Rufus Griswold, a rival of Poe's who unfortunately was responsible for writing the obituary which gives us this unflattering image of Poe.

But back to Edgar's relationship with John Allan. There was likely additional tension between them once Edgar found out his adoptive father had not one, but two mistresses, and that he paid for the schooling of some of the offspring from those other relationships. It's not hard to imagine Edgar's resentment as he constantly fought to get funding for his own schooling. Edgar was also very fond of Francis Allan and being the romantic and sensitive soul we sense from his writing, I would imagine he held an additional grudge against John for that infidelity. There is evidence John Allan cared for Edgar when he was younger, so I found it likely he would want Edgar to take over his warehouse and import business.

Robert Stannard was indeed a friend of Edgar's although we don't know how close they were. What we do know is Edgar was quite smitten with Robert's mother, enough that he did have her in mind when he wrote the poem, "To Helen." When Jane Stannard died in 1826, Edgar was deeply affected. She would be one of many women for whom Edgar cared deeply to die prematurely. There's no great mystery as to why so many of Poe's stories deal with the loss of a beautiful woman.

The most fascinating thing I learned about Poe which I did not know before doing the research for this book, was that Elmira Royster, the young girl living near Edgar in Richmond, was the true love of his life, even more, it seems to me, than his love for his child bride Virginia Clemm. I don't doubt Edgar loved Virginia and was devastated by her death, but his relationship with Elmira is far more interesting to me. When Edgar first meets Elmira in my story, she asks him if he actually swam six miles up the James River as she had heard. This would be quite a feat for anyone, much less a fifteen-year-old boy, but it is believed to be a true story, and Edgar was reportedly "quite athletic." This tidbit shatters the stereotyped image of Poe I had always imagined of a weak, withdrawn misfit.

Elmira and Edgar did fall in love just prior to Edgar's departure to attend the University of Virginia in Charlottesville. They promised to write each other as I recorded in the last pages of my story, and apparently, they both did. But Elmira's father, who disapproved of Edgar's social status as the biological son of two actors, David and Elizabeth (Liza) Poe, hid Edgar's letters from his daughter, and kept Elmira's letters from being posted. So the two lovers, receiving no replies from their letters, each surmised the other had fallen out of love.

Years later, after Virginia had died, Poe returned to Richmond and reunited with Elmira to discover that she had lost her spouse as well. Their courtship resumed and they became engaged. Poe reportedly was never happier than at that point in his life. It makes his death so much more tragic, having occurred on a business trip to Baltimore and Philadelphia where he also planned to get Maria Clemm, his mother-in-law, and bring her to Richmond for his wedding to Elmira. (I know. Weird, right? But he and Virginia had lived with Mrs. Clemm for years and they had remained close after Virginia's death.)

As you most likely know, the circumstances of Poe's death are a great mystery, one that I won't address here. (Possibly another book? Let me know what you think.) But I did want to share with you some of the content I included about Edgar's life that really happened.

So, what about Poe's stories and how I incorporated them into my book? The following is a list in chronological order, chapter by chapter, with a brief summary of each in case you need a refresher of what it was about, or perhaps as an enticement to enjoy it for the first time if it's unknown to you.

Chapter One

"William Wilson" delves into themes of identity and morality through the haunting encounter of a man with his malevolent doppelgänger, culminating in a disturbing revelation." In Poe's story, this double first appears when the narrator is a schoolboy and reappears throughout his life, essentially driving him crazy. As with many of Poe's stories, the reader must ultimately question this narrator's sanity, even to the point of wondering if there is a double at all. Is William Wilson really just grappling with his own conscience? Is he consumed with guilt to the point of madness over his selfish and self-destructive behavior, failing to live up to the standards exemplified by his better twin, the standards he knows he should be following? I think that device works really well; I have no quarrel with it at all.

Still, I flipped the story to a degree, since Poe's narrator is really a much worse person than his double. I thought it would be interesting to have young Edgar discover a double who projected a much more sinister threat, an evil creature of unknown origin whose sole purpose seems to be to torment an innocent Edgar. In some inexplicable way, Edgar's dark twin seems to cause all of the horrifying events which unfold during that summer. I hope to leave the reader wondering where this Dark Edgar came from. Is he a demon who can just assume Edgar's appearance whenever he wants? Or could Good Edgar have unintentionally created him somehow? What is Dark Edgar's purpose? And regardless, which Edgar will prevail? Would his friends and family even realize if Dark Edgar won out?

"The Raven" recounts the haunting visitation of a mysterious raven to a grieving narrator, who is driven to madness by the bird's ominous repetition of the word "Nevermore," thus exploring themes of loss, mourning, and the relentless grip of sorrow upon the human psyche. I played with the idea––and I bet some of you thought of this too––of having a raven be Edgar's companion instead of the one-eyed cat, but the cat won out. I can't say why; it just did. So instead, the raven became Dark Edgar's accomplice, perhaps his avatar, and in the most practical sense, a harbinger any time "something wicked this way comes." (Yes, that's an appreciative nod to Ray Bradbury. And Shakespeare, of course.)

"The Black Cat" explores the descent into madness and guilt of a narrator plagued by the consequences of his violent actions, revealing the dark undercurrents of human nature. The story Robert tells Edgar about the black cat that appeared at his house, and the explanation for why it just has one eye is borrowed directly from Poe's story. I felt Edgar needed a companion aside from his human friends, a mentor of sorts, that could assist him through this frightening time, and what could be better than a cat who speaks to him telepathically? I've had cats around for most of my life, so creating snarky dialog for one is pretty easy. I named her after the title character of another of Poe's stories, the description of which follows. You might see some slight connections from that story as well.

"Morella" deals with themes of death, obsession, and the supernatural as a grieving husband is haunted by the memory of his deceased wife, whose mysterious return leads to a shocking revelation about their intertwined fates. A beloved woman returning after her death, reincarnated in another form, is about as much of a connection as I can draw between Poe's Morella and mine. But I liked the name and wanted the cat to bear the name of one of Poe's ghostly women.

Chapter Two

"The Cask of Amontillado" recounts the chilling tale of Montresor's meticulously planned revenge against Fortunato, luring him into the catacombs of his family estate under the guise of sampling a rare wine. The setting of this story was impossible for me not to include. I imagine most people are familiar with the plot, too, so I hoped readers might begin to suspect what would happen to Edgar before he did. I gave the Richmond apothecary to whom Edgar is delivering the wine Montresor's name as a further wink to the original story.

Chapters Three and Four

"The Fall of the House of Usher" develops themes of mental deterioration, entwined with atmospheric gothic elements, as it chronicles the demise of the Usher family and their ancestral

home. I changed the family name of the brother and sister in Poe's story (*Tamerlane* was the title of Poe's first published work) and gave my episode a totally different ending since I believe most readers might know this story so I could surprise them when the house *doesn't* fall down. Edgar also gets glimpses in his panicked attempt to reach Robert midway through the chapter of scenes from other Poe stories, images which foreshadow events to come.

It really was fun to put myself into this iconic haunted house. I can't help but think that my description of it may have been influenced a bit by Roger Corman's 1960 film version of the story, although there was no conscious effort on my part to do so. (Corman's film strays greatly from the original story as do most of Corman's other movies loosely based on Poe stories. But then, who am I to judge?)

Chapter Five

"Berenice" scrutinizes the descent into obsession and madness through the lens of the protagonist's fixation on his cousin's teeth, culminating in a horrifying denouement. Teeth! What a horribly wonderful element to use as a focus for a horror story. I had to incorporate that into my tale, so I put a bag of them on Elmira's porch for the trio of friends to find at the end of the chapter. Dark Edgar has a fascination with Elmira's teeth and at the end of my novel, Edgar's thoughts go strangely to her smile, specifically her teeth, once again. That does not go unnoticed by Morella.

Chapter Six

"The Oblong Box" navigates themes of curiosity, secrecy, and the macabre as it unfolds a tale of suspense surrounding the mysterious contents of a peculiarly shaped vessel during a sea voyage. The name I gave to the man whom Edgar is to meet at the warehouse, Cornelius Wyatt, comes from Poe's story. For Edgar, whose memory of a recently desecrated grave is still fresh, the mysterious arrival of an oblong box might likely contain a body, so the nightmarish hallucination caused by Dark Edgar which transforms a shipping crate for a grandfather clock into a coffin seems quite plausible. A ticking clock features prominently, too, later in my novel at the Valdemar Hotel and also foreshadows the threat of the swinging, descending pendulum in the last chapter.

"Some Words with a Mummy" satirizes contemporary American society through the comedic premise of a resurrected ancient Egyptian mummy engaging in dialogue with a group of intellectuals, offering commentary on cultural practices and scientific advancements. The tone of this story is totally different than what's happening in Chapter Six of my book. I wanted primarily to utilize the same process Poe describes for his character to reanimate a corpse. The device in both stories was known as a Voltaic pile, an early form of battery. In Poe's story, the corpse, an Egyptian mummy, actually talks to a group of people, but as I wanted a scene with more horror, I thought it would be frightening to have the corpse jerked about like a marionette, with Wyatt, revealing himself to actually be Dark Edgar, grinning and cavorting madly about in the rafters of the warehouse, manipulating the corpse just as he was figuratively manipulating Edgar.

Chapter Seven

"Metzengerstein" explores themes of obsession, fate, and the supernatural as it follows the tragic downfall of the titular character, whose ancestral feud leads to a series of eerie events culminating in his fiery demise. The plot of this chapter has very little to do with Poe's story other than the fact that the lascivious carnival owner in my story shares the name of Poe's main character in his. Both Metzengersteins, Poe's and mine, have a fascination with horses, though, and the final image of Poe's story, the suggestion of a burning horse and rider glowing in the clouds, was one I definitely wanted to end this chapter with.

Chapter Eight

"The Tell-Tale Heart" peers into the psyche of a narrator plagued by guilt and paranoia after committing murder as he recounts the meticulous execution of his crime and the haunting sound of his victim's heartbeat. I can't imagine any fan of Poe not being familiar with this story——it's a favorite for many and certainly is one of mine. Obviously, I didn't want to simply re-tell Poe's tale, and yet I wanted Edgar to experience the terror of Poe's narrator without having to actually kill anyone. A dream solved that problem while still furthering Dark Edgar's role in the overall story. And there's a twist at the end of the Chapter Eight that goes beyond "The Tell-Tale Heart."

A quick word about using dreams...Yes, dreams can be overdone in horror, but given Poe's familiar line, "All that we see or seem is but a dream within a dream," I trust that I can be forgiven for utilizing dreams so much in this book. I often play with the idea that dreams are just a way of experiencing an alternate possibility, one of many other worlds of experience just as real as what we generally assume, perhaps falsely, to be the only reality.

Chapter Nine

"The Premature Burial" explores the theme of fear and obsession with death as it follows the narrator's harrowing experiences and vivid imaginings of being buried alive, reflecting on the horrors and anxieties associated with premature interment. I was surprised when I re-read this story in preparation for writing the novel that it isn't really so much a story as it is a narrative of a character who has a phobia of premature burial recounting various accounts of people who allegedly had been buried alive. The device described in this chapter whereby someone who has been mistakenly presumed dead and interred in a coffin could alert others to their predicament was a real product offered by some undertakers, as Poe mentions in his story.

Chapter Ten

"The Facts in the Case of M. Valdemar" presents a chilling narrative of mesmerism and its consequences as it recounts the experimental attempt to prolong the life of a terminally ill man, revealing eerie and grotesque outcomes beyond scientific comprehension. I love the premise of this story so much! The idea of cheating death by putting someone in a state of hypnosis is so thrilling, especially when it goes horribly wrong. I gave my hypnotist the name Gordon Pym, the protagonist of a fascinating adventure story by Poe (not really horror––Poe wrote in other genres as many of you know) and gave the name Valdemar, the man who is hypnotized in Poe's story, to the entire hotel where the hypnotism show takes place, and where Edgar experiences the events that lead to the climax.

Chapter Eleven

"The Masque of the Red Death" depicts a tale of hubris and mortality as Prince Prospero attempts to evade a deadly plague by secluding himself and his courtiers within a fortified abbey, only to face a gruesome reckoning when a mysterious fig-ure appears amidst their extravagant masquerade ball. Like the deathly robed figure in Poe's story, Dark Edgar leads Edgar through multi-colored halls in the hotel. Instead of a red masque, Dark Edgar first wears a yellow mask as Edgar has succumbed to Yellow Fever in this chapter. The yellow, green, and blue halls are reminiscent of the differently colored rooms in Prince Prospero's castle. As Edgar moves through time, witnessing scenes from his past, present, and future, he also hears voices of characters from the stories he will later write, as he did in the chambers below the apothecary's shop in Chapter Two.

Chapter Twelve

"The Pit and the Pendulum" follows the horrifying ordeal of an unnamed narrator as he navigates the torturous chambers of the Spanish Inquisition, confronting imminent death from a descending pendulum blade and the encroaching walls of a pit, illustrating themes of terror, survival, and the indomitable will to live. The parallels to this story are obvious. The absolute darkness of the chamber containing the pit is the most frightening part of the book for me. It is the void I believe we all face at some time or other––our confrontation with the idea of oblivion, the end of our existence––and Edgar's surrender and literal leap of faith seems like something we all ultimately have to do. To find that Edgar is still restricted in the chamber with the pendulum requires Edgar to depend on his own resolve, his inner strength, which becomes a pivotal moment in his development from boy to manhood.

Chapter Thirteen

"William Wilson" serves again in Edgar's final confrontation with his nemesis. The ending of Poe's story overlaps a bit with mine, but the two serve entirely different purposes. Poe's narrator's obsession with his double is self-destructive, whereas Edgar is freed (perhaps) with his final meeting with Dark Edgar. Both stories suggest the duality, the potential for good and evil, that lies within us all.

I would love to hear what you thought of *Edgar* and whether you would be interested in seeing the story continue into Poe's later years. I'm toying with that idea, so your comments would be helpful. You are welcome to email me directly at author@davidallenvoyles.com and, of course, you're always invited to communicate with me via Instagram and Facebook.

Don't forget to get on my free mailing list where you can get *Dark Cycles* delivered to your email inbox on the first of every month. I assure you, it's not like any other newsletter (there's fun, free stuff in every issue.) You can find the link on my website at davidallenvoyles. com and download a free, original story, *Captain Buchanan's Return*, that you won't find anywhere else.

ACKNOWLEDGMENTS

Harry Lee Poe's biography, *Edgar Allan Poe, An Illustrated Companion to His Tell-Tale Stories.* (Metro Books, 2008) provided most of the background information I needed in order to develop Edgar's relationship with the Allans and his friends Elmira and Robert, as well as his life in Richmond in general. Harry Lee Poe is a cousin of Poe's and serves as Charles Colson Professor of Faith and Culture at Union University in Jackson, Tennessee and has served as president of the Poe Foundation. The book contains removeable replicas of handwritten letters, drafts, and other documents which make exploring its pages even more enjoyable.

I edited slightly the one-sentence summaries of Poe's stories after querying for them in ChatGPT, the chatbot created by OpenAI. Using Artificial Intelligence for creative purposes is controversial, and for good reason. I believe my usage of it for research ("Did American houses in 1826 have screen doors?") and in creating those summaries is a legitimate use of AI, but I must also say that I deplore the idea of AI-generated fiction being passed off as literature.

I'd like to thank Bambi Sommers once again for her tremendous editing, and my writer/creator friends, Polly Schattel, Andrew Clark, Jason Stokes, Anna Ray, Jacqui Castle, Shawn Burgess, and Bryan Lienesch for their excellent and insightful feedback after reading early drafts of *Edgar*. Thanks also to my dear, old friends (yes, we go way back but, damn it, we *are* old) Scott Conrad, Sue Key, Jim Munden, and my brother, Steve Voyles, for their constant encouragement and feedback.

Thanks to Dave Dick for his excellent illustration of young Edgar, Morella, and the raven which appears on the cover of the book. You should all check out Dave's other "dark art" online. Google "Dave Dick Illustration."

Many, many thanks to my son, Josh Voyles, who made an incredible gift for me after reading an early version of *Edgar* that I'll always treasure, a handmade, bound collection of his original art inspired from my story and Poe's.

And as always, special thanks to my wife, Ann, not only for her invaluable role as first reader/editor, but as my companion through life, without whom I'd be lost.

OTHER BOOKS BY DAVID ALLEN VOYLES

*Visit **davidallenvoyles.com** for links to these books and download a free original horror story while you're there. Follow David Allen Voyles on Instagram, listen to the author read some of his stories on the Dark Corners podcast, and join the **Dark Corners** Facebook page for author updates and other horror-related topics.*

The Thirteenth Day of Christmas and Other Tales of Yuletide Horror

David Allen Voyles revives the tradition of telling Yuletide ghost stories with his collection of twelve original, frightening ghost tales and one novella, all set in the Christmas season. You'll find a wide array of supernatural entities within these stories, from traditional ghosts to modern twists on familiar Christmas characters like Santa and Krampus.

Tales from the Hearse

Voyles evokes his past role as Virgil Nightshade, the storyteller and ghost tour host, with this collection of thirteen stories of the macabre. One can easily imagine riding in the back of his 1972 Cadillac hearse through a spooky graveyard listening to him tell his tales of horror just as his customers did in Asheville, NC. If you love ghost stories, haunted houses, and walks through the graveyard, climb in the hearse and take a dark ride with David Allen Voyles. Just make sure your doors are locked.

Witch-Works

Children die in Maria Bay in disproportionate numbers. They always have.

If anyone suspected Harold O/Bannon and the Black Cat Toy Factory (aka the Witch-Works), they kept it to themselves. In 1954 the factory was destroyed in a fire. When Daniel learns of his father's death and returns to the home he had fled years before he finds he is intimately involved in O'Bannon's dark designs which have spanned generations of mystery, murder, and horror.

Wraiths of the Appalachian

When Eddie Bowen quit his job, threw a sleeping bag into the back of his Volkswagen bus and headed out onto the highway, he had no idea what horrors awaited him. With no specific destination in mind, he surprises himself by following the directions of a crackling voice that speaks directly to him through the static of the vintage radio. With a mysterious canine companion who seems more wolf than dog, Eddie finds there is something much more terrifying behind the Appalachian campfire stories he heard as a boy than he ever could have imagined.

www.ingramcontent.com/pod-product-compliance
Lightning Source LLC
Chambersburg PA
CBHW060907140726
47996CB00001B/153